It Happened on Fifth Street

A Tale of Forgotten Heroes

By Robyn R Pearce

Book 1 in the Freedom Series

**It Happened on Fifth Street: a tale of forgotten heroes
Book 1 in the Freedom Series**

First published 2020 by GettingAGrip Publishing
R.D.4, Pukekohe, 2679, New Zealand

ISBN   Ebook 978-0-473-52051-9
ISBN   POD 978-0-473-52050-2

A catalogue record for this book is available from the National Library of New Zealand

Cover design by Nick Castle
Layout by AtriTex Technologies P Ltd
Print and digital versions available through Amazon
For bulk supplies for schools, contact the publisher.

Visit the author's website at https://www.robynpearce.com

To Peggy, who introduced me to Alf
Without you, this book would never have been

and

My grandchildren
The fight for truth and freedom is your heritage

Freedom is a heavy load, a great and strange burden
for the spirit to undertake …
It is not a gift given, but a choice made, and the choice
may be a hard one.
URSULA K. LE GUIN, *The Tombs of Atuan*

PART ONE

Chapter 1

Abigail
Auckland January 2015

I was snuggled up on my bed reading, our ginger cat Macavity asleep beside me, when the door opened and my mother's head appeared. A savory smell of baking followed.

'Abi, are you doing anything right now?'

Summer holidays were always like this – frequent interruptions to do jobs. I sighed. Put my library book down on the bed.

'Muuum, I'm always doing something.'

'Well, apart from texting friends or having your nose in a book. Could you help me by running a pie over to Aunt Hanna, please? I promised I'd drop something round this afternoon for her dinner but an urgent job has just come in.' Now it was Mum's turn to sigh. 'I'd really appreciate it, love.'

Got to hand it to her. My mum could make an instruction sound like I had a choice. Yeah right.

'Do I have to? I'm sooo close to the end.' I flicked the remaining twenty pages.

'If it's no more than fifteen minutes. Early dinner tonight – I've got a meeting. It's really your turn to cook, but I've made us a pie too.'

It was only a couple of blocks round to Great-Aunt Hanna's place. Normally I zipped round on my bike, but with a pie to carry I had to walk. She was a sharp old lady with a heap of entertaining stories, some of them quite racy. For an oldie, she was pretty cool.

I walked by the wide front entrance of her sprawling old villa and round to the back of the house, passing the garage that now only housed a lawnmower and garden tools. (How she'd hated the doctor taking her driver's license off her.) Stomping up the wooden steps to the back porch, I navigated past the usual litter of gardening shoes, gloves and small tools.

'It's me,' I called, walking in without knocking. Either Mum or I called in several times a week and the back door was seldom locked during the day.

Aunt Hanna peered over the top of reading glasses perched on the end of her button nose. Strands of white hair dropped out of her untidy bun. She held a letter in her age-spotted hands and a mess of old papers littered the battered mahogany dining table.

'Abigail, you're a welcome sight. I think you'll be rather interested in this.' She gestured at the pile of papers.

I left the pie on the bench and sat down at the table to see what was taking her attention.

The late afternoon summer sun poured in through the high sash windows in her dining room, highlighting the dust on a mess of yachting and flying trophies jumbled up on the carved sideboard. It also lit up my favorite photo of her. A dark-haired beauty leant against an oak tree in full summer leaf, a quiver of arrows slung across her slim shoulders and an archery bow in her hand. She was giving a sultry come-hither smile to the camera. No wonder she'd scored so many boyfriends in her day.

Outside, red, pink and white dahlias created a splash of color in front of shimmering silver birches. The quiet rustle of the leaves and the smell of fresh-cut grass drifted in through the open window. Aunt Hanna loved her garden; spent more time outside than on housework and cooking. Hence the pie. Mum knew that her sparrow-framed aunt sometimes skimped on meals.

'What do you know about America in the 1800's, dear?' Aunt Hanna looked up at me.

'Not much, but the teacher said we're starting on US history next term. Why?'

'Did you know that we've probably got some American relatives?'

'No,' I replied in surprise. 'Never heard that before.'

'Our Burnett ancestors, though English-born, also lived for some years in America. They were your four times grandparents. I don't know much about them, except that some of their children were born in the States, others in England, and the family ended up here in New Zealand, settling in Whanganui in 1856. I believe they left parents, brothers and sisters in America.

'Why didn't I know that?'

'Over the decades we've lost touch. That's why I've never bothered to mention it. I don't know if even your mother knows about them. However, these letters,' she waved her hand over the documents scattered on the table, 'might reopen some connections, especially with the internet these days. They look interesting.'

I was curious. 'But how come you've just found this stuff now? And why did they leave America?'

She gestured to a battered-looking tin trunk on the floor. 'This old thing's been in my junk room for years. It was tucked behind stuff my mother squirreled away. She lived through the Great Depression and her favorite saying was, "It might be useful one day." She rarely threw anything out. Over the years I've found a few treasures amongst the dross.

'I looked inside this trunk years ago and noticed it was just old papers. For the longest time I've been meaning to get into it and see what she thought was worth keeping. When it rained yesterday, I finally decided to pull it out.'

'Any treasure or dark family secrets? Any scandals or murders?'

'Well, I'm not sure yet. From a couple of letters I've scanned, *something* was kept a secret by the older family members. Have you got an hour to give me a hand? I'm trying to sort this mess into date sequence before I start reading the contents.'

I didn't need a second invitation. My friends often teased me, but I liked jigsaw puzzles and sorting things into order, and at school I was a library monitor.

A small brown envelope was lying in front of me. I pulled out a thin white wrinkly page, almost like tissue, with a small blot of ink in one corner. The writing was surprisingly legible. I quickly scanned for the date.

'Oh, wow! This is really old!'

Heads together, we studied the piece of paper.

5th street, Cincinnati, Ohio
January 14th, 1837

Dear Joseph and Mary Anne
I have hard tussles with my neighbors all around, but I tell them – as long as I have an English tongue in my head and English blood in my veins, I will speak. My doctrine is (and they can't get over that), 'I hold these truths to be self-evident – that God has endowed man with inalienable rights, among which are those of life, liberty and the pursuit of happiness. Not the Red man; not the Yellow man; not the Brown man; not the Black man; not the White man – but Man.'

But said one of my neighbors, 'The Nigger is not a man.'

Said I, 'In order to be a consistent Anti-Abolitionist you are obliged to deny one of the best senses God Almighty has given you, your own precious eyesight.'

I regret to say that Abolition does not go ahead here in Cincinnati.

Joseph, your mother does not wish me to be involved. She is afraid of the consequences of upsetting our neighbors, that it will damage our trade, but I think her real fear is of my activities being discovered by the law enforcers. I cannot sit back and observe the inhumanity to be seen on every street corner of this place without doing something. Your sisters are in agreement with me. They're even attending the Abolitionist Church.

I urge you not to share this letter with Alfred. There is great danger in what we do here. Your brother is too young to be trusted with this matter just yet. His thoughtless quick tongue might betray us to those who wish to harm our endeavors.

Your ever-loving father, Cornelius Burnett

I looked at Aunt Hanna, gobsmacked. 'What was going on, do you think? What's abolition? Where's Cincinnati? And it sounds like the family are not all living together, don't you think?'

Aunt Hanna rested her knobbly hands on the table.

'Girl, so many questions! Why don't you ask that phone you're always playing with?'

I reached to pull my mobile out of my pocket. She grinned. 'I'm teasing. I suspect the letters might give us the answers to who was living where, and why. Although,' she paused as her hand hovered over a pile of letters, 'you might still like to look up abolition and the location of Cincinnati when you go home. I could tell you, but I know you don't have a lot of time and I'd rather have your help with this lot.'

I started to sort with her. Our concentration was occasionally broken with an exclamation of surprise or a quick chat about which heap to put something on. Some letters were still in envelopes, often with the date scrawled in pencil on the outside. We didn't bother to open those; just put them in their year pile. Most letters were folded neatly, without envelopes, and had to be opened to find the date on the first page. We ended up with piles from 1829 to 1886 and some of the handwriting was hard to read, but we quickly became familiar with the style of the regular correspondents.

We also found advertising for theatre productions, cuttings from newspapers or journals, the occasional picture or photo, odd scraps of paper that looked as though they'd been torn out of an exercise book or off a pad, and some formal-looking documents.

An hour later the letters were sorted. As I pushed annoying wisps of ponytail back behind my ears, I looked at the piles spread all over the table.

'Reading all these isn't going to be quick. Where do we start?' I asked.

Aunt Hanna sat back, took off her glasses and rubbed a hand across her face, depositing a sheen of ancient dust from the letters across her wrinkled cheeks. Casting her eye over the table, she smiled.

'I like the 'we', dear. You'd like to help uncover their story?'

'Oh yes.' I was hooked. I really wanted to know about these long-dead relatives whose blood I carried in my veins. 'I've got plenty of time while it's summer holidays. We don't have the money to go away, now it's just Mum and me.'

I paused. Forced a cheerful voice. I knew Aunt Hanna worried about us. 'And I like a mystery.'

'That's great. I'd love your assistance.'

She looked more closely at the heaps. 'Interesting! Most stacks are of similar size, except between 1840 and '41. Why less in those years, I wonder?'

'I could take some home to start reading tonight, if you like. What if I start earlier than 1840 and see what I can find out?'

'That's a great idea. I'll find a tin to put them in. I saw something in the junk room.'

While she ferreted around in her back room, I picked up one of the newspaper articles we'd put in a separate pile. It was headed up ***Freedom Journal, Issue 25, April 1858.***

Just then Aunt Hanna came back with a biscuit tin. It looked nearly as old as the letters, with a few dents and scratches. However, the picture on the lid was still clear – a grumpy-looking old woman with big boobs and double chins, covered to her neck in a black dress. An ugly white bonnet did nothing to improve her appearance.

She chuckled, gesturing at the old lady. 'A souvenir tin celebrating 50 years of Queen Victoria's reign.' She loaded in a few letters, then went back to her piles.

I started to read the yellowing newspaper still in my hands. My eye had been caught by the author's name – Alfred Burnett. Wasn't he the one whose father didn't trust with dangerous information?

Chapter 2

Abigail
Auckland January 2015

The story was titled:

Part I: *In Which I Come Face to Face with Slavery for the First Time*

By Our Correspondent, Alfred Burnett

It was the summer of 1834 and our family had decided to leave dangerous, dirty, disease-ridden New York for a safer life in the prosperous small city of Utica, in upstate New York. The best way to get there was by steamer up the Hudson River to Albany, and then by packet, a narrow passenger vessel, on the Erie Canal.

New York's North River piers, at the beginning of the wide Hudson River, were a noisy, crowded and exciting place for a nine-year-old boy. They seemed to stretch for miles. People everywhere, scurrying like a disturbed ant nest. Boats and ships of all shapes and sizes, tied up alongside the wharves. A forest of masts with ropes and wires clinking in the breeze, their wooden arms reaching to the sky. Gangplanks reaching from boat to shore. Pulleys rattling as burly men heaved on ropes, and big boxes, freight and even livestock being hauled or lowered in and out of the holds of the ships.

Many vessels couldn't reach the wharves, so they were rafted up to those that could. Sailors and dock workers, rolling heavy barrels and carrying boxes of produce, scurried across other boat decks to reach their own. How they didn't trip over all the hawsers, long ropes and springers stretching from boat to boat, I did not know.

Seagulls screeched. People shouted. Horses and mules pulling carts and carriages neighed, brayed and snorted when other animals and vehicles got too close. The sharp crack of flicking whips split the air. Sailors of every color called to each other in strange languages. Iron wheels rumbled on stone cobbles, masts and ropes creaked and groaned, and boats shifted and swayed with the flow of the tide.

The smells of a sea port are different from city smells. I knew tar and hemp, the salty tang of the sea, and the sharp odor of fresh dung from the livestock being driven between ship and shore. But many other aromas I could only guess at.

I was busting to explore the wildly exciting scene. Mother had other ideas.

'Stay here, children,' she said firmly to me and my six-year-old sister, Jane. 'I don't want to lose you in this crowd.' She even enlisted the help of the aunts and uncles who'd come to farewell us. More than once, poised to escape on an adventure, I was pulled back by my braces.

As I stood, surrounded by relatives, my eye was caught by a dark-skinned lad of about five years. He was dressed most unusually for a small boy. A white collar and cuffs contrasted with his black hands and face and frizzy-tight short black curls. Yellow stockings, matching blue pantaloons and jacket trimmed with gold buttons. Shiny black shoes with huge buckles. I couldn't help staring. I'd seen some black people on the streets of New York, but never one dressed like a toff. He was struggling to carry a yappy white dog with a red ribbon and a silly coat.

A white lady was a couple of steps in front of him, dressed in silken frills and furbelows like nothing I'd ever seen the women in our family wear. She was carrying only a parasol and a reticule. She'd turned around and was scowling at the child's attempt to manage the dog. Behind the boy was an anxious-looking young colored woman in workaday clothes, loaded up with baskets. Behind them were three porters, sweating under stacks of heavy trunks. When the lady stopped, the little procession was forced to halt.

She snarled, 'Hurry up, Eli. For goodness' sake! Control that dog! I'll give you a whipping if you don't move faster. I should have left you in Charlotte.'

He looked scared. Shrank from her angry voice. At that instant the dog wriggled out of his arms and came running in my direction, its leash dangling. It was the work of a moment to grab it. The frightened child scurried toward me.

I handed him the leash.

'Thankee, young massa. I be for a beatin' for sure.' Angrily, his mistress marched back. He cringed. It was as well that I stepped aside. I felt the wind from her raised arm as she landed a mighty cuff round his ears. He almost lost the dog again as he reeled from the blow.

I stood there, mouth agape, as they moved off. My twenty-year-old brother Thomas was standing beside me. I turned to him in puzzlement. He answered my question before I could ask it.

'That child, and the older girl carrying the baskets, are slaves, Alf. Many slave-owners treat their slaves like dogs. Judging by what we just saw, that dog is probably better treated than the child.'

This was a new term for me. 'What's a slave?'

Thomas frowned. 'It's when a person is owned by someone else. To their owners, slaves are property. They buy and sell them just like a dog or a horse, a house or a farm.'

I was shocked. 'How can that be possible?'

'Slavery has been a dark side of nearly every civilization since the dawn of time, often as a result of war. In America it's common in the southern states, but because of human greed, not war. Most slaves in this country – black men, women and children – originally came from Africa, or their ancestors did. In most cases, it was other Africans who kidnapped them and sold them to white slave traders. It's a terrible practice.'

My jaw dropped, but I was too young to fully understand the enormity of his words. Instead, I focused on the scene in front of me.

'Why is that little boy dressed up so fancy?'

'He's a house slave and that woman's page boy, so she's given him flash clothes to make her look good. Don't be deceived by the clothes. He'll be at her beck and call nonstop – probably sleeps on a mat at the foot of her bed in case she wants anything during the night.

'Although yon little boy, being a house slave, will live in a nice house and be dressed well, he'll never get to play like you. His mistress will have him running after her every whim, fetching and carrying, and waving a fan over her for hours when it's hot. If she wants to beat him black and blue for the slightest misdemeanor, there's none can stop her. You saw how she hit him. She has the power of life and death over her slaves.'

I looked up in shock at Thomas. 'Why doesn't his mother stop the lady treating him so bad?'

'It's highly possible that child has been sold away from his mother, in which case he'll be lucky if he ever sees her again. But even if she's owned by the same people, she's got no say over how her little boy is treated.'

I struggled to take in what Thomas was telling me. 'Why haven't I seen slaves before?'

'Because it's now against the law in the northern states, thank goodness. From what we just heard, I'd say that woman lives in the south and is passing through New York on a visit. Southern people often travel with slaves to attend to their needs.'

'Why don't the slaves just leave?'

'The punishment for running away is horrendous. They're whipped and worse. I don't want to give you nightmares, so I think we'll leave it at that.'

My head was spinning with the nasty details when we heard a horn blow. It was our steamer. I forgot the plight of the little black boy as the crowd of excited and jabbering people began to move.

Watch for the next exciting episode: Danger on the Hudson

Just then my mobile pinged. I glanced at the screen. 'Oh bummer. Mum's wanting to know when I'm coming home. We've got to eat early so she can get to a meeting. Better dash.' I grabbed the Queenie tin, kissed my aunt goodbye, and headed home.

Chapter 3

Abigail
Auckland January 2015

As soon as Mum left for her meeting, I cleaned up the dishes, then carried the tin to the carefully wiped-down table. Aunt Hanna had stressed the importance of care with the fragile papers.

Eagerly I lifted the lid. What mysteries might I uncover? Opening one of the envelopes, I pulled out a couple of small sheets of paper. A brown coin with a hole through it fell out. 'United States of America' was imprinted on one side and '1795' on the other, but the rest was very hard to read. I put it to one side.

The letter was by the same writer as the one I'd read at Aunt Hanna's.

5th street, Cincinnati, Ohio
September 14th, 1837

Dear Joseph and Mary Anne
Please do not share this with Alfred.
Last night we had a close shave. The sheriff and his deputy came knocking on the kitchen door, demanding admittance. Only your mother was in the room. Thanks to the good Lord, I had just left the house with the items they were seeking and your mother had only five minutes earlier disposed of evidence, into the fire. When asked where her husband was, she was able to say, quite truthfully, that he had just gone to church. And so I had — but not the church the sheriff would have expected.

But more of this I won't expand on just now. You know on which church door I was knocking.

I turned the page. The writer then talked about the price of sugar, molasses and eggs and how much they'd taken in sales.

He finished with, '*The store is doing well. Cincinnati has far more opportunities for our family. I do wish you and your wife, and your brother Alfred of course, would come west to join us. I know Utica is a pretty little town, but this place is going ahead by leaps and bounds and now one of the largest cities in America. And I could certainly do with your assistance, both in the business by day and the business by night.*

Your loving father, Cornelius Burnett.

Well, something mysterious was certainly going on.

For the next hour I ploughed through more letters. It seemed that both families had bakery and confectionery businesses, but there were no obvious clues as to just what Cornelius was up to. Some letters were from other family members in New York and England. Another son, Thomas, lived in Syracuse and was also working as a baker. Joseph, the oldest son, and his wife Mary Anne, were living in Utica, apart from the rest of the family. A younger son, Alfred, the writer of the article I'd read at Aunt Hanna's, was living with them.

I needed a map. I'd vaguely heard of Cincinnati but where the heck was Utica? My American geography was very sketchy. Google Maps showed it was about two hundred miles north of New York but still in New York state. Then I logged in Cincinnati. Discovered they were just over six hundred miles apart and the shortest route from Utica to Cincinnati was about nine and a half hours by car. How long would it have taken in 1837? I didn't know enough about travel back then to be able to work it out. Certainly no cars and modern multi-lane highways! Horses for sure, and boats round the coast and on lakes and big rivers. And there'd been several mentions of a canal. Were there trains back then?

So many questions. But the big one was what Cornelius wanted kept from Alfred. I couldn't wait to see Aunt Hanna tomorrow and hear whether she'd found out more. I yawned. Time to get some sleep.

As I packed the letters away in the tin, I spotted the old coin again. That would look quite cool as a pendant. Something a bit different from my girlfriends' bling. I remembered a fine black plaited cord tucked in the back of a drawer. Aunt Hanna had given it to me some years back to string a trinket I'd bought at a school fair. The cheap plastic thing had gone in the bin ages ago, but the cord had been worth keeping.

I decided to wear the coin to Aunt Hanna's in the morning and see if she noticed it. I carried it into my room, threaded the cord through, and slipped it over my head to test the length.

Suddenly I felt dizzy. Was I fainting? I tried to clutch the edge of the chest of drawers. Failed. The room vanished. A deep blackness overtook me.

When I came to, my head ached. My limbs felt floppy. I shook my head, confused. Looked around.

What the …

Staring at me in shock was a boy younger than me, probably about twelve, a messy mop of brown hair dangling into his hazel eyes, a snub nose, freckles splotching his broad cheeks and square face. His old-fashioned clothes would have looked good on Oliver Twist or the Artful Dodger. Heavy woolen half-pants, long stockings pulled up to cover his knees. A short-waisted jacket loosely thrown on, buttons undone. Underneath, a plain brown cotton shirt. Heavy scuffed black lace-up boots.

He was standing beside an open drop-leaf writing desk with a key hanging out of the lock. In one hand he had a letter.

24

Chapter 4

Alfred
Utica October 1837

Joseph was downstairs in the hot bakery with Sam, his assistant. From the sweet smells wafting up the stairs I guessed they were preparing another batch of lemon drops. We'd had a run on them in the store over the last couple of days.

I was at our well-scrubbed pine table, puzzling over my arithmetic book. Nearby, my brother's wife Mary Anne bustled around. She pushed a couple of pieces of long-burning wood into the fire box, shoved in the damper to slow the fire, and shifted her soup pot to the back of the black stove.

'Alfred, I'm just off to Bleecker street market to see if Mr de Jong has a nice piece of pork for our supper. If I'm more than half an hour, please stoke the fire and give the soup a stir, there's a good lad.'

I looked up from my study, happy to be distracted. There was a test on Monday but I hated arithmetic. 'Are you sure you don't want me to carry your basket?'

Mary Anne laughed. Lifted her woolen shawl from the chair beside me, then reached for her plain blue weekday bonnet hanging on the peg by the back door.

'Good try, little brother. You know what Mr Dorchester will say if you don't know your numbers. Best you concentrate on your study.'

With that she picked up her wicker basket and was gone, out through the kitchen door. I heard the garden gate slam behind her as she stepped out onto Genesee street.

I looked down again at the book. It was so tedious. I'd rather be almost anywhere but sitting in our kitchen.

I wondered what my friend Seamus was up to. Not doing boring sums, I'd hazard. Mr O'Leary probably had him digging potatoes or helping with the animals. We hoped to go fishing at our favorite spot after supper, down where the bend in the Mohawk River came close to the town and the Erie Canal. It would just be my luck if his Pa kept him to his tasks. A slave-driver, that man. Said they needed every penny. It was amazing he let him come to school at all.

Could I sneak in half-an-hour reading *Robinson Crusoe?* With Mary Anne out of the house and Joseph busy, who would know?

And then an idea struck. Last night I'd noticed Joseph slipping a letter into his writing desk in the parlor. When I asked if it was from our parents, he fobbed me off with a vague remark about boring business documents and sent me to help Mary Anne with the dishes. I just knew he was keeping something from me. With no-one around, now I could find out what. I gave in to temptation.

As I stepped across the hall I stayed close to the wall to avoid the creaky board in the doorway to the parlor. I didn't want Joseph coming upstairs to see what I was doing, for we didn't generally go in there during the day. The key was sitting in its usual spot, on a nail behind the highly polished walnut writing desk with its fancy scrolls and inlay of mother-of-pearl. I unlocked the lid, pulled out the supports and opened up the lid. Sure enough, an envelope was thrust into one of the empty partitions. And yes, the scrawled address was in our Papa's big writing. How odd that Joseph didn't share it with me. A letter from Cincinnati was normally read and discussed over the dinner table by the three of us.

I pulled out the two pages and started to read.

5th street, Cincinnati, Ohio
September 14ᵗʰ, 1837

Dear Joseph and Mary Anne
Please do not share this with Alfred.
Last night we had a close shave. The sheriff and his deputy
came knocking on the kitchen door, demanding admittance.

What! How dare they keep secrets from me.

Suddenly, I heard a heavy thump. I whirled around, heart in mouth. Had Joseph caught me prying?

To my shock, sprawled on the floor as if she'd been thrown, was a strange girl, probably a few years older than me, dressed most oddly and looking stunned.

'The saints preserve us! Who are you? How dare you come into our house uninvited?!'

She sat up, looking terrified.

She stuttered, 'I … I don't know. I was just about to get ready for bed and suddenly things went black. Next minute – I landed up here.'

Her accent was unusual. A little like my parents' voices, but different; they'd never lost their Englishness. I have a good ear for different voices and am often in trouble for mimicking others, but she sounded like no one I'd heard before.

Her clothes were bizarre. A loose-fitting black garment I guessed was meant to be a shirt, of a style I'd never seen a woman wear. Glittery white writing splashed across the front, saying 'SEIZE THE DAY'. On her lower limbs, outrageously on show, peacock-blue ragged inexpressibles with holes all over them. The rips were such as you'd see on an urchin boy's garments, but no urchin I'd ever seen would be so colorful – their clothing was only ever dirty gray, brown or black hand-me-downs. Her feet were bare but clean, rather than calloused and dirty like the few children who ran around unshod. I'd never before seen anyone clad this way, and as to a girl wearing inexpressibles – how unseemly! I couldn't imagine what my family would say.

She looked around as she began to scramble up from the floor. 'Who the heck are you? And where am I?'

I glared at her. 'I asked first. You can't just walk into our house. Who are *you* and why were you on the floor?'

She staggered, leaning on Joseph's piano as if her balance was poor. She was taller than me. Her long hair was tied back with some kind of string. No ribbon. No bonnet. Bits of fair fly-away hair were loose around her thin face. All in all, she looked like a vagrant.

Her terror faded to confusion as she glanced around the room.

'I didn't walk in. I just found myself here. It felt as though a giant hand picked me up and threw me. I'm as surprised as you.' She rubbed an elbow.

I stood, hands on hips, waiting for more explanation. She took a similar position. It was a stand-off.

Finally, she broke the impasse. 'I'm Abigail. From Mt Eden.'

'Mt Eden? Is that in New York?'

'Of course not. It's in Auckland. Why would it be in New York?'

'Where is Auckland? I've never heard of any town by that name.'

She looked stunned. 'You haven't?'

Consternation washed her face. She scanned the room again. Peered hard at my clothing. I was a bit offended. For sure, I wasn't clad in my Sunday go-to-church clothes, but I was a lot more presentable than her. I had on my old grey knickerbockers, the ones with patches that I kept for weekends. My brown shirt had the buttons respectably done up to the chin. I'd thrown on my worsted short jacket this morning as well, for a tinge of autumn was in this morning's cool wind. For sure, my leather boots were on the shabby side, but show me a boy whose boots don't look the same. My woolen stockings weren't falling down; I'd just pulled them up and tucked them under the bottom of my sit-down-upons a few minutes earlier. In fact, I was far more suitably attired than this peculiar and entirely under-dressed stranger.

Her next questions surprised me even further. 'What country is this? And what year is it?'

Had she taken leave of her senses? 'Are you jesting? It's America, of course. In the year of Our Lord, 1837.'

She crumpled into my brother's armchair. 'Oh shit! That's terrible. What's my mother going to say! I'm supposed to be putting out the cat and going to bed.'

It was my turn to be shocked. 'Such language!' Then I noticed an old coin dangling from a cord around her neck.

'Where did you get that coin? I've got one exactly the same in my bedroom.' Anger surged through my body. I yelled, 'You're making this all up! You're a thief.'

'No!' she replied, indignant. 'I just found it in an old envelope. I was going through some old family letters and it fell out. I put it on a thong. Oh …. ' Her odd-sounding speech slowed for a moment. 'The last thing I remember was putting it over my head.'

She looked around the room, bewildered. 'I was in my bedroom at home.'

We were both as confused as each other.

She gathered her wits a bit ahead of me. 'What's your name? And what town is this?'

'I'm Alfred Burnett and this is Utica, in upstate New York.'

If she hadn't been already sitting, I think she would have fallen to the floor again. Her face went white. Her mouth dropped open.

'Oh my God! We're related. I'm from your future. I've just been reading about you. My name is Abigail Burnett, and I was born in 1999, in Auckland, New Zealand. It's now January 2015 where I'm from.'

Now I collapsed, on the chaise longue. 'Do you think I'm a fool! That's not possible.'

'Well, I didn't think it was either, but here I am. I've seen television stories about this kind of thing. I just thought the writers and producers had good imaginations.'

I looked at her blankly. 'What's television?'

The girl didn't immediately answer. Then, 'It's a screen that beams moving pictures and information from anywhere round the world. Almost everyone has at least one in their homes, and some houses have them in nearly every room. And you can watch it on mobiles and computers as well.'

This was going from mad to madder. I couldn't even imagine what she was blathering on about.

She saw my bewilderment. Paused a moment, then spoke.

'The world's very different, nearly 180 years into the future. I'll really confuse you if I try to explain everything.' She didn't notice my irritation at being treated like a small child.

'The thing I'm most interested in is how I'm going to get back home. My mother will be beside herself if I'm not safely tucked up in bed when she gets back from her meeting, and nowhere to be found.'

Anxious adults – that was something I *did* understand.

She saw the letter in my hand. I'd quite forgotten it, in the bewilderment of the last few minutes.

'Do you mind if I look at that?' she asked as she reached out her hand.

Still trying to decide whether she was crazy or I was, I passed it over. I didn't think it possible, but she looked even more startled as she glanced at the first few lines, all I'd had a chance to read before being so dramatically interrupted.

She looked over at me. 'I just read that letter about an hour ago! My great-aunt has a whole lot of old family letters in a tin trunk.'

'You're lying!'

'No, I'm not. Here,' and she passed it back. 'There's two pages. You know I've not looked at the second page. I'll tell you what it says. The writer talks about the price of sugar and molasses. He wishes the reader and his family would come to Cincinnati, and it's signed, 'Your loving father, Cornelius Burnett'.'

I quickly scanned it. She was right.

We stared at each other, dumbfounded.

Chapter 5

Alfred
Utica November 1837

I couldn't dismiss the evidence in front of me; there was a weird girl in our parlor, with an impossible story. For a few minutes neither of us said a word, as we tried to make sense of the enormity of the situation. Then, my stunned brain kicked back into life.

'My sister-in-law will be back soon, or my brother's going to walk upstairs from the bakery. Will they ever believe your story? And, I'm not supposed to know about this letter. I don't want them to find out I've been snooping. If we use this as evidence, I'm in trouble.'

'What about *my* trouble? I'm the one tipped arse-up into nearly two centuries before my time. I'm more worried about how I'm going to get home than what your brother thinks.'

I ignored her rough language. Stared hard at her slender figure, vivid blue eyes, and her very odd and unseemly collection of clothes. As I looked, an idea struck.

'Could your arrival here be anything to do with that coin around your neck? It looks exactly like mine. Are you *sure* you're not a prankster or thief?'

She started to protest but I wasn't taking no for an answer. 'I'm going to see if my coin is still in my room, and you're coming with me.'

I put the letter back in its not-so-secret place, shut the desk and returned the key. Grabbed her hand and pulled her after me into the hallway. I dared not leave her in the parlor.

We climbed the dark wooden stairs. Our house was rather large for just three people, though it had not seemed so before my parents and three sisters removed to Cincinnati the year before. As a result of this change in family arrangements, we had an empty bedroom and I now enjoyed the big room that used to house my three sisters.

'Surprisingly tidy for a boy,' said my accidental companion as we stepped into my sun-filled room at the back of the house.

I went straight to the three shelves Joseph had put up. My box of tin soldiers and few precious books were on the top shelf and the rock and curio collection took up the two lower shelves so I could easily sort and arrange them.

It only took a quick look at my small selection of old coins to see that the one I wanted wasn't there. Just to be sure, I scrabbled through the arrow heads and other small artifacts gathered from where the Indians used to camp, down by the Mohawk. Then I checked my colored stones. No coin.

Joseph reckoned the few coins I'd found had probably dropped from pockets of foremen or engineers when they were building the Erie Canal. I'd found this one when Seamus and I built a fort down by the canal.

I knew mine had the head of a woman with a cap behind her head. On one side 'Liberty' was engraved on the top and '1795' on the bottom. A small hole had been drilled above her head. Joseph had explained that these small coins were no longer in circulation. Figured someone had used it as an ornament.

I glared at Abigail. 'Let me have a closer look at that coin.'
Leaving it around her neck, she held it out for inspection.
'That *is* my coin. You're a thief!' I was furious.
'Hold up, kid. Calm down.' She explained how she'd found it in the envelope, and decided to try wearing it. Then more about her Aunt Hanna, the tin trunk and the family letters.

I didn't know what to do. If I could imagine the unimaginable, it sounded vaguely plausible.

She sat down, uninvited, on my bed. 'Alfred, I promise you. Everything I've told you is true.' She patted the spot beside her. 'Sit down and let's think what we can do about this.'

I plonked down beside her, keeping a careful distance. I didn't trust her.

She took a different tack. 'Are you interested in history? Looking at your collection, it would appear so. 'Cos, here's the thing – so am I. I'd really love to know what it's like to live in your times, and I'm super curious about what happens to your family. Well, *our* family, actually.'

'And I want to know more of the bizarre things you began to talk about downstairs,' I replied cautiously. 'But you can't stay. There's no way to hide you, even in the spare room. Mary Anne would quickly notice if food went missing. And you can't walk down the road dressed like that. You'd be in prison for vagrancy quicker than the time it takes to rattle a beggar's cup.'

She looked offended. 'I don't *want* to stay! And I'm not a vagrant. These ripped jeans are all the rage. My mother thinks it's silly to pay for jeans with holes in, but the really cool girls love them.'

I guessed that 'jeans' was her word for the tattered inexpressibles on her lower body. I pointed downward. 'You mean lots of women display their limbs like that?'

She snorted with amusement. 'Kid, you're nuts! If you mean legs, why don't you say so?'

I was shocked. 'You mustn't say 'legs'. No polite lady or girl would use that word!'

She put back her head and laughed. How I hated people laughing at me.

'Well, thank God I live in the 21st century. If you're referring to my jeans, I wear them most of the time, except when

I go to school. And my school skirt only comes to here.' She pointed to above her knees.

I shook my head. Scandalous!

Suddenly, she exclaimed, 'I've got an idea. Maybe, if I keep the cord but give you the coin back, I'll be able to get back to my own time, hopefully before my mother comes home. I had no problem handling the coin by itself. And tying the cord to the coin didn't do anything odd either. It wasn't until I put both over my head that I suddenly landed up in your century.'

I thought about this. What if her idea of separating the coin from the cord caused her to disappear as dramatically as she arrived?

She continued, talking so fast I had to listen extra hard to understand her odd accent. 'We know the coin ends up in my time. Maybe,' she paused, 'if I connect up the two objects again and slip them over my head, I might be able to come back to you whenever I like. That way, we can keep learning about each other's lives.'

She saw me hesitating. 'But even if we never meet again, aren't you pleased that your family story is being rediscovered in the 21st century?'

Silly question – of course I was. 'So, what *is* known about us?'

'I know hardly anything yet, sorry. Aunt Hanna and I just started sorting the stuff in her tin trunk today. But we're onto it – I'll be able to tell you more when I come back – if I can.'

She paused, then added, 'You might be able to help speed up the process; not everything's obvious from the letters. And, together we might be able to work out what your father's keeping from you. For a start, we noticed a lot of letters for the period between 1836 to 1839. After those dates, for a couple of years there were less. Did something change in your family in 1836?'

I explained about the rest of the family moving to Cincinnati last year.

'Why do you think your father wanted to move there? I mean, like, he was prepared to split up his family. That's pretty major.'

I paused before answering. 'He rattles on about how much easier it is to make a living, but I'm sure there's something else no-one will discuss with me. I do get riled when they treat me like a child.'

Abigail smirked. 'Well, you *are* a kid.'

'I'm not a kid. I wish you'd stop calling me that. It's a baby goat.'

She patted my arm. 'Relax, Alf. I'm teasing. But aren't children called kids?'

'Not that I've ever heard. It sounds right strange.'

With a shrug of her shoulders, she let the subject go. More seriously, she continued, 'Let's think about what we know. That letter you had in your hands when I landed up in your front room talked about nearly being caught by the sheriff. And in another one your father was getting pretty hot under the collar about abolition. I haven't had a chance to find out what that's all about.'

'Oh, if it's to do with abolition, he's been drumming on about that for ages. Before he removed to Cincinnati, he talked about it all the time. In truth, he got a bit boring. When my Pa gets churned up about something I mostly stop listening.'

Abigail frowned. 'Could it be abolition of slavery?'

'Yes, I think so,' I replied. 'Something's going on, but no-one goes into details. Why do you ask?'

'Well, I know America had slaves back in the day. Oh, and today I also read an article you wrote in 1858, about the first time you met a slave. You became quite a good writer. Or,' she looked confused, 'should I say you *will* become a good writer.'

I laughed. 'Really? My teacher would be impressed! He's always growling at me for sloppy spelling and grammar. What's the article about?'

'A little slave boy called Eli, who almost ran into you on the dock at New York. Your family was about to board a steamer to Albany.'

'Oh, I remember that very well. Did I write about the explosion?'

Abi looked at me, startled. 'No. It finished when the passengers were called to board the boat. What explosion?'

I leaned back against my pillow, getting comfortable as I prepared to tell the story.

'It was the most terrifying thing I've ever seen ...'

Chapter 6

Alfred
Hudson River 1834

It took some time to get everyone aboard the huge paddle steamer, but finally the bosun blew his whistle, the gangplank was raised, and with a blast of its horn the boat left the North Pier. We waved to our New York relatives until they were out of sight. Then Mother entered the ladies' saloon with the girls. I was told to stay with the men.

I was too excited to sit for long in our lounge. Once Father started reading a newspaper, I went exploring. Up and down the stairs connecting the decks I ran, keeping my head down when I went past the ladies' saloon.

Up top, above the saloons, was a promenade deck. Many passengers were enjoying the view as we headed north up the broad Hudson River. On either side were the housings of the two paddle wheels and, at the back, two towering funnels. Once I understood the layout of the boat, I went back to my favorite spot – watching the huge paddle wheels encased in their steel caging. The paddles dug deep, churning up the river, non-stop round and round. Spray, foam and water were pulled up by the blades and then, as they reached the top of their cycle, torrents of water spilled back to the river. Slurp up, splash out, tumble down. Swish, swoosh, kerchunk, kerchunk, kerchunk. On and on and on. Clank, thud and grind of the engine; the rhythm of falling water; the sharp smells of oil, coal, wood smoke and river water – I could have stayed there all day.

An hour or so later, Father and my brothers came out to keep me company. Father pointed to a smart double-masted sailing boat, its white sails trimmed to the wind. People were crowded on its deck and cockpit.

'If we were on one of those we'd take at least three days to reach Albany, and up to nine if the wind is contrary,' he said. 'On this fine vessel we'll be there in just over a day, or maybe a day and a half, depending on the steamer's speed and how long it takes to move passengers and their goods off and on at the landings. Steam power is a magnificent invention.'

'But Pa, not all steamboats are safe,' argued Joseph. He and his bride, Mary Anne, were traveling with us, for he and Father were going into business together.

'That's quite true – if you've got a captain who fancies himself as a racer. I asked around before I chose this vessel. I'm told our captain is a steady fellow. Doesn't put his boat or the lives of his passengers at risk.'

'But Papa, surely it's good to get there faster,' I piped up. 'Racing sounds like fun.'

'Not if you push your boat so hard that the boilers blow up.'

Father had scarce finished his sentence when two steamers came apace up the river behind us. Smelly black smoke and red sparks poured out of their smoke stacks. Even above the beat of our engine and the pounding churn of the wheels, we could hear the roar of their engines and shouts coming from both boats.

'You want to know about racing? Watch these fellows,' said Father, pointing behind us.

As the two rivals drew near, our vessel moved closer to the shore, giving the dueling boats more room.

I felt a slight list of our boat as the people on our decks surged, first to the side and then forward to watch as the competitors raced past us. We did the same; it was so exciting. We could see men grabbing logs of wood from the piles on the decks, hurling them to the stokers in the engine rooms. Passengers on both boats shouted and cheered as first one boat, then the other, drew ahead. Soon they were a quarter-mile in front of us.

Then, for a moment, the smoke from one of the boats became even blacker and more dense. Suddenly – a terrible bang. Pieces of wood and metal flew into the air. Flames shot out from the middle of the boat. Above the roar of the explosion we heard screams. Men, women and children were thrown into the water. In moments, the back of the boat started tilting down. The bow followed a few minutes later. With terrifying speed, it disappeared, taking those closest with it. They didn't rise again. Cries and shouts came from all over our boat as we stared in disbelief at the lethal whirl-pool ahead.

Pieces of wood torn from the boat, baskets, clothing, firewood from the deck – all littered the river. And people. Bodies. Everywhere. Some splashed. Others didn't. Couldn't. Planks burned. Slicks of oil coated the water.

As we steamed swiftly to the scene, our sailors and many of the men, including my father and brothers, raced around looking for anything they could use to help people stay afloat until they could be rescued. Women and children crowded the rails, aghast.

'Run up to the top deck, Alf and Jane,' Father yelled. 'Out of the way. Quick.' We did as we were told. Found a spot immediately above our family.

Once we got close to the wreckage and people in the water, our boat's engine was shut down and the paddle wheels stopped. Men leaned over the rails. They began to haul survivors aboard.

The competing boat slowed but it had been going so fast, it took ages to come back. By then, our vessel and nearby sail boats had already saved a good number of survivors.

On the higher deck we could see more. I could scarce breathe for the horror of it. People were grasping or half-lying on anything that floated. A few started swimming to the nearest shore, a couple of hundred yards away. And then I started noticing the ones who didn't move. A tiny girl, her face half-blown off but a white bonnet still around her neck; a large woman with no head, blood pumping from the neck and ripped petticoat flounces trailing behind; a leg with a boot but no body; a man floating face-down in the stream, blood coloring the water around him. Everywhere there were bodies.

Debris began to bounce against the side of our boat. I saw a small boy in a blue jacket clinging to a thick plank of wood, only a couple of feet off our side. It was the child from the dock.

'Thomas,' I shouted to my brother below. 'It's that little slave boy, Eli.' I couldn't just watch. I ran down to join them, Jane hard on my heels.

Joseph and Thomas threw him a rope. He held to his board tight as an oyster on a rock. The rope thumped back against the side of the boat. They threw again, yelling at him to reach out. Again, he did nothing to grab it.

'What can we do?' said Joseph. 'He's too scared to let go.'

Father looked at Joseph and Thomas, all togged up with their laced-up boots, jackets, ties and tight-fitting inexpressibles. 'There must be a way.' Then his eyes lit on me in my looser-fitting clothes, easily removed low-sided boots, no tie and a jacket that could be shrugged off in an instant.

'Alf, you can swim. If we lower you down, could you could tie the rope round him? Once we've got him to safety we'll haul you up.'

Mother was about to argue but stopped. She could see sense in the plan.

I never hesitated. In moments I was stripped down to my breeches. In less time than it takes to tell this tale, I was in the water beside Eli. I trod water as I tied the rope under his skinny arms. Thank goodness my brothers had taught me knots as we'd sat around the parlor fire on long winter nights.

He was crying. 'Oh young massa, I think I goin' to Jesus this time, for shure.'

'He's not ready for you yet, Eli. We'll have you safe in no time,' I told him. Waved at the family to haul away. Took my turn at looping an arm over the plank.

Thin-shanked yellow-stockinged legs, now without their fancy black shoes, rose above my head. Short minutes later I was beside him, the two of us dripping on the deck.

Mother took charge. 'Sarah, would you please help Alf. I'll look after this little fellow.'

She stripped off Eli's wet clothes, rubbed him down briskly with a towel and put him into my spare set of clothes; one of the girls must have fetched them while I was taking my unscheduled swim. He was a lot smaller than me; the trouser legs and shirt cuffs had to be rolled up. Then she wrapped the shocked and shivering child warmly in a blanket.

'My sons tell me your name is Eli,' she said kindly, taking the little boy on to her lap and giving him a good cuddle. 'Is that right?'

He nodded, wordless.

'Do you know where you were traveling to or who your mistress was planning to visit?'

'I be goin' with Miz Gerard an' Hetty,' he stuttered through blue lips, 'but I don' know where they be an' I don' know where us be goin'. I couldn' see 'em. An' I los' the dog agin.' He knuckled tears out of his eyes, trying to be brave.

'Well dear, there's lots of people helping. Other boats might have picked them up. You're safe with us for now.'

Sarah, Mother's helper at fourteen as well as her namesake, gave me a big hug as she helped me towel off. I had to stay in my wet trousers but at least my shirt was dry. 'Well done, little brother. You did a good thing there.'

Our men were called to help pull other survivors aboard, while we stood in a circle around Eli and Mother. After giving him some of our sandwiches and lemonade, Jane and I were left to look after him in the ladies' saloon while Mother and the girls went to aid others. Mother was great in an emergency. Quite unflappable.

I fished my wooden Jacob's Ladder out of my bag and tried to entertain him. It helped a little. At least he stopped crying. After about ten minutes his teeth stopped chattering. But he didn't want to talk.

A crew member put his head in the door. 'Please take all survivors to the main saloon so they can look for their families.' As he walked away I heard him mutter, 'If they're still alive, God help them.'

We helped Eli wrap the blanket securely around his shoulders and walked with him into the main cabin.

The room was overflowing with people, many of them lying injured on benches, tables or even the floor. Two men with shirt sleeves rolled up, doctors I guessed, were working with the injured and giving instructions to helpers, our mother and big sisters among them. As we stood, wondering where to go, a steward ran past with an armful of grey blankets. Shocked and exhausted survivors sat, sprawled or lay wherever they could find a spot without getting trodden on.

Pools of dirty water, river weed and blood were being ground into the fine carpet. All was noise and confusion. Rescuers assisted more people in, then raced back to their posts. I heard a man say to his companion as they dashed past, 'Time's running out. Most of them can't swim.'

We moved into the room, clear of the doorway. I wasn't sure where to go. Eli scanned the room. Suddenly he gave a glad cry, dropped the blanket and ran across the room, wrapping his arms around a shivering young woman sitting on the floor, slumped against a wall. It was the plainly dressed older girl we'd seen on the wharf, carrying the baskets.

'Hetty, Hetty, you 'live!'

We followed our charge. The slender young woman looked as overcome as the child. With a shriek of thankfulness she pulled him into a tight embrace, getting his (well, my) dry clothes wet. 'Oh baby, you here. Praise da Lord.'

'Here miss, take our blanket,' said Jane, who'd stopped to pick it up.

'Thank 'e, miss.' As she wrapped it around her shoulders, Hetty looked up at us. Looked again – at me. 'Ain't you da boy on dock, back in da city? This a good thing you done, helpin' this chile.'

Cuddling Eli, she said to him, 'You jus' rest here now a bit. Hetty try an' think what us gonna do. Miz Gerard be drownded. I seed her go down – her petticoats too heavy.' She looked frightened. 'We all on our own. Don' know nobody.'

This was too big a problem for me and Jane. 'Miss, I'll get my father. He might be able to help,' I said.

We found Father, by now resting against the rail with our brothers, watching the scene. The only people left in the water were beyond our help. Smaller boats, lower to the water, were continuing the dreadful task of hauling in bodies and body parts.

As we gabbled our story, we didn't notice an interested listener. A tall sailor, almost as dark-skinned as Eli, was coiling ropes just behind us.

'Pa,' said Thomas, 'I believe the child and young woman are slaves, from what I observed back in New York. If their owner has drowned, what will become of them now?'

'Scuse me, genl'mens. P'raps I kin help. We has people 'long the river what helps our folks in need. Would you mind takin' me to dis young woman?'

We led him to Hetty, then stepped back to let them talk. As the sailor spoke quietly, Hetty's look of despair faded. First she looked disbelieving, then came a smile. Whatever he told her, it seemed it was good news. I wondered what it could be.

Chapter 7

Alfred
Utica 1837 and the Hudson River 1834

'Oh my God! What a terrible thing,' gasped Abigail. 'You were very brave, Alf. And fancy it being the same little boy you'd seen back in New York! Then what happened?'
I continued my tale.

Our next stop was Peekskill, but much later than expected. It was awful to see the shock and fear of the people waiting on the dock as we got close enough for someone to call out the news.

The dock workers quickly threw up a cordon to keep the crowd back. The survivors were assisted off first. Next, our disembarking passengers. Then male travelers, including my two brothers and father, helped the sailors off with the corpses our people had been able to reach. They carried them to a shed on the dock. No-one could see who they were, for someone had covered their faces with white table napkins. As they passed, people fell silent. Then, a woman pushed out of the crowd, screaming.

'That's me man. Them's his boots.' She threw herself on the body, forcing the men to lay their sad burden down. Another woman came out of the crowd. Pulled her back so the grim unloading could continue. Others started to sob and wail.

Onboard and out of the way, I sat on a seat with my mother and Jane, watching for Eli and Hetty. Once the tragic procession had left the boat, I noticed the big sailor helping them descend the gangplank. No-one took notice of two blacks, the man carrying a small child, as they quietly stepped clear of the chaos on the dock.

They disappeared from view for a few minutes. Then I spotted them again, talking to a humbly dressed elderly colored couple who stood a little apart from the crowd. The old lady gave Hetty and Eli a big hug. Her husband shook the hand of their rescuer, who then headed back to our ship. The four quickly disappeared.

'What do you think happened to Hetty and Eli?' Abigail asked.

'That's a curious thing. I asked my mother but at first she didn't answer. Just held Jane and me tight. But something Thomas had said, back in New York, was worrying me, so I asked again.

'Mama, what happens to a slave if their owner dies? Eli and Hetty don't have any money. Who will look after them?'

'She'd sighed, then replied, "Normally they're bequeathed to someone in the family. Or they're sold at auction. They're considered part of the estate of the person who's departed."

'Then she added, "I'm sure that sailor's friends will get Eli and Hetty to safety. It might not be where they thought they were going. I have a feeling they'll be very happy in their new situation."

'It seemed an odd thing to say. I quizzed her, but she would say no more. I believe she knew more than she was telling.

'I had horrible dreams about that day for a long time, but I'm real glad that we were able to save Eli. And find someone to help him and Hetty. I felt good about giving him my clothes, too. Mother was the only one bothered that I had no clean garments 'til we reached Utica four days later.'

Abigail sighed. 'You'll probably never know what happened to them. Let's go back to the original question – what your father and brother are keeping from you. So, your father doesn't like slavery?'

'I'd put it much stronger than that. He *hates* slavery.'

She replied, 'In another letter by your father that I read today, he sounded very cranky. If I can remember it correctly, he was saying that everyone had the right to life, liberty and the pursuit of happiness – all men, no matter their color. Then he went on to say how he didn't think abolition would go ahead in Cincinnati. I think this secret must be something to do with abolition of slavery, Alf. Let's see if we can piece it together. When did your father first start talking seriously about abolition?'

'I remember well. It was when Mr Gerrit Smith invited him to an abolition convention here in Utica. About two years ago …'

Just then we heard a door shutting downstairs.

'Oh no. That'll be my good-sister home,' I said.

'Damn! Sounds like I'd better try and go home – if I can,' said Abigail. 'We haven't got very far on your family secret yet, have we!'

'And you've not told me anything about the future, except that I can write a good article,' I sighed.

She touched the coin. 'Well, fingers crossed this little trick works again, and I can come back soon. If there's a next time I'll tell you more about my world, and you must remember to tell me about that convention.'

We heard Mary Anne call, 'Alf, where are you?' Footsteps began to ascend the stairs.

Abigail looked at me. 'Here goes, kid.'

I gave her a dirty look.

She giggled. 'Sorry. Forgot you don't like being called that.'

With the cord still over her head she swiftly started to detach the coin.

'Hold the coin, Alf. I don't know exactly at what stage the magic happens,' she urged.

Sure enough, the second it was completely free of the cord, with the tips of my fingers holding it tightly, Abigail disappeared. I sat there blinking, looking at the coin in my hand and the dent in my quilt where she'd just been sitting. If I hadn't seen it with my own eyes, I would never have believed it possible.

Thirty seconds later, Mary Anne poked her head around the door. 'What are you doing up here, Alf? You forgot to stoke the fire. Just as well I wasn't away long or we'd not have the soup ready for luncheon.'

I mumbled a reply that, thank goodness, she took little notice of, for I could not have made an intelligent response. Mary Anne was used to me forgetting my chores, but this was for a very different reason. My head was flipping somersaults in disbelief.

Tucked in bed that night, as I played back the events of the day and the discourse with my strange visitor, I thought again of the day Mr Gerrit Smith and my father went to the Bleecker street convention.

Chapter 8

Alfred
Utica October 1835

I was engaged in one of my favorite after-school jobs, re-stocking the candy jars, when a tall man of middle years walked in. He had a strong face, firm mouth, a beak of a nose and a determined air. Father was behind the counter.

'Good afternoon. My name is Gerrit Smith. And you're Mr Burnett, I presume? You've a fine business here.'

They talked for some time. I took little notice. All I remembered later was some reference to a convention and that Father sounded interested.

At dinner time Father mentioned his visitor.

'Did he buy any cookies, Papa?' asked Ann. She was a couple of years older than me, and took a keen interest in our daily sales.

'No, child. He's one of the wealthiest men in the state and a very important man around these parts. His cooks make all the breads, biscuits, pastries and pies he and his family could possibly ever consume. However, he did purchase some marzipan and candied orange peel for the children of his staff. He'd ridden the thirty miles from his Peterboro property to meet with Mr Alvan Stewart, the lawyer. With time to spare for his appointment, he wandered into our store.'

I chipped in. 'You seemed to have a fine discourse.'

'Indeed. I feel honored to have met him. He's very well-known for his generosity to worthwhile causes. He was interested to hear my views on the abolition of slavery.'

'What did you say?' queried Sarah.

'That I hate the very idea of slavery but am not yet fixed in my ideas as how best to halt the vile practice. We were in complete agreement about the immorality of it. No man should be the property of another. But the best way to stop it is a topic of hot debate.'

'So how can it be stopped?' Sarah wanted to know.

'There are three main ways. Immediate abolition. Then there's gradual abolition, as happened here in the northern states. Thirdly is colonization – sending them back to Africa. I'm not sure yet as to which is best. Thus far, Mr Smith's thinking is that we should help them return to their original homes. To that end, he's a member of the Colonization Society but, like me, he's open to hearing other ideas.'

This started a spirited discussion around the table. I didn't bother to join in. Instead, I thought about what bait I might try next time I could get away fishing. Seamus had shown me a good spot beside the new Chenango Canal. From one of its backwaters you could see the dirty coal boats going to and from Pennsylvania. But, much more importantly, trout fair begged to jump on a fellow's line. It was very useful having so many good waterways all close to Utica.

I came out of my reverie to hear Father say, 'There's been a lot of argument recently about the Abolition Convention to be held here next Wednesday. Apparently, they want to form a New York State Anti-Slavery Society. I've heard a number of our customers talking about it. Seems many of the leading citizens of the city don't want any truck with abolitionists. Some of them accept colonization, the method Mr Smith has some understanding of, but they're not in favor of immediate or even gradual abolition across the whole country. They hate abolitionists. Say they're extremists and bad for business.'

Sarah, chin in hand, leaned forward. At fifteen she took after our mother, not only with her quick mind but also her fair hair and piercing blue eyes. 'I heard that the abolitionists are struggling to find a venue. They wanted to hold it in the Court House but there was too much dispute. Many residents feel strongly that the hall of justice should not be desecrated by such a radical meeting.'

'Yes,' Father replied. 'Mr Smith and I discussed that. He's curious to know what all the fuss is about. I am too. So he invited me to accompany him to the convention. He's interested to see how their opinions marry up with his beliefs on the matter. It's only right to give these people a fair hearing before I firm up my thinking.'

Mother frowned. I could tell she was thinking about the work he'd not be doing on a business day. 'So, if they're not allowed to hold it at the Court House, where are they meeting, Cornelius?'

'Just round the corner. At the Bleecker street church. Don't worry, Mother. I can get a good amount of work done before I go out. I don't imagine it will go on for too long.'

Mother looked even less happy. 'Are you sure you want to attend such an event, Cornelius? You know this is not the time to be getting distracted, just when the business is getting nicely established.'

She should have known better. Anyone suggesting my father shouldn't do something was sure to send him in the direction they didn't want.

Little did any of us realize that Father was a week away from being permanently distracted – for the rest of his life.

The day of the convention, October 21st 1835, I had a heavy head cold.

'No school for you today, Alfred,' said Mother firmly. She saw my look of delight and added, 'But if you're too sick to go to school, you're too sick to wander around. Bed for you, and I don't want to see you unless you're down for the privy or your lunch.' I didn't waste breath arguing.

Actually, it wasn't too much of a hardship. I was reading *Peter Parley's Story of the Trapper* and had just reached the part where Daniel arrived back at his camp and found his son had disappeared. Maybe stolen by Indians. Propped up in bed in my night shirt, I was deeply absorbed when I heard unusual noises coming from the direction of Bleecker street. With my room at the back of the house, I often heard church bells. This was certainly not them. Putting down my book, I sat up and listened. Men's voices. Shouts and yells.

In a flash my clothes were on and I was downstairs. Next, a check for inconvenient adults. Joseph was in the store; that exit was blocked. It had to be through the back door. I peeked into the kitchen. At that moment Mother had her back to me. Pot mitten on her hand, she was bent over the oven, inspecting something delicious-smelling. Our midday dinner, no doubt. I slipped silently past, out the open back door. Round to the front garden. A quick jump over the low fence. In a twinkle I was at the corner and turning into Bleecker street.

From there I could see a big crowd of men, and a few women, outside the church. They sure looked riled up. I wriggled my way to the front. Ignoring the yelps of annoyed people as I jostled them, I clambered up the steps to peer through the big central door into the crowded building.

In the pews, the attendees were on their feet. Half-way up the aisle I spotted my father on the edge of a row. He and many others were waving fists angrily. People all through the building shouted. No-one listened. Hymn books and other small items were thrown. At the front, below the pulpit, about twenty-five men were arguing. Some of them were even fighting – in a *church*!

As I stood there, trying to make sense of the scene, there was movement in the throng behind me. I looked back to see people being shoved out of the way by a group of tough-looking fellows carrying a long fireman's ladder. They raised it against the church wall and two started climbing, encouraged by their supporters. Were they going to rip off roof tiles and throw them at the people inside, I wondered?

A man beside me gasped as the ruffians started to climb. Forcing his way inside, he dashed up to the group at the front. I saw him tap one of them urgently on the shoulder. In moments they were both back on the step. The new man almost stood on me as he addressed the rowdy crowd with a strong clear voice.

'This is private property. Please respect it. We don't want violence and damage to a holy building. I ask you to go back to your own affairs and allow us to attend to ours.'

To emphasize his point, he stepped over to the ladder and gave it a shake. The watching crowd laughed as the would-be trouble-makers sheepishly began to climb back down.

But then the mood of the people changed again. A big chap with bushy side-whiskers and a watch chain over a drum-tight belly wobbled importantly up the steps to confront the speaker. Forced to step aside, I tumbled down into the tightly pressed throng below. Several whacks and shoves from irate observers landed on my head, shoulders and legs as I fell. The fat-bellied man shouted out his message so the people behind could hear.

'The peace of this city *is* our affair. You damned abolitionists are a threat to it. We demand you get these people to leave, or we will continue. Your church is causing trouble by harboring these fanatics. If you allow them to carry on, we make no promises to protect your property. We are determined that Utica will not be tainted with this fanatical behavior.'

The ranting on both sides continued for some minutes. Then I heard a loud voice inside, shouting above the noise.

'All persons who wish to attend this convention without disruption are welcome to assemble at my home in Peterboro tomorrow.'

Surely Mr Smith was giving that invitation? He was the only one in Peterboro with a mansion big enough to hold such a crowd.

People started flowing out of the church like a dislodged swarm of bees, buzzing with anger. I made myself scarce. A conversation with Father's belt around my nether regions did not appeal. I skipped back home, entering by the garden again. Mother thought I'd just been to the privy.

The next day Father was absent from the breakfast table and didn't return until I was in bed. I put the incident out of my mind and went back to my own concerns – fishing, swimming, finding more treasures for my growing science and curios collection, school and diverse tasks for the bakery.

Six days later I was in the parlor laying the fire; the nights had started drawing in and we often sat there in the evenings. Some papers had been left on Father's chair. A quick look showed they were proceedings of the re-convened convention held at Peterboro. I stopped to read. Apparently Mr Smith had been elected as chairman. He'd decided that colonization was out; immediate abolition was the course he'd chosen to put his support behind. So much for being only an interested observer!

His speech to the delegates was reported.

My hatred of slavery always existed and always will. We have and hold probably between five and six million slaves in the United States. I will fight the institution that makes this thing possible as long as I am able and when I can no longer fight, I will bequeath the contest to my children. I don't expect to live to see slavery abolished, but the wicked institution will and must go. Slavery and liberty cannot exist side by side; one of the two must surrender.

From then on, Father became increasingly absent from work. He had many meetings with Mr Smith, Mr Alvan

Stewart and Mr James DeLong, another wealthy businessman with a big home on upper John street. Other men began to call into the store, not to buy bread, cakes or sweets, but to talk to Father in low voices. They would never state their business when customers were in the store. He'd step outside to speak with them, or they'd exchange a few quiet words and be gone.

For the next ten months events continued on pretty smoothly, at least for me. However, I often overheard arguments between my parents. It seemed that Mother was concerned about Father's focus, or lack of it, on our business. But they'd always bickered so I took little notice.

Then came major upheaval, with the move to Cincinnati for all the family except Joseph, Mary Anne and me. I didn't really understand why they'd shifted. The official story was that Cincinnati, with a population of 40,000 as opposed to Utica's 8,000, had much better opportunities for a big family. But I suspected there was more to it, for one Sunday I heard Father talking to our minister on the church steps. Something about being called to till the fields of a mighty endeavor. I did not take his meaning.

He spotted me listening. 'Alf, go home with your mother.'

As I came up behind Mother and Joseph I heard her say, 'I wish we were staying here where your father has fewer opportunities to poke his nose into trouble.'

'What trouble?' I piped up from behind.

'Alfred, where did you spring from? I thought you were with your father.' She looked secretive. Didn't answer my question. Nothing further was said on the matter in my hearing.

Chapter 9

Abigail
Auckland January 2015

'Yowch,' I spluttered, as I found myself sprawled on the floor again, but this time it was *my* floor. I was back in my bedroom. This landing on my bum was becoming a bit tiresome; at this rate I'd have a bruised backside.

How much time had passed? I looked around my room. My cell was still on the bed where I'd thrown it. The library book I'd finished earlier was where I'd left it before walking round to Aunt Hanna's with the pie. Everything looked just as before. Except for one thing. No coin.

I scrambled to my feet, checking the time on the phone as I did. To my amazement, it was still 10pm, the same as before I did my *Back to the Future* impersonation and landed in 1837. How did that work? I'd been gone nearly an hour. Had I imagined the whole thing? I looked down. Only the thin cord was hanging round my neck.

I ran out to the dining room. Scrabbled through the letters, looking for the coin. Nothing. Where was it? Back to my bedroom. Gave a sigh of relief when I found it sitting innocently on the bureau beside my hairbrush.

I finished tidying up, put the coin carefully in a small earring bag in my jewelry box, the cord well away from it in another drawer, and took my over-stretched brain to bed.

As I lay there, running through the events of the day, I tried to make sense of what I'd just experienced. Could I tell anyone? Mum would be sure I'd taken leave of my senses. She had enough to worry about. It was only six months since Dad had died and we both missed him dreadfully.

Could I tell Aunt Hanna? She was pretty broadminded, but this little escapade was way out there. I didn't want her to scoff or disbelieve, or worry that I was doing dumb things like drugs. So, I hugged my adventure to myself.

Sleep did not come for a long time.

On waking, my first thought was that I'd had a *very* vivid and unusual dream. But – I knew it wasn't. I reached for my phone, to check out the unusual name Alfred had mentioned just before I did my vanishing act. What was it? Oh yes, Gerrit Smith.

To my shock, I found him! He became a really big deal in the fight to end slavery. There had indeed been an anti-slavery meeting in Utica in 1835 disrupted by a mob; the experience caused Smith to become totally hard core about the issue. Maybe it had the same effect on Alf's dad?

I felt really weird. Here was I, Abigail Burnett, a teenager in an ordinary life in quiet little New Zealand, and yesterday I'd talked to a boy who must have died well over 100 years ago. I had to know more. I finished a quick breakfast, then looked in on Mum, already at work in her office.

'I'm just biking round to Aunt Hanna's. Anything you want me to take?'

She looked up from the designs spread over her desk. An empty coffee mug suggested she's started early. She was much tidier than Aunt Hanna. A file holder of paperwork was neatly to the side of her big screens and a line-up of awards for graphic design decorated one wall of her office. Through the window, morning sun lit up the dark green trees on the side of Mt Eden, its summit showing above our neighbors' expensively restored bungalows.

'All good here, love. Just bring back the pie dish if you wouldn't mind,' and back to her work she went.

I was pretty lucky with my mum, not like some of my friends. She was firm but fair. Gave me a lot of freedom, but expected to be obeyed about things like curfews. Maybe because she was only twenty when she had me, people often asked if we were sisters. Mum would look pleased, while I tried to hold back a snort of disagreement. I suppose it was a compliment to her youthful looks. Mind you, sometimes her dress sense was a bit dire. No-one would accuse us of shopping at the same places, that's for sure.

Grabbing my back pack, I loaded in my Grumpy Queenie tin with the letters, hesitating over the coin but eventually left it safely in my drawer.

Aunt Hanna was tying up tomatoes when I walked round the side of the house.

'Pop the kettle on,' she called when she saw me. 'I'll just finish up here.'

Her coffee was nearly cold by the time she wandered in. 'Sorry, pet. I couldn't help dead-heading the dahlias as I came past. They don't keep flowering into the autumn if I don't cut the spent flowers off quickly.'

I didn't care about dead flower heads; I was itching to know more about dead relatives. Except they didn't seem dead anymore, given I'd been chatting to one yesterday.

'From what I've been able to find out,' I was careful what I said, 'I think there might be something to do with abolition of slavery going on. Did you get time to read any more letters last night?'

'I started further back,' she replied. 'Decided I might as well get the story straight so I could work out who everyone was and where they all connected. The main letters are between various members of the Burnett family. The parents who emigrated from England to New York city were Cornelius and Sarah. Father took most of the boys in 1830, and went back for his wife and the rest of the children during summer, 1831. Of their eight children, two died before they'd been in New York three years. One daughter got scarlet fever, a killer back then, and the next year one of their sons, described as gifted, was taken by cholera.

'After that, Sarah couldn't wait to get out of New York, convinced that the airs of a big city were killing her family. She was on the right track, except it was more likely the water; the sanitation standards of those days were terrible. Sewage often contaminated the drinking water, and dirty streets and effluent flowed into the rivers and waterways.'

She shuddered. 'I hate to think of how smelly and dirty the cities and towns were in those times. These days we kick up a fuss if the slightest hint of pollution hits our water supplies, or our rubbish doesn't get collected on the right day.

'But what about your research? Was there anything interesting in the letters you took home?'

I nodded. 'I've solved one puzzle. The reason there's more letters from 1836 is, that's when the parents and daughters moved from Utica to Cincinnati. They left behind three sons. Joseph, the oldest one, and his wife Mary Anne, carried on the business in Utica. Alfred, the youngest boy, remained with them. Thomas, the second son, went to Syracuse. He was working for another baker.'

I shared what I'd discovered about the distances and gave a brief overview of the various family matters discussed in the letters. I so wanted to tell about my surprise visit, but didn't dare. It was just too crazy.

We finished our morning tea and went to her dining table, still covered with papers. She reached for a document set apart from the many piles.

'I've found another article by Alfred. It was underneath the cardboard that lined the bottom of the trunk.'

Chapter 10

Abigail
Auckland January 2015

Ireached for it eagerly. It was another instalment from the same magazine as before – the **Freedom Journal.** This time it was *Issue 27, June* 1858. For a moment I wondered where *Issue 26* had gone, but quickly realized it must have covered the explosion. So – it didn't matter. I'd heard it from the source!

Part III: *In Which I Am Introduced to the Erie Canal But Lose My Parents*

By Our Correspondent, Alfred Burnett

[In our last instalment we left Alfred and his family, in 1834, relocating to Utica, upstate New York. After the paddle steamer disaster on the Hudson River they'd watched little Eli, whom Alf had rescued from drowning, and his fellow slave Hetty, being assisted ashore by a helpful sailor. The steamer they were on then continued on to Albany.]

Once we disembarked at Albany it was time to meet this mighty Erie Canal everyone kept talking about. I looked around the landing stage and boat harbor in surprise. What could all the fuss be about? How could these low-slung long skinny boats and the narrow strip of water leading away from the crowded landing be as important as I'd heard? It looked like a boring ditch in comparison to the wide waters we'd just traveled. Perhaps the detractors who scathingly referred to it as Clinton's Ditch had the right of it. I wondered if Governor Clinton cared.

To be sure, there was noise and bustle. Loaded carts came and went. People shouted. Animals were chivvied and chased by men with sticks and barking dogs. But there were no big vessels, nor huge black clouds of smoke pouring from tall stacks, except from the steamer we'd just left.

'Papa, where are the engines?' He'd taken me for a stroll along the landing to keep me occupied. We fellows seemed to spend a lot of time waiting while women fussed about their boxes, bags and cloaks. We threaded our way past piles of freight, huddles of people, laden carts, crowded carriages and deep and dusty storage sheds.

'No modern machines on these boats, Alf,' he explained. 'It's all horse or mule power.' He gestured to a line of animals tethered further back from the boats, most with noses in feed bags. Their tails flicked constantly, trying to dislodge the hovering flies attracted by manure and sweat. Some boys, many of them in shabby ill-fitting clothes, tended the animals. Others squatted in a circle round the back of a shed and out of the wind. If I wasn't much mistaken, a marble game was in progress. I marked the spot. If I could escape parental eyes, maybe I could get in a game. My marbles were always in my pocket.

Having reached the end of the main landing, we turned back. As we strolled past the horses and mules again, Father said, 'You'll be surprised how quickly ground is covered with these critters, even though they generally pull the vessels at only about four miles an hour. They could go faster, but they're not allowed. Too much speed damages the walls of the canal. If the packets weren't so packed with folks heading west, they'd be quite a pleasant way to move through the countryside.'

'Why are we traveling on a boat instead of the road?'

'Because roads are so uncomfortable and expensive. I'd far rather go by canal. It's a lot easier on the body than being jarred and jolted through potholes, deep mud and rocky roads on a stage coach. On a packet, weather permitting, you can get out and stroll along the towpath if you feel crowded. None of that in a stage coach. There you're either riding outside in all weathers or squashed inside with smelly strangers.'

The rest of the family came back into view. Mother beckoned us over to where the seven of them stood with their hand luggage. She had her organizing look.

'After all the drama we've just gone through I need a good night's sleep in a proper bed, Cornelius. I don't know what you want to do, but the girls and I will take the train to Schenectady. I'd rather have a one-hour train ride than sit for at least twenty-four hours on the packet as it ascends that big series of locks. Alf can come with us. Joseph, would you like to be our escort?'

Joseph hesitated. Mary Anne gave her husband a sweet look and just like that, he agreed. I resolved not to be so attached to my wife's petticoats when I grew up.

'I'm for the Cohoes Falls on the packet, Mother.' Father spoke firmly. 'I want to see those twenty-seven locks.'

'Oh, can I go with Father?' I pleaded.

'I'm not keen. How do I know you'll behave yourself and not go wandering off?'

'Oh, let him come, Sarah. It'll be good for him. The Erie Canal is one of the greatest engineering feats of modern time. The Eighth Wonder of the World, many call it, and the system of locks they've developed to get up the Cohoes Falls is a significant part of that reputation.'

I looked up hopefully at Papa. He didn't often stick up for me against Mother's wishes.

She sighed. Crossed her arms. 'I don't much like the idea, Cornelius. Will you be able to keep a close eye on him? You know how he's always dashing off on a whim. I have the devil's own job to keep track of the child. And when you get talking to someone about your enthusiasms, you forget to notice what he's up to.'

Father looked as annoyed as I felt at being called to task. I fidgeted as I listened to this irritating discussion. How I wished they'd stop talking about me as if I wasn't there.

'What about me?' asked Thomas, standing solid and patient. 'Shall I go with Pa?'

'I'm just getting to you, son.' My mother would have made a good sergeant major had she been a man. 'I want you to travel on the line boat with our household goods. I know you and Joseph saw that everything was loaded, but I worry about a careless crew member unloading some of our boxes at the wrong town.'

I overheard Joseph whisper quietly to Mary Anne, 'It's as well no young women are likely to be on Thomas's boat, else I would still fear for our possessions.' She chuckled.

'Perhaps I could go with Thomas instead,' I piped up. He still remembered what it was like to be forever under the eye of interfering adults. He didn't talk down to me and I could pretty much do what I liked when I was with him.

Mother gave me one of her 'don't mess with me' glares. Just then the call came for all train passengers to depart for the terminus.

'All … right,' she reluctantly agreed. 'Sort it out between the two of you. But for goodness' sakes, don't let him wander off. Alfred, you mind your father.'

Joseph and the women hurried to grab their carpet bags. With a flurry, they were gone.

Father and Thomas looked at each other. Looked at me. 'I think you should be with me, Alf,' said Father. 'But wait here near the agents' offices while I go talk to our captain.'

'I need to go back to the line boat and make sure they can take me, let alone a small boy. I'd be happy to take you, but the captain might not want any more passengers,' said Thomas. He headed off to a different jetty, where his boat was loading the last of its freight.

I looked around. On one side was a big group of fair-headed people, all speaking at once in a strange language. A roly-poly lady, blonde braids twisted tightly around her ears, handed out biscuits from a box. Nearer the wharf two little children played tag around the legs of a small family group. As their game took them very close to the water's edge, they got a sharp reprimand and a slap from an anxious mother.

I stood there for a few minutes. Father and Thomas were taking a long time. No-one was interested in me. Perhaps those boys round the back of the shed would still be playing marbles. Picking up my bag, I wandered back along the landing to see if I could get into the game.

'Hey boy, ya wanna play?' said one of the bigger lads, glancing up to see me watching.

No second invitation was needed. I was in like a robber's dog.

Within a few minutes I'd scored a couple of beauties. Then my best aggie marble was captured by a dark-haired skinny boy of similar age to me. We were playing for keeps. I wanted it back. I focused more. Engrossed in the game, time passed.

Our group started to dwindle. From time to time a shout came from one of the boats, or someone would pop their head around the corner of the shed to summon one of the boys. Whoever was called would pocket his marbles, untether his animals, and head away.

'What boat are you on?' casually asked Hughie, the boy who'd won my aggie. We were about to play another round. I was still trying to get it back.

'I don't know. My father and brother are deciding that.'

Come to think of it, they'd been gone a long time. I stood up and peered round the corner of the shed, back to where Father had told me to wait. Seagulls squabbled over some crumbs but the waiting passengers had disappeared. I took a few steps to get a better view. Gazed around.

Where were my father and brother? I couldn't see either them or the boats they'd each headed to.

Suddenly I felt really scared. What if I'd been left behind? I had no money. No food. Now it looked as though I had no family or transport either. I knew no-one and I was in a strange town.

Hughie glanced over. 'What's up?' he called.

'I think they've left me behind.' My voice wobbled.

He pocketed his marbles, including my aggie. 'Come with me. My family runs one of the freighters. We live on the canal so I know most of the boats and crews. We'll find them.'

I remembered to pick up my bag from where I'd safely tucked it and scurried after my maybe-rescuer.

A few queries later, my worst fears were realized. My father's packet and the line boat carrying Thomas and all our possessions had both gone. I was all alone. Gulp. I hoped any onlookers would think it was dirt I was rubbing out of my eye. What would become of me?

I looked anxiously around. Turned back to Hughie.
He'd disappeared too.
I sat down on a convenient bollard and cried.

Watch for next month's exciting episode:
Alfred Earns His Passage

I looked over at Aunt Hanna. She was holding a magnifying glass, using it to peer at a page of handwriting.

'You don't have any other boxes with old papers, do you?' I asked. She didn't answer.

I tried again. 'Aunt Hanna, can I interrupt you?'

'Oh sorry, love. I'm just trying to make sense of this one.' She showed me a very odd-looking letter with words running over the top of each other. 'Have you ever seen a letter like this?'

I hadn't.

'In the old days, when paper was scarce, or to save expensive postage, they sometimes did this. The writer wrote on the page in the normal way, and then turned the paper sideways to write at right-angles down the page again. It's called crosshatch writing,' she explained.

I peered at it. 'Good luck on that one! Sooner you than me!'

'I'm getting there. Once you get used to the writer's style it gets a *little* easier.' She gave a wry smile. 'What did you ask?'

I repeated my question.

'Now you mention it, there might be another trunk. I caught a glimpse of something underneath a pile of cartons in the old kauri wardrobe when I hauled this one out. Forgot about it once I started digging in here. Let's go and look.'

She got up slowly. I hoped I wouldn't be so creaky in the joints when I was an old lady.

A big free-standing wardrobe was against the back wall in her junk room. Underneath the layers of dust and old peeling varnish I could see swirling patterns of what might be beautiful wood if it was cleaned up. She'd inherited the house from her mother, so I guessed everything in the room was pretty much as it looked when her mother died, with the addition of thirty more years of dust and neglect. She directed me to pull out some saggy cardboard boxes. Sure enough, tucked away in the dark back corner was another trunk of similar vintage to the first.

Excited now, we opened it and peered in. A treasure trove? Or a collection of rubbish? A mix of old books and shabby magazines met our eyes. No letters that we could see, but who knew what was underneath the top layer. We lifted the trunk onto the shabby chaise longue pushed back near the door and started to lift out books, checking the titles.

We were only at the second layer when Aunt Hanna said, 'I've got something. Look at this.' She held out a small cloth-covered black book, with faded gold lettering on the spine. Squinting a bit, I made out, *Water-bound Adventures of a Young Voyager by Alfred Burnett.*

I opened it eagerly. 'Oh look. The same chapter titles as the articles!' At the bottom of the title page we read, 'First published in serial form in *The Freedom Journal*'.

'That'd be right,' said Aunt Hanna. 'It was common in those days for a newspaper or journal to break a longer story into segments and run it over several weeks. And many books were first published in instalments – most of Charles Dickens' titles, for example.'

It was the work of a moment to flick through. The story I'd just read was the third chapter.

We grinned at each other in delight.

Chapter 11

Abigail
Auckland January 2015

The book was easier to hold than the pages I'd just finished so I wandered into the lounge and stretched out on the squishy old leather sofa, leaving my aunt to continue her cross-hatched deciphering task. As I opened the book, the musty smell of old paper wafted out, hinting at deeds and adventures of long ago. I flicked past the first three chapters – repeats of what I already knew.

It felt really strange to be reading the words of someone who was just a kid when I met him yesterday, in 1837.

Chapter IV: I Am Rescued – But Work Is Involved

'Hey sonny, got a problem, have we?' A gruff voice spoke above my head. A wiry weather-beaten man chewing a smelly black pipe was standing over me. Hughie was beside him, grinning so widely I could see the gap in his front teeth. I knuckled away the tears, hoping Hughie hadn't noticed.

'This is me dad, Alf. He's good at fixin' things.'

'Best you come with us, son. We're off up the canal in thirty minutes. If your father and brother are not long departed, we'll find them when we get to the Cohoes Falls. In the meantime, you can make yourself useful.'

He strode over to a long narrow boat. We had to trot to keep up with his long stride. Three fellows in the middle of the boat were tying down barrels with thick ropes. Washing flapped on a line stretched back and forth across the back deck. A thin column of grey smoke curled up from a skinny chimney pipe.

'Hey, Ma, we got company,' he called as he stepped aboard.

A moment later a grey-haired woman popped her head up from below. Resting her freckled forearms on the deck, she looked around.

'You mean this young fellow with our Hughie?' A hint of a smile flicked across her lined face. 'You managed to get yourself left behind, did you? Bring your bag down here, luvie.' She disappeared again.

Perhaps I was in luck. These strangers seemed both kindly and unbothered by my predicament.

I stepped on to the back deck and followed her down, curious to see what it was like below. The ladder ended in a small crowded cabin. At the back end was a tier of five bunks. The space between each was only just enough for a small child or thin person to squeeze in like a sandwich. On the front wall, at the opposite end, an odd arrangement of folded-down wooden frames and canvas was attached.

To one side of the narrow room was a small table littered with kitchen utensils, carrots and onions. Beside it, a black cauldron simmered on a pot belly stove, reminding me how long it had been since my last meal. On the other wall of the cabin a series of narrow shelves were loaded with plates, cups and other kitchen and food items. Boxes containing who knows what took up more than half the remaining floor space. A few stools were pushed under the table. Apart from the hunger-making aromas coming from the battered cauldron, the room smelt of wood smoke, pipe tobacco and musty clothes.

Hughie's mother wiped her hands on her apron. 'I'm Miz Wetzel. Put your bag over on the boxes, sonny. We can stow it in the stable later if you have to sleep on board. It's a touch crowded in here, for sure. Now, pop up and help Hughie so we can get away. With luck we'll soon meet up with your family.'

Bag disposed of, I scooted back up the ladder. Hughie was waiting. 'Come on, Alf. We're off to fetch the hayburners.'

'What's a hayburner?' But he'd gone. I had to run to catch up.

Back where my problems had begun, Hughie untied the ropes of four mules, some of them still munching hay. Ah, the answer to my question.

After checking all halters and lead ropes were secure, he gave me charge of two of the mules. Taking the others, he led us all back to the boat.

'Just wait here with your mules while I put the resting team in the stable. Sal's got the white nose. And this one,' as he affectionately rubbed the back of the tallest, 'is Hurry Up. She's a cunning old gal – don't believe in working too hard. We're always telling her to hurry up.'

I gulped. I hoped the animals couldn't tell that I was scared. Would they run away? Would they nip? Cautiously, I reached out, copying Hughie. I was surprised at the harsh thickness of Hurry Up's coat.

I took a closer look at Sal. Intelligent soft brown eyes looked back. She nudged my shoulder gently with her soft nose, as if to say, 'I won't hurt you.' Hurry Up hung her head, crunching sloppily on a few strands of sweet-smelling hay. The other two moved forward to wait their turn at the horse bridge, happy to go aboard. All Hughie did was hold the tail of each one to keep them steady while they clip-clopped swiftly up the gangplank and disappeared into the bowels of the boat.

A few minutes later my new chum emerged minus mules but with arms full of a confusing jumble of leather, chains and rope. He threw everything down on the hard-packed ground at my feet. Our family just hired carriages or wagons when we needed them, so I wasn't much help, except as admiring audience.

As I watched him lay out the harness, lines, chains and heavy wooden bars he called whiffletrees, my curiosity got the better of me.

'Why a stable on the boat?'

Hughie looked at me as if I were stupid. 'The mules can't work without rest. We change them over every fifteen mile.'

Silly me – how obvious.

Thirty minutes later, animals harnessed up and load finally secured, his father gave a signal.

'Alf, I'll get you to walk up front with Sal. She's the leader,' said Hughie as he passed me Sal's halter. 'Hurry Up follows her.'

He moved to the back, clicked his tongue and shook the reins. With a jingle of chains Sal and Hurry Up leaned into their harness. The slack lines, running from the whiffletrees and traces to the boat, took up. With no fuss, the heavily laden boat smoothly and quietly pulled away from the landing. We were off, but not quite in the manner I'd imagined. Was I to walk all the way to Utica? My family would never believe it, but I was earning my passage. If only they could see me now!

Thoughts of my family raised another matter. My father rarely disciplined me with a birch or strap, but I suspected that this misadventure would classify as a punishable offence. I tried to shrug off concern regarding the state of my backside once he and I were reunited. After all, there was no point in worrying about future pain until the certainty was upon me.

Chapter 12

Abigail
Auckland January 2015

Aunt Hanna decided to rest her eyes. 'I'm going out to the garden for a bit of light relief,' she said. Weeding never seemed like light relief to me – I'd far rather be reading a book!

I grabbed a drink, then back to the sofa to carry on with Alf's crazy adventures. I couldn't imagine my mother leaving me behind in a strange place, but perhaps, with a big family it wasn't so hard to do.

Chapter V: I Work For My Passage on the Erie Canal

At first, I concentrated hard on my task of leading Sal along the towpath, until I realized that, in reality, Hughie had full control of both mules from the back. An occasional command and a tweak of the reins was all that was needed. Maybe I wasn't quite as necessary as I fancied?

Once we were out of Albany it was quiet on the towpath. Just the jingle of harness and the hiss of water under the bow of the boat, nearly three boat-lengths behind. Birds chattered in nearby trees and low-growing shrubbery; occasional clouds cast welcome relief from the heat of the sun. I became more confident as the first mile turned into two.

I called back to Hughie, 'What happens at night? Where do you tie the boat up?'

'We don't. The boat never stops unless we're off-loading or taking on a new load. Same as the passenger boats. No money to be made tied up to a landing.'

'You mean someone walks the mules all night? Don't you all get tired?'

'It's just the way it is. No point complaining – no one would listen, least of all me Ma and Pa. They've been brought up the same way. This is a canaler's life. 'Tis useful to have a big family, it must be said. Me little sisters and brothers take turns as well, all except the little tacker. On the canal we learn to be hoggees almost before we're out of clouts – well, by age three or four – as soon as we're able to walk at a steady pace for an hour or so. The little ones don't do a full four-hour shift like me. It's not so bad a life, strolling along the canal, unless it's raining and blowing.'

'What about winter storms? Or if it's snowing?'

Hughie snorted with amusement. 'Have you ever seen a boat moving through ice?'

I looked back at him, puzzled. Was this a trick question?

By the look on his face, I'd said something funny – or silly.

'How do you suppose boats move through ice, Alf? By the time the canal be iced up, we be tucked up warm and dry in our winter accommodations. A really big freeze can crush boats.'

I felt really dumb. Changed the topic quickly.

'Do the fellows up there take turns leading the mules?' I pointed to the three men who'd been manhandling the barrels when I so unexpectedly joined the boat. Now they were sitting in the bow of the boat, two of them smoking pipes.

'Nah. Me oldest brother Davie is the second steersman and Pa's offsider. He's the dark one, same as me. Ma says it's the Irish in us. The fair man with the bushy red beard is Olaf the Swede. The big black fellow is Elijah. They're both bowmen. It's their job to help keep the boat straight, look out for snags and any other obstructions, and to load and unload the freight. Soon you'll not see Davie and Olaf. The boat works on shifts or tricks of four hours. Once the boat's settled they'll get to bed. Pa and Elijah swap with them later.'

'Elijah gave me a fine hello. He seems friendly.'

'He's like part of the family now – bin with us nigh on four year. He says he's a freeman, though I know he used to be a slave in Kentucky.

Perhaps he ran away. Pa don't enquire too closely. The stories Elijah tells about how the slaves be treated, it'd turn your guts. Depends how long you bide with us, but if you're lucky you might get him to spin a tale or two.'

Slave stories? All I knew about slavery was what I'd just learnt since leaving New York. I tucked his comment away for later consideration.

Something else perplexed me. 'Where does everyone sleep?'

Hughie laughed. 'The men and Davie sleep in the crew cabin, up front. Me second-eldest brother Fred, the other hoggee, is nearly strong enough to start doing the heavy work. Then he'll shift up there too. At present, Ma and Pa, Fred and the rest of us all sleep in the aft cabin.'

'I only saw five bunks. Where do you all fit?'

'There's three more bunks open out when the family goes to bed. Mebbe you didn't see 'em.'

'Are they the wood and canvas things hanging down the wall?'

'For sure. When you join your boat you'll find many more of 'em. They're a useful way of bedding people without taking up space during the day.'

Suddenly, round a bend in the canal another hoggee and his mules appeared. They were on our path and coming our way, pulling a loaded passenger packet. Land's sakes, what was I to do?

I was on the verge of panic when Hughie called forward.

'Steady as she goes, Alf. They'll make way for us. We have right o' way.'

Sure enough, a few minutes later the approaching team almost stopped, the man on the tiller steering for the opposite bank. Their momentum kept it coming until they were almost abreast of their animals. Their lines went slack, sinking out of sight under the water. We kept our path and speed and, to my surprise, our boat passed over the other lines without a hitch. Quick greetings were called between the canalers and their hoggees as we passed by. I breathed a sigh of relief. No tangled traces or run-away mules, no embarrassment for me in doing the wrong thing.

Hughie called to me a few minutes later.

'Alf, round the next corner we'll come to our first lock. I'll tell you what to do when we get there.'

I didn't like to tell him I had no idea what a lock was. I'd been about to ask Papa when all the fuss about boats and trains happened. The only locks I knew were in doors or on luggage. Somehow I didn't think this was what he was talking about.

Around the corner the canal pinched in. Tall rock walls towered above us. Several boat lengths in front, huge wooden gates blocked the way. How strange. How could we proceed? Then I noticed we were about to pass another set of solid wooden gates. These were open, one on each side of the entrance to the narrowing section. A tubby man stood on a low bridge over the top of the shut gates. He appeared to be waiting for us.

Hughie called from behind. 'Keep going until we get past the open gates, Alf. Then stop and wait for me.'

Sal and I pulled to a halt as instructed. I pretended I was in charge, but I must reluctantly confess that the mule stopped by herself. She gave me a look, as if to say, 'You only think you're the boss. Leave it to me, little boy.'

I looked back to find Hughie unhitching the boat lines from the mules while the boat drew level under its own momentum. Then, to my surprise, he threw our pulling ropes onto the foredeck. Elijah coiled them neatly, then picked up a long pole. As I watched, a tall slightly-built boy whom I'd not spotted before ran forward to midships with another pole. Maybe that was Fred. Then I noticed Miz Wetzel and two of the younger children also pick up poles and space themselves along the sides of the boat.

As soon as the boat passed the first set of gates, they began to slowly creak shut. It was like watching a mighty mountain shift. I stood there with my mouth open.

Hughie came alongside with Hurry Up. He laughed to see my jaw drop. 'Have you not seen a lock before, Alf?'

'Never. It's amazing, but I don't understand how it works.'

'We couldn't go up or down hill if we didn't have locks.'

'I still do not comprehend.'

'A lock allows water levels to be changed. Think of it as a movable dam. These gates we're going past will soon be shut. Then we'll be

closed into a narrow chamber with gates at both ends. The man up on the little bridge is the locktender. Once the gates behind us are shut, he opens valves that bring water into the lock, or let it out if you're going downhill. When the water is the same level as our next section of the canal, which in this case is higher, the gates in front will open and we'll go forward.'

I looked down at the crew and family, all standing alert with poles in hand. 'So why the poles?'

'There's quite a surge of water as the water changes levels. Everyone has to stand ready to fend off. The current often pushes the boat too close to the walls. Sure way to spring a leak. Or some other damage. Sometimes people get hurt too. That's why our baby brother is tied to the top of the cabin.'

I looked at the little child on the roof of the rear cabin. At the front of the mule team I'd been too far away to observe that he didn't move far. Now I was right beside them, I could see he was wearing a harness and tied to a running line across the top of the cabin. He uttered no squawks or complaints. Instead, he seemed as fascinated as me by the clang of the huge gates shutting and then the bubbling whoosh of water as an invisible device allowed gallons of water to pour into the lock.

For a while the boat floated stationary, except it rose higher and higher. Then the pressure of the incoming water pushed it slowly forward, closer to the front gates. About thirty minutes later, Elijah threw Hughie back the lines, our mules were re-connected and we prepared to move forward as soon as the boat was released.

About an hour into the journey, two of the younger children were detailed to relieve Hughie and me so we could eat. I was grateful to rest my legs. You'd not think walking along a flat path would be so tiring. Maybe it was because I was unused to staying focused for so long. At least, that would have been my mother's opinion, I knew for sure.

'Stay up top, lads. I'll pass your dinner up. It be right hot down here,' called Mrs Wetzel as we stepped aboard.

Hughie and I flopped down on the roof of the cabin. Standing on the ladder, his mother handed up tin plates of lamb stew and vegetables, with a hunk of fresh corn pone to mop up the gravy. We ate with *our plates on our laps, legs stretched out, watching the trees and water slide gently past. Hughie's burly father said little, his hand occasionally moving the long tiller handle to keep it a pace away from the side of the canal.*

Our meal over and back to slowly walking along the canal towpath with the mules and Hughie, I thought about the day's events. None of my family, except me, had to work for this day's dinner. I could have taken a fast and exciting train ride and by now be relaxing with my sisters at a boarding house. Or I could have enjoyed the scenery as I cruised along with either Father or Thomas.

It was pleasant strolling along the canal on a fine summer's day but perhaps Hughie's life of apparent freedom wasn't always fun. I began to wonder about times of rain, cold, thunder and sleet. Some of the boys I'd played marbles with were poorly dressed. Tatty old boots. Dirty and skinny. I had good clothes. Comfortable well-made shoes. And I'd never gone to bed hungry.

Chapter 13

Abigail
Auckland, January 2015

I was pulled back into the 21st century by my aunt's voice.

'Did you hear me, Abi?' Aunt Hanna was looking at me, amused. I'd been so deeply absorbed in Alf's adventures that I looked at her blankly.

She repeated her question. 'Would you like to stay for lunch, dear?'

'That would be lovely, thanks,' I answered, still thinking about what I'd just read. It was entertaining and I'd learnt more about my impulsive and somewhat scatterbrained young/old ancestor, depending which century I was in, but there were still many unanswered questions.

As Aunt Hanna made a salad from the lettuce, radishes and tomatoes fresh out of her garden and I grated cheese to sprinkle on top, I asked, 'What do you know about slavery in America, Aunt Hanna? Alf's mentioned it in his stories and it's talked about in the letters.' I kept my more direct source to myself.

'Just clear a space on the table and, while we eat, I'll tell you what I know,' she said.

Once we were seated, I went back to the subject.

'Was slavery allowed in the whole of North America back in the 1800s?'

'I'm pretty sure it wasn't legal in the more industrialized northern states by the time the Burnetts arrived in the country. The predominantly agricultural south was a different story. It remained part of everyday life down there until the end of the Civil War in 1865.

'How could *anyone* think slavery is okay?'

She sighed. 'As you get older you'll see how people can be manipulated by smooth talking shysters. Advocates for slavery claimed that anyone with even a small amount of African blood wasn't really human, and didn't have feelings like white people. Laws legitimized it. Society supported it. And preachers quoted verses from the Bible to justify it.'

I looked up in surprise. 'That's not very Christian.'

'I agree, but if you take things out of context, it's amazing what you can find in the Bible to support any manner of whacky beliefs.'

'Do you think that's what Cornelius was talking about in the first letter we read? When he was angry that a neighbor said a nigger was not a man.'

'I'm sure,' Aunt Hanna agreed. 'Problem was, that wrong thinking gave license to anyone with a cruel streak to do what they liked. In many, if not all, of the slave states there was no legal limitation to the horrible things they could do to their slaves. They were just property. No sensible owner of a horse or dog would treat their animals in the way many slave owners and overseers treated those poor suffering people.'

Horrified, I asked, 'Everyone in the south was like that?'

'Certainly not, but whether the owners were cruel or not, slavery was a deeply entrenched way of life. Even those who didn't like it found it hard to extricate themselves. Many owners of large plantations believed they couldn't afford to farm without overseers and slave labor.'

I thought about Eli. 'But they can't have just been in the fields, surely? Eli and Hetty, in Alf's first article, must have house slaves, don't you think?'

'I'm sure. The wealthy slave owners took their personal slaves wherever they went. I imagine Hetty was that's woman's maid. She would dress her, do her fancy hairstyles, clean up after her, wash and mend her clothes – whatever the mistress wanted.'

'Dress her?' I laughed.

Aunt Hanna smiled. 'The upper-class women wore very fancy clothes. They had to be laced tightly into corsets, buttons were often up the back of their dresses, and they wore layers of garments. It would have been hard to get in and out of some of their clothes.'

She saw me pull a face. 'Be glad you don't live in those times. You'd not be running around in shorts, T-shirt and bare feet or sandals in summer. At your age you'd probably be working as a maid, all buttoned up in a starched dress and pinafore, stockings and leather shoes or boots, no matter the temperature.

'The work done by servants in the north was done by slaves in the south. All the manual work – washing, cooking, cleaning the house, preserving food in the summer, sewing clothes by hand, mending, gardening – all done by slaves. Forget labor-saving machines, ready-made clothes, electricity, big supermarkets with convenience meals and tinned and frozen food. Running a home and family was hard and tiring work.'

I grimaced. 'They'd spend all day doing the housework.'

'Exactly,' replied Aunt Hanna, who was on a roll. 'Which is why the women who could afford it were happy to let others do the hard work. In the south, even the housekeeper who managed the domestic staff and day-to-day issues was often a slave. And black women were also the wet nurses and nursery maids. In many families, they pretty much brought up the children of their owners.'

'What on earth did the mothers do with their time, if they weren't doing the housework or looking after their children?' I asked.

She shrugged. 'They certainly weren't working outside the home, especially if they were married. That was deeply unacceptable for a woman with any social standing. For most, their days were occupied with visiting, playing music, painting, reading. I suspect many were bored out of their brains. It's a different topic, but the women of the times had no more rights than the slaves. Couldn't vote. Were the property of their husbands. They lived comfortable lives if they had a good husband, but their options and opportunities were very limited.'

'That sounds super boring!' I said as I finished my salad.

'Oh yes,' agreed Aunt Hanna. 'And if they had a mean or cruel husband, they were trapped. We're lucky we live in our times, Abigail. In fact, the women's rights movement became quite intertwined with the abolition movement, but that's a story for another day.'

Chapter 14

Abigail
Auckland January 2015

Once the kitchen was cleaned up, Aunt Hanna said, 'I'm just going to pop out and thin the carrots. You're welcome to stay and keep reading.' She clapped her floppy old sun-hat on her white hair and headed for the back porch.

That suited me. I sprawled out on her comfy old leather couch to read a bit more of Alf's book. I wanted to learn as much as possible about him and the family before I tried to return to his time.

Chapter VI: In Which I Am Reunited with My Family

Although I enjoyed strolling along the path with my new friends Sal, Hurry Up and Hughie, I began to worry about Father and Thomas. By now they'd probably had a chance to talk to each other at one of the locks. They probably thought I was still back in Albany. What if one of them got on another boat heading to Albany and passed by without spotting me? The more I thought about it, the more vexing the matter became. I'd had several intimate conversations with Father's bell. Chances were, this would be another of those times. I did not anticipate a pleasant outcome.

About three hours after we'd left Albany, we approached the first of the Cohoes Falls locks. It was now that I was released from my duties and told to walk up beside the locks to see if I could spot either Father or Thomas.

I hadn't gone far when I observed two men walking fast in my direction. Oh dear, my moment of reckoning approached. Here were my father and brother – heading back to Albany on the towpath. I could tell, even at a distance of many yards, that my father was as mad as a March hare.

I think it best if I draw a curtain over the reunion. It is sufficient to report that I preferred to stand rather than sit, for the next some hours.

It was late afternoon by the time Father and I reached his vessel, a couple of locks further ahead than Thomas's slower one. It was embarrassing to step aboard the boat with my bag; it seemed that the small number of fellow passengers, who'd also chosen not to take the train, knew of my misadventures. I tried not to mind the joshing.

For the next hour or so, Pa and I wandered up and down the towpath admiring the tumbling waters of the Cohoes Falls and watching boats progress through the locks. I did find it of interest, as my father had anticipated all those hours ago, back in Albany. With my unscheduled experience as an assistant hoggee I also now had a much better understanding of the skills of the boat crews.

Even though slow, there was much to see and remark on. The canal was crowded with all manner of boats. Flamboyant packets used the colors of the rainbow to attract the eye of potential passengers. Pink, blue, yellow and red seemed to be their favorite choices. Sedate line boats, carrying both passengers and freight, were of more serviceable colors. And the hard-working freight boats reflected the goods they carried; the coal-carriers were especially dirty, but those transporting animals and agricultural products didn't bother much about their looks or cleanliness either. All were standing to for their turn at every lock in both directions.

Suddenly I spotted a familiar boat waiting to enter the next lock. 'Look Pa, there's the Wetzels.' I waved enthusiastically. Hughie, standing beside the mules, waved back.

Father strolled back to talk more with the parents. Hughie and I had time for a couple more rounds of marbles. I won my aggie back just as Father returned.

'Time to rejoin our boat, young 'un.' He gave my curly mop an affectionate rub. I think I was almost forgiven for giving him such a fright.

'Don't forget, Mrs Wetzel,' he called as we turned to walk back up the path. 'Look us up whenever you come through Utica. Just give us a few weeks to set up, and then, whatever bakery items you want – every time – are on the house.'

Back on our packet it was time to prepare for bed.

It was now that I saw how the Wetzels' extra bunk beds worked, for this boat had many of the same devices. The crew showed us how to lift the long canvas fittings, until then laid flat against the wall, and turn them into hammocks by tying their attached ropes to hooks in the ceiling. Once each set was put up, the hammocks and the seat below created a three-tier dormitory all along the sides of the boat.

I'm unsure if 'bunk' was the name you could truthfully bestow on such narrow fixtures. They were not much wider than a coffin. If a large person happened to be in a top one, I feared for the person below; canvas stretches and there was but little room between them, even before a sleeper climbed in. But more of that to come.

It was not a comfortable night. I didn't sleep well, not because of the skinny canvas bunk, but due to the discomfort of my tender rear. It was still smarting from the close encounter with my father's belt.

The other matter of note to mention on this slow ascent of the Cohoes Falls was the food. At supper that night, Papa nearly lost a tooth. The meat, whatever it was, was beyond tough. The cook would have profited from lessons with Mrs Wetzel. It was better than going hungry, but not by much.

The big thing worrying me was Mother. I could guess her reaction when she heard of my unscheduled departure from Albany. This I was not looking forward to. She had a very fierce tongue when annoyed. The next day, as we were getting close to the top, Father found me leaning out the window of the main cabin, idly watching the hypnotic swirling water of one of the last locks. He took a sideways glance at my glum face.

'Son, Thomas and I have agreed that we won't inform your poor mother of your misdemeanors. She would be most distressed. You've been punished sufficiently. However, do NOT let me down again. Wandering off like that was beyond stupid and could have had a very bad end. You gave us a terrible fright.'

Was I relieved! This was very good news.

It was much later that I realized they had an ulterior motive. It wasn't just me who would be saved a tongue-lashing. Who had gone off without checking my whereabouts?

Ah well, we men had to stick together.

Chapter 15

Alfred
Erie Canal 1834

Chapter VII: 'Beware, Low Bridge'

Twenty-seven locks in quick succession, to raise boats up one hundred and sixty-five feet, creates a long slow bottleneck of boats. The next day was well advanced before we were reunited with the rest of our family. They were eagerly waiting at the Schenectady landing with the rest of the passengers when we pulled in, looking rested and ready for the final eighty miles of our exodus.

First to board were all the women, shown to the ladies' saloon. This sounds fancy, but really it was just a small extension of the big main cabin. A flimsy curtain between the two sections was tied back for day-time use. Then the men boarded. As more and more people stepped on, the vessel began to feel very crowded. The first men commandeered the padded seats alongside the sides. The next group perched on the tables in the middle. Some sat on their luggage. The rest had to stand. I was told to remain beside my father until we were underway. He was taking no further chances with me.

A crew member stood just inside the cabin, instructing all new passengers to pile bags down the middle of the cabin and under the tables. No wonder we'd been warned not to bring more than one small carpet bag each. My spare clothes had walked off at Peekskill but the rest of my family each had one change of attire. A blanket each and activities to fill the hours took up the remaining space in our bags. The parents, Joseph and Mary Anne, had writing materials to catch up on correspondence. My mother, two older sisters and my good-sister Mary Anne had their knitting and embroidery. Joseph and Father had books.

My little sister Jane went nowhere without her doll and a cat's cradle string. And I had my Jacob's Ladder and my marbles, which now again included my favorite aggie.

There was one other highly important item – the food box. I watched to be sure it didn't get misplaced in the pile of luggage. I hoped some of Mother's good victuals remained.

'Welcome folks,' said the captain when everyone was aboard. 'There's just a few safety rules. Parents, please keep your children under control. No-one is allowed to remain on my stern deck. You may only use it to access the cabin roof, which you're welcome to use once we're underway. You're also welcome to walk along the towpath if you wish to stretch your legs.

'Now, this is most important for those sitting up top. When I call 'Low bridge', for those on the roof of the cabin, if you're sitting on a box or chest, get off your seat and sit down as low as you can. If you hear 'Very low bridge', lie down. Some of the bridges we pass under are dangerously low.'

Father leaned down and spoke quietly in my ear. 'You're not going up there without one of us, Alf, so don't even think about it.'

Tarnation. He'd read my mind!

However, I was up there soon enough, along with my whole family. Everyone wanted to get away from the stuffy and smelly conditions inside. Not all our fellow passengers paid as much attention to hygiene as my mother. The cabin reeked of garlic, tobacco, whisky, and seldom-washed clothes and bodies. Thank goodness it was a mild afternoon with a light breeze to keep us cool. We stayed up top for what remained of the day. It was very pleasant with sun slanting through the trees, casting long shadows across the boat and making tiger stripes on our bodies.

Every now and then a 'Very low bridge' call came from the captain. I chuckled to watch elderly fat men clutching cigars and hats and old ladies in their bustles and bows casting themselves face down as the boat scraped under low bridges. I turned my head from side to side as we glided through, hoping to see some of the larger bottoms scraped by the brick structures just above our heads. There were some very close calls.

I mentioned the food box earlier. Most travelers started their journey with provisions of some kind, in order to save money. With such a large family we were no exception. Our box had been well stocked when we left New York. However, with the dramatic delay on the Hudson, it was almost empty. I began to worry. Even I was not keen to rely on the culinary skills of the packet cook, having chewed my way through the grisly tough stew that nearly cost Papa his tooth and the rubbery porridge we'd been served at breakfast.

'What do we do for food when ours is all finished, Mother?' I asked as I munched on an apple from the bottom of the box.

She smiled, amused at my concern. 'Don't panic. You won't starve. A lot of the lock-keeps sell vegetables, fruit and eggs, but we've no way to cook on the boat. However, I hazard that we'll soon come to a village with a general store selling prepared food. Or, a bumboat might come alongside.'

'What's that?' piped up Jane, playing beside me with her doll.

'A boat selling supplies. A floating store.'

Sure enough, beside the next lock were several buildings, including Mother's hoped-for store. Next to it was a bakery, so the whole family came ashore while the crew worked through the lock. Mother and the girls were on a mission to restock the provisions; Pa and Joseph wanted to check the bakery items. I was obliged to follow my father.

As we approached the buildings, Mary Anne laughed, pointing to a sign above the store door.

'Look there, family. A fine promise, don't you think?'

Looking up, we read: 'If We Don't Have It, You Don't Need It.'

When we rejoined the womenfolk ten minutes later and I gazed around the shelves, I figured the store owner was telling the truth. You could have provisioned a home, a blacksmith's smithy and a farm with the immense range of goods for sale. However, and more importantly as far as I was concerned, there was enough food to satisfy our needs. Back on the boat, fresh bread and Cornish pasties from the bakery, and ham, cheese and fruit from the store, filled our bellies. I took a peek into the food box and relaxed; we'd get to Utica the next day without being reduced to short rations.

As evening closed in, it was time to prepare for sleep. Problem was, with so many people crammed into the boat, it was clear that not everyone was going to have a bed.

The women and girls disappeared behind the curtain, now pulled firmly closed. For some time we heard rustling and titters but no man was brave enough to walk through. How they arranged their affairs I cannot tell.

But I can tell you about my own experience – and it wasn't good.

The tiered bunks were hoisted up again. Perhaps some had paid more in order to have a bunk, for some men went to the sausage-like fixtures with an air of expectation. My father told me to wait. I watched in fascination as a portly fellow with a huge belly squeezed, with great difficulty, into a middle berth across from us. The canvas stretched most alarmingly, nearly reaching the man who'd claimed the seat below. The top berths were only inches from the low roof of the cabin. I pitied the poor men who had to clamber up there. Not only was it difficult to get up but, as I discovered the following day when listening to them, bad air and oppressive heat made it very difficult to sleep.

The next surfaces to convert to beds were the tables. But this still left people without beds. What was to do?

'It's the floor for you, Alf,' said Father. He'd secured a table and was about to use his bag for a pillow. He looked down at me retrieving my blanket and noticed a dilemma. Marbles and a wooden Jacobs Ladder, all that was left in my bag, didn't exactly make a soft resting place.

He pulled out a couple of his spare garments. 'Put these in your bag, son, then get yourself down here below me, with your feet out into the aisle.'

Joseph had to stretch out beside me, but being so much taller, was most uncomfortable. His feet were up against one line of seats and bunks, his body squeezed between luggage stored under the table, and his head bang up against the central partition.

It was hard to find a comfortable position on the hard and dirty wooden floor, no matter how much I wriggled around. And my face was far too close to dropped food crumbs and people's stinky boots. I sat up and looked around the big room as one after another the oil lanterns were put out. In the half-light the fellows looked like odd-shaped loaves of bread laid out for inspection on the counter of a really untidy bakery.

It took ages to get off to sleep. People tossed and turned, moaned and groaned. Then, eventually the snores began. If it weren't so uncomfortable, I could have been entertained by the sounds, somewhat akin to a very badly tuned orchestra. Deep rumbles, high-pitched snorts, and the drum-beat of oft-repeated mid-range snores rolled and rumbled through the saloon.

But it got worse. I had finally dropped off into a restless sleep when suddenly the whole room, and probably the whole boat, was rudely awoken.

First a loud but smothered noise.

Then, 'Hey, get off,' shouted my brother.

'Ow, stop it!' and similar cries came from a couple of other voices on the other side of him.

I sat bolt upright. With moonlight coming through the windows and a slither of light from the steersman's lantern on the back deck, I saw a melee of struggling bodies. Then someone struck a lucifer and a lantern burst into light.

The canvas of the fat man across the way had given way, dropping him onto the man below. That poor fellow, almost suffocated, had managed to extract himself. The only place to go was on top of my brother and his near neighbors.

Sleep was a long time returning.

The next morning brought another moment of high drama, at least for the person concerned. A popular daytime pastime was to stroll along the towpath ahead of the boat, and then re-board at the next lock or bridge. Some of the men had the habit of waiting at a convenient bridge, hopping down onto the deck as the boat slid quietly underneath. On one occasion a large woman joined them. She was a jolly soul – not at all prim and proper. They all readied themselves to descend to the boat as usual, except this time it was more than a small step down; the bridge was somewhat higher than most. To facilitate the descent, the men hung down from the bridge so they had less distance to drop. The heavy woman, long skirt flapping in the breeze, imitated them. However, when the moment came for her to drop the foot or two to the deck, her nerve failed. The boat glided serenely on while she hung by her fingers, suspended over the water and shrieking with fear.

What a circus. The hoggee had to pull the team to a halt. The captain steered the boat into the side of the canal. Men jumped off and ran back to the bridge where she still hung desperately, fingers going blue with strain. It was only with many men pulling and puffing that she was finally dragged up onto the bridge again and escorted back to the boat. Some passengers hid their mirth; others were not so kind.

At the end of that day we arrived at Utica, our new home. The journey had been entertaining, but I was ready for more space, my mother's good cooking, less adults keeping a close eye on me, and a bed.

Chapter 16

Abigail
Auckland January 2015

Woken by the weekly rubbish truck clearing the bins out on the street, I lay in bed thinking about what I'd learnt. What was the next step? I thought of the coin, now safely housed in a new container. On one of my searches in Aunt Hanna's junk room I'd found a really old tobacco tin of her grandfather's. If my calculations were right, he'd have been Alf's nephew. It felt right to house a coin with such magical properties in an artifact once handled daily by someone so close to Alf's time.

I imagined the coin, tucked safely into its tin, whispering, 'Don't leave me here. Let's have another adventure.'

Could I risk the time-travel trick again? Who knew where and when I'd end up? I now knew more about Alf and his family, at least the early part of his life, but the real mystery was unresolved. We were still no closer to the family secret.

My biggest worry about going back again was how to blend in. I couldn't return looking like last time. First stop, Mr Google. It took a while to find what an ordinary girl might wear. Most of the pictures were of the kind of gear Aunt Hanna had talked about. I shuddered. Fancily-dressed women in very ornate dresses, unbelievably small waists, impractical shoes and ridiculous hats. I didn't have a maid to button me up in those impossible clothes and I sure couldn't do it myself. Plus I didn't know where you'd find such things, outside of a costume hire place or the wardrobe section of a film production company. No spare cash to go down that route. And I was absolutely not going to squash myself into a corset, even if I had one.

To my relief, I finally found pictures of servants and farm girls in plain waisted ankle-length dresses, buttoned high up the front, almost to their necks. Long sleeves were often rolled up as they worked. On their heads they wore simple cotton bonnets or caps tied under the chin. One website said that most working-class women had only two dresses per season, one for daily wear and a good one for church, so an apron was almost always worn. For footwear, clunky boots were common.

What about young girls? I was only fifteen, quite slim and small for my age. I might just get away with looking like a child. The girls all had long hair, but tied up in prissy bows and ribbons. The long hair was sorted, but ribbons? Not something I'd normally be seen dead in. Tricky, but I didn't want to look too impoverished. Maybe there were some in the wrapping stuff Mum kept for Christmas presents? And thank goodness, the girls' dresses were less fussy than the women's. A number of pictures had plain cotton dresses, more like the servants' garments. Some were waisted but others hung loose from the shoulders.

What did I have that would look vaguely acceptable? Starting from the bottom, my Doc Martens. Thank goodness they were black – the purple ones Mum refused to fork out for would *not* have helped me blend in.

A dress? I hardly wore dresses and certainly nothing that would have passed for acceptable in the late 1830s. I smirked at what Alf would say if I turned up in one of my short party frocks. But Mum's wardrobe might have something suitable. I'd have to think about it some more. Time for breakfast.

As usual, Mum was already at her desk when I wandered into the kitchen.

'Morning, sleepyhead. What are you doing today?' she called when she heard me rustling around in the pantry.

I took my bowl of muesli into her office, plonking down on the spare chair while I ate.

'Mostly hanging around home today. Reading, calling my girlfriends, checking out a few more of Aunt Hanna's letters.'

A thought struck. I needed to offer a reason to be out of the house, in case my cunning plan succeeded but I didn't come home as swiftly as last time. 'Oh, and I might go for a bike ride to see one of the girls, if anyone's home.'

'All good. If you do go out, just text me to say where you're going. Okay?'

'Sure. What's on your 'to-do' list?' I asked, hoping I sounded nonchalant.

'Two client meetings. They'll take most of the day. I'm away in half-an-hour. Will you be okay on your own?'

I smiled to myself. Perfect. But not to look too happy, I gave a snippy reply. 'Mother! I've been looking after myself while you go on appointments since I was thirteen.'

Once she'd driven off, I went on a raid of her clothes. Nothing hanging in the wardrobe looked at all suitable. Like me, she mainly dressed in tops and jeans or leggings. What to do?

And then inspiration struck. I remembered the white cotton full-length and long-sleeved nightie she wore in the winter. It might pass muster. She'd be unlikely to miss it at this time of year. We didn't have any suitable aprons – of the two hanging in the kitchen, one was plastic, with 'Chief Tucker Mucker Upper' in bold writing. The other, although cotton, had a picture of the Eiffel Tower, which wasn't built until 1889. We had nothing that would blend into Alf's world. I'd have to manage without.

What else? A shawl? It would help cover the nightie and who knows what time of the day, or month of the year, I might land in. My sweatshirts certainly wouldn't do. Mum had a big selection of shawls. I found a plain black shawl she hardly ever wore and hoped that it wouldn't look too modern. The bonnet, like the apron, I gave up on. Hoped I'd get away with my hair not covered. Young girls didn't seem to wear hats unless they were going out.

By 10 o'clock I was prepared. I covered the possibility of being out of the house when Mum returned by making a quick phone call to my girlfriend Felicity.

'Hey Fliss, I might come over to hang out later. If I don't show, don't worry. I've got some stuff to do. It could take longer than I think.'

I felt a bit underhand telling fibs; I had a completely different destination in mind.

Chapter 17

Alfred
Utica October 1837

I was doing a delivery for Joseph, heading down Genesee street, just a block from our shop in the middle of town, when a couple of my school mates spied me.

'Hey Alf, what sweeties ya got?'

This was a normal greeting, and one of the reasons I never had problems making friends. The only problem I *did* have was how many sweets I could filch without a smack from the makers of said treats.

A few minutes later, depleted of loot, I spotted a packet boat loaded with passengers and coming up the canal. The proximity of the town's canal landing to our premises was one of the reasons Father was so happy with our location.

'Sorry lads, gotta go. They might need help in the store.' It was common for passengers to come to us for supplies and I was under strict instructions not to loiter if I was on duty – a regular Saturday morning occurrence.

When the rush of customers was over, Joseph and I went back downstairs, leaving our assistant in the shop. Joe was teaching me the fine art of confectionary-making.

He gave a nod of approval as we carefully cracked the last pieces of toffee and put them in the big bowls used to carry sweets upstairs.

'Once you've run that lot up to Miss Rous, bring in another load of firewood. Then you can stop for the day. I can't start on Mrs Zimmer's order until Sam gets back from market. It takes a lot of sugar, cream and eggs to make four pounds of macaroons and the two three-quart pyramids of ice cream she wants.'

I was glad to stop. It was a warm day, even though late autumn, and the bakery was nearly at summer heat. On really hot days the two ovens and the ever-burning stove turned the windowless room into a furnace.

As I stacked the wood beside the ovens I asked, 'When do you think you'll be able to build the new bakehouse in the back yard, Joe?'

'I'm hoping for have enough cash saved by next spring. I'm not keen to go through another summer with this setup – we near melt into a puddle, it's so hot and humid. I can't wait to get windows and a door so we open up to any breeze.'

I cast a thought to the strange girl who'd landed in our parlor a week ago. In her time, I wondered, had they come up with any new way of keeping cool?

And, would she come back? I'd kept a close eye on my coin; it looked just as normal – a bit tarnished and insignificant – resting on my curios shelf. Had I dreamed it? But I knew I hadn't. Hard as it was to believe, I had to accept that she was from my future. Nothing else made sense.

I'd tried to find the place she said she was from, in Joseph's world atlas in the parlor. The atlas was quite new – published in 1832. Only on the front page, which showed the whole world, could I find a small clump of islands named New Zeeland, on the other side of the world, way down in the lower part of the Pacific Ocean. The nearest land was a much bigger country, named New Holland. No towns showed on either country. Just a few capes and islands were named. South of the two main islands of New Zeeland was a tiny dot in the ocean, named Lord Auckland Islands. Was that where she lived? I was greatly jumbled in my thoughts. Tried to push her to the back of my mind.

Bakery chores finished, I walked into the kitchen as Mary Anne was fastening her bonnet over her blonde curls. As she tied the ribbons under her chin she said, 'Can you shell these, Alf, before you do anything else?' She pointed to a big bowl of peas on the table. 'There's someone I needs must get a few supplies to. I'll be about an hour.'

Just when I thought I'd get time to myself! I stifled a groan.

My sister-in-law spent most of her time cooking our meals, cleaning the house, buying provisions at the market, taking in sewing for others, and making and mending our clothes. Most of the mending was mine, I have to confess. Trees and river banks can be rather hard on garments. Oh, and taking tea with her friends and going to meetings. I'd heard her mention the Bible Society, the Missionary Society and lately she'd also been going to a new one, the Anti-Slavery Society. I didn't know what they talked about at all these meetings, but it seemed to keep her occupied.

As I turned to acknowledge her request, I saw the cloth laid on the top of the basket had slipped. Underneath it was one of Joseph's old shirts. I'd expected to see some of our bakery items – bread, for instance, or vegetables from Joseph's well-tended garden. But who would need a faded old shirt of my brother's?

'Where are you going?' I asked, trying for casual interest.

'Just some folks who have need of a few provisions,' she replied. 'No-one you know.' Quickly she grabbed her basket and scooted out the door.

Her vague reply piqued my curiosity; I have a good nose for a secret. Mary Anne was usually very chatty about her activities, but of recent times I'd sensed she was holding out on something. Joseph was in on it; they would often change the topic when I entered a room.

I decided to follow her.

I waited for the click of the gate. Waited a bit longer, to give her a head start. Then, figuring she'd had enough time to get nearly to the next street, whichever way she was heading, I also walked out the door.

I looked both ways. A few people were going about their business. Mary Anne was turning into Bleecker street. I caught a glimpse of her trim back and the skirt of her blue cotton day dress swaying as she disappeared around the corner. I skipped out the gate and ran to spy her next change of direction. Waited again. When she was almost out of sight I followed to the next corner. For fifteen minutes this cat and mouse activity continued. She walked further and further away from the center of town, into the poorer areas.

And then, to my great confusion, she turned into the lane leading to Hayti, the Negro quarter. Darn it. A skinny white boy like me would hardly blend in. Nor did Mary Anne, but clearly that didn't bother her; at that exact moment she disappeared between the shanties as though she had a right to be there.

Everyone who lived in that crowded cluster of dilapidated houses was a shade of brown or black. I couldn't say I was visiting a friend; she knew I didn't have any Negro boys as friends. I don't know if they got any book learning some other way, but they didn't attend any of the schools I knew about. And I only ever saw black children playing down by the river at the tail end of a summer's day. Never during work or school hours. Always keeping to themselves. I'd not given much thought to where they went or what they did during the day. Did they have their own school? Or no school? Perhaps even the little ones had to work?

For a moment or two I stood at the corner, studying the nearest buildings and the people moving between the shacks and along the narrow lane, hoping for a clue. Of the buildings I could see, many were scarce more than old bits of wood stuck together any old how. I'd heard Joseph say they were made out of left-over debris from the new railway line, stuff scrounged from building sites, or even rubbish thrown away. What on earth could Mary Anne be doing down there? Something to do with one of her committees, maybe?

A couple of bigger boys noticed me. Looked a bit threatening, as if they were about to come and punch me for being nosy. I turned for home, really perplexed.

Chapter 18

Alfred
Utica October 1837

Back at home, I finished shelling the peas. It wouldn't do for Mary Anne to realize I'd followed her. I was about to take the empty pea shells out to the compost heap when I heard a thump and an 'Ouch' behind me. I swiveled around, hoping against hope that this was a rerun of last week. Yes! My heart leaped with both shock and delight. That girl was here again, my coin around her neck as before.

'You're making a habit of this,' I blurted out. She was sprawled on the floor, next to the table, tangled up in a shapeless white garment, thick black boots sticking out below.

She sat up, rubbing her head. 'Ow. That bloody hurt.'

I frowned. 'Your language hasn't improved, but at least you're a bit more decently clad than last week. Although,' I added, 'your dress is still unusual.'

Abigail snorted. 'I did my best. Be grateful – I'm trying to blend in.'

'Well, your lower limbs are covered, thank goodness. You won't risk arrest for indecent exposure this time.'

All I got in reply was a disdainful glare.

In hopes of further visits, I'd prepared a plan.

'Let's go out to my tree house. If you're found in the house, I'll have to explain how you got in. But if we're in the garden, I can say I saw you looking over the fence and invited you to come in through the side gate. Our story is that you're a canaler girl, having a stopover in Utica while your parents get repairs done to their freight boat 'cos it got damaged at the last lock. All manner of people from different places come through here – that should stop questions about your clothing and funny accent.'

Abigail nodded. 'Good thinking, mate.'

'You have some very odd expressions,' I said. 'But let's not worry about that. I needs must get you out of here.'

I took her out the back door, past Joseph's carefully tended rows of beans, peas, cabbages and potatoes, to our big elm tree near the back fence. It gave welcome shade on hot days. We stepped under the branches and I proudly pointed up.

Joseph had helped me build a hut soon after we settled in Utica. It was mostly made of timber offcuts from when he and Pa did the renovations at the shop. Seamus and I spent a lot of time playing there when we could escape our chores. A tin roof kept off the rain, a hole covered with sacking served as a window so we could spot any Indians or other enemies, and I had a rope ladder that could be pulled up through the trap door if under attack. I even had a shakedown bed of sacks and old linen scrounged from Mother and Mary Anne. When I could sneak away with a book, it was my favorite hideaway. Staying indoors was a sure recipe for being given more jobs.

As quick as squirrels, Abigail and I were up the ladder and safe from prying eyes amongst the rustling autumn-colored leaves.

'Hey, Alf,' she said as we settled in. 'You know I told you I'd found your story about the little slave boy on the wharf in New York? Well, you wrote more articles – and they were turned into a book! That article I'd already read became Chapter One. The next chapter is the story of the explosion that you told me and how you and your family saved Eli. And about the sailor helping him and Hetty. The next two chapters, and I've just read them, are how you got lost at Albany, rescued by the Wetzels and became a hoggee for a few hours. Then about riding the packet to Utica after your father found you. You've got a good eye for interesting detail. Sometimes you're quite amusing.'

I tried to look modest. 'Well, my teachers don't think so.' Aping my grumpy master, Mr Dorchester, I pumped out my chest and in a fair imitation of his gruff voice said, 'Alfred has ability, but we see it infrequently. Instead, he wastes his time entertaining his classmates.'

Abigail laughed out loud. 'Wait 'til you're a famous writer. Then you can stick it to them. Maybe you'll even become a comedian, and get paid lots of money.'

It was my turn to laugh, but I tucked the idea away. Right now, I was more interested in what I put – what I was going to put – in this book she was talking about. 'Did I write about Joseph and me taking a visit to the parents in Cincinnati? We only got back a few months ago. I experienced some wonderous things.'

'I don't know – haven't quite finished yet.'

'I'm sure to have described it. Since you can read about it there, let's not waste time talking about that. Tell me about life in your time.'

Abigail opened her mouth, as though about to argue. Quickly, I added, 'No-one else can tell me about the future. Pleeease.'

My head nearly burst as she tried to give me a word picture of her world. The machines they traveled in by land and sea – I couldn't believe how fast they moved. And when she said that people could get from England to America in about ten hours, in metal machines she called planes, I glared at her.

'In 1830 that journey trip took my family ten weeks. You're playing me for a fool? That is NOT possible!'

She just sniggered at me. I was so angry I felt like pushing her out of the tree hut.

'By 1900, many machines will have been invented. Life in my time is pretty easy in comparison with yours, or so my Great-Aunt Hanna tells me.'

I looked at her doubtfully. 'Give me an example.'

'Sure.' She thought a moment. 'I know. How much time does it take your sister-in-law to wash and dry the clothes?'

'I don't exactly know, but Monday is washing day and she's busy on it near the whole day. If the weather is bad, she's occupied with laundry the next day as well.'

'What do you mean?'

I looked at her in surprise. 'Getting it dry, silly.'

Now it was her turn to look surprised. 'How?'

'It gets hung on the hoist in the kitchen. Often heavy items are still draped above us when we have our supper. We have to duck under the sheets and towels and Joseph sometimes gets tangled up in his own damp work clothes. The only other thing Mary Anne does on washing day is to cook our meals, and they're simple. We rarely get a dessert on a Monday. And I have to help with more chores. Monday is not our favorite day. Mary Anne is always tired and a bit cranky by the end of it.'

A little smugly, Abi replied, 'We just put the dirty clothes in a washing machine, add soap powder, flick a switch, push a few buttons, and walk away. In less than an hour – job done. Mum likes to dry our clothes in the fresh air if it's not raining, but on wet days we use our clothes dryer. That takes about the same amount of time as the washing machine. Within a couple of hours we can be folding the clothes and putting them away.'

I could imagine Mary Anne's disbelief at this impossible tale.

Abigail then tried to explain something called electricity. I could make no sense of her explanations, but the things they were able to do because of it made me sour with envy.

'I can't begin to understand how this works,' I said. She'd just finished talking about a dishwasher. 'Mary Anne and I are the dishwashers in our family. And it takes a lot of time to wash pans, trays and pots down in the bakery as well. I do some of that – I work an hour or so downstairs after school most days, as well as Saturday mornings.'

'What about heating and cooking?' she asked.

'Wood and coal for the stoves in both kitchen and bakery all year round, and also the parlor and bedroom fires in the winter. We buy supplies from a merchant, then Joseph and I stack them in the woodshed. My job is to keep all the wood baskets topped up. It's not fun in the heavy snows.'

She smirked. Tried to make me believe that houses could be both warmed and cooled with this strange electricity thing.

'You mean you can cool a room down as well?' I thought of the sweaty conditions we had to deal with in the bakery during summer.

I was still trying to absorb these miraculous inventions when she changed topic.

'Alf, I've been thinking about this big secret your family's keeping from you. So far, the letters I've read don't tell me much, but do you think it could be to do with slavery?'

Frustrated, I said, 'They just clam up when I'm around.' I told her about Mary Anne's odd destination just that morning. 'She's definitely hiding something from me. Since she went to Hayti I can only think it must be to do with colored folk. No whites there.'

Abigail looked puzzled. Then she threw me a bombshell. 'If it's to do with slavery, you'll be pleased to know that in my time it's ages since America has had slaves. Although it's not perfect by any means, people of any race, color or faith are supposed to have equal rights with whites in America now. In 2009 your first black President, Barack Obama, was sworn into office. Elected not just once but twice. He's half-way through his second term now.'

My jaw dropped open. 'Really! If I told that to anyone, they'd say I was out of my mind. That is the most unbeliev-able of all the crazy things you've told me.'

Abigail grinned. 'Well, aren't you the lucky one, to know something that no-one in your lifetime will ever see. But why don't you think a black man could be an American President?'

'I've never seen a black man in any important position. Only white men make decisions and run things.'

'Not in my day. In most countries of the world, people of many nationalities and religions share positions of influence. And that includes women. Many women are heads of state, presidents or prime ministers – whatever label their country uses. In New Zealand we've had two, and there's sure to be more in the future.'

Everything I knew was being tipped on its head. I'd never even heard a woman speak out at a public meeting or in church. I wondered again if she was just a clever trickster and a mighty good liar.

She wasn't fazed by my look of disbelief. Instead, she said, 'School starts again in a few weeks and we'll be studying American history of the 1800s. I'll be at full attention!'

Then she added, 'I don't know if I'll always be able to come back into this time and place. Time doesn't go at the same speed for me. When I got home last time not even ten seconds had passed in my world, but I was with you for about forty-five minutes. And in my world, I was here yesterday, but you say it's a week later. I don't know why that happens or what causes me to arrive on a particular day. Maybe it's something to do with what I'm reading when I put the coin on. And so far it seems to be just you I come to – we must be connected somehow.'

Just then I spotted Mary Anne coming through the garden gate. Judging by the way she carried her basket, it was empty. I pointed. 'Sssh.'

'Might be a good time to try my disappearing act,' she whispered. 'Grab hold of the coin.'

As I held the coin between my fingers she deftly separated it from the black cord. As soon as the two items were parted, as before, she vanished. Only a small rush of air lingered briefly in the tree hut.

Chapter 19

Abigail
Auckland January 2015

Back home and changed into shorts, I decided to finish Alf's little book – Aunt Hanna had let me bring it home.

***

Chapter VIII: The River Boat Pilot, and Westward Travel

In August 1837, to my delight, my brother announced that he and I were to take a visit to Cincinnati. He had things to do there and Mother wanted to see me. We left my sister-in-law Mary Anne and Miss Rous running the store, and our journeyman, Sam, downstairs with the pots, pans and hot ovens, turning out bread and biscuits, cakes and confectionary to please the palates of Utica.

With just a carpet bag each, Joseph and I rode the Erie Canal packet to Buffalo. There we changed to my favorite transport, a paddle steamer. I was glad to stretch my legs again, with space to roam the vessel without restrictions as we followed the shoreline of Lake Erie, all the way to Cleveland. I was less than excited to transfer there to another narrow packet on the slow and winding Ohio Erie Canal. For four days we meandered south, traveling from the top to the very bottom of the state of Ohio, slowly ascending and descending 146 locks and 14 aqueducts – I counted them! It was a novelty at first, but I soon became weary of the slow progress, especially the many hours it took to ascend the first 42 locks between Cleveland and the hilltop town of Akron. All that to cover only 35 miles!

You can imagine how excited I was to finally reach the famous broad waters of the Ohio River, at the junction town of Portsmouth. I couldn't wait to board the next paddle steamer, on the final leg of our journey.

At regular intervals along the river we passed landings on both the Kentucky and the Ohio sides with huge piles of wood neatly stacked ready for customers. Every now and then we were the customer, pulling in to replenish our fuel.

A magic moment happened at one of the refuel stops. I had wriggled into one of my favorite hiding places on the top deck, watching the action on the dock. Well, I thought it was a hiding place. Men formed a chain, sweat dripping off them like rain as they threw heavy chunks of wood up to our lower deck. The owner of said wood kept tally. Our first mate kept a watchful eye on his men. Meanwhile, the pilot took a rest. He was outside his wheel house, his chair tipped back on two legs. He'd propped his feet up on the rail, enjoying the pleasant airs while puffing on a well-blackened pipe.

I was engrossed in the scene below when I heard a gruff voice.

'Hey, young 'un. Come here.'

I swung around to see who'd spoken. It was the pilot. Oops, here was trouble.

Reluctantly I approached, scuffing my feet. I lifted my head to find piercing grey eyes scrutinizing me. His wind-weathered ruddy face was fringed by a full white beard. Removing his pipe from the furze bush of whiskers, he gave his red-veined nose a good rub, scratched his beard with short stubby fingers, then gruffly spoke.

'Why ain't you down on the lower decks with the other young 'uns?'

I hung my head, momentarily stunned into silence. I could see my freedom to roam coming to an abrupt end. I peeked at his face. He didn't look cross. Rather, it was an enquiring kind of look.

He spoke again. 'What brings you up here so much?'

'I'm sorry sir. I was trying to keep out of the way,' I mumbled.

'No harm done.'

For the third time, he asked, 'What brings you up here so much?'

Taking heart from his friendly manner, I looked squarely at him. 'I want to be a paddle steamer pilot when I grow up.'

'Why?'

I forgot to be intimidated as I answered, 'I love to watch the wheels. And the sound of the engines. Oh, and the whistle.'

He chuckled. 'It's not all high adventure, you know. Do you think you could manage the many hazards, such as shipboard explosions, fires, snags, ice and changing levels of water? It's not enough to just work with what you see. River channels constantly shift. You have to know where the snags are. And the sandbars. You're constantly trying to gauge the depth of the water and the strength of the current. You must learn the landmarks and be able to navigate through night, fog and driving rain with little or no visibility.

'In winter you have ice. If you don't judge its onset correctly you can become stranded for months and the ice damages the boat. In the summer you have droughts that cause the water levels to drop dangerously. Nobody goes anywhere if there's not enough water. I can tell you, the passengers get right cranky if they're stuck on a sandbar when they're of a mind to get to their business in Cincinnati or Louisville. Or they might be fixed to continue on down the Mississippi to Memphis, Natchez or New Orleans. And the people waiting for their freight complain mightily to my owners if their goods don't arrive when expected. Much harder to pilot a river boat than a lake steamer.'

He stopped himself. 'Don't mind me. Whether river or lake, we pilots have a great life. We're never long in any place. Meself, I'm rather partial to the freedom.'

Just then he heard the mate call, 'Ready to depart'. He tapped his pipe out on the rail and stood up. 'Off you go, lad. I don't mind a keen fellow coming up here but just be sure to keep out of everyone's way.'

I descended to the lower decks to find my brother, with a grin as wide as the Atlantic.

We Reach Our Destination

Two days later we arrived at Cincinnati. Squashed up behind wide-skirted ladies and tall whiskery men with beaver top hats and broad shoulders, I couldn't get near the rail so jumped up on a seat for a better view.

Running up the slope away from the river were row upon row of houses, mostly brick, all jammed up next to each other. They were so close that I could imagine neighbors leaning out their windows to shake hands with the occupants of the next house. Or maybe they didn't like to be that friendly?

Joseph laughed as he watched my awe at the size of the place. 'Cincinnati is a very important city for commerce, brother.'

From my vantage point it looked as though a lot of the commerce happened right there on the huge waterfront. I could barely see from end to end of the landing, crowded with river boats of all types. People, horses and wagons seemed to be going any which way. The chaos of the scene made sleepy Utica with its wide streets and large gardens seem like a country estate. But as we drew closer, a most unpleasant smell hit me.

'What's that awful stink, Joe?' I'd noticed something similar several times on the journey, always when we'd been in or near large towns, but this was worse than usual.

'It'll be the drains, or lack of them. In such a big city people and animals live squashed up close together, many with no gardens or back yards to dispose of their rubbish. Mother has mentioned sewage problems, you might remember. She said that open drains run through the streets and discharge into the river. They carry much of the waste – slops and the dung from horses, free-running dogs and the hundreds of pigs roaming the streets. Even though the pigs eat much of the waste, and night carts take away the human excreta, big cities always smell pretty bad.'

If I were ever to live in this city, I resolved that I would only swim and fish upstream of the drain outlets!

Folks clustered around piles of merchandise, coming or going off the fleet of boats. Barrels were stacked up in big heaps on the landing. Drays of pumpkins, corn and other farm produce were pulled up as close to the wharves as possible. Other drays were surrounded by a haze of flies. I later found they carried pork from the many abattoirs nearby, packed and salted into barrels. Even though there were no raw slabs of meat, the smell was a magnet to the unwanted pests. Much pork was exported from Cincinnati, according to Joseph. So much so that the city was known as Porkopolis – not a very flattering term, methinks.

And the noise! Draft-horses lined up, waiting their turn; the horses patient, their drivers not so. The wagoners at the back bellowed for the people in front to move along. Dogs barked and honks and squeals of fattened pigs, being driven onto or off boats, rose above the rumble of other traffic.

It was good to spot my sister Ann in the crowd, no doubt sent by our mother in hopes that this might be the vessel we were on.

I was pulled out of the story by my mother's voice at the back door. She'd just driven in.

'Abi love, are you there?'

'Yep,' I called.

'Can you help me with the groceries, please?'

The next chapter would have to wait.

Chapter 20

Alfred
Utica October 1837

Mary Anne was at one of her meetings and I'd been sent to the garden to dig the last potatoes of the season. Joseph took pride in growing enough root vegetables in his garden to last through winter, and these potatoes were destined for the cellar.

As I dug my fork into the soft soil, dislodging the weeds allowed to spring up late in the season, I heard, 'Hey, Alf.'

There, leaning over the garden fence, stood Abigail. Her hair was tied back with a ribbon and a patterned blue shawl covered the same shapeless white garment as last time.

I ran to the gate. Looked around. No watchers, thank goodness. It would give any passer-by a terrible fright to see a girl just suddenly appear at their feet. I ushered her quickly in.

'Tree house?' she asked.

'For sure. But I can't be too long, or Joseph will want to know why there's not many potatoes in the sack.'

We clambered up. It was a couple of weeks since her last visit and the late autumn leaves had started to drop. Soon the hut would be visible to all who bothered to look, although the hut walls meant we could only be seen if an observer stood immediately below.

As was becoming our habit, first we traded dates. It had only been a day in her time, but two weeks in mine, since we'd met.

'Yesterday I read your story about traveling to Cincinnati,' she said.

I laughed. 'The size and smell of the place quite took me by surprise. But it was good to see the family – the first time in over a year. Mother and my sisters fussed over me. Fair wore me out with their fidgets and nonsense! Papa was glad to see me too, but what I heard a couple of days after we'd arrived, when he thought I wasn't in earshot, gave me pause. His reason for missing me wasn't the same as Mother's.'

Abigail gave me a questioning look.

'I heard him tell Joseph I was old enough now to join him fulltime in the bakery. Said that he liked my quick wit and sharp mind and could do with a bright young fellow in the business. I don't often get praise from my parents so I was feeling quite proud – until Mother burst my bubble.

'She was cross. Told Father I wasn't mature enough yet, and that my teachers still say I'm not putting enough effort into my lessons. Wants me kept to my studies for a few more years.'

Abigail chuckled. 'My aunt says eavesdroppers never hear good of themselves. Just remind me, when exactly did you do this trip?'

'A couple of months before you first landed on our parlor floor. Tell me, in the book you're reading, did I write about the black man who came to lunch?'

'I don't think so. I haven't quite finished it yet, but I did look at what was coming next. The next chapter seemed to be all about your journey home.'

'What a journey that was! Dreadful in parts, and splendiferous at the end.' I was about to start on the splendiferous parts when Abigail stopped me.

'Sorry to interrupt, Alf, but I can read that in the book. What's this about a black man?'

'It was an odd thing. I'm still trying to make sense of it, truth to tell.'

We were at lunch in the kitchen, three days after Joseph and I arrived, when we heard a knock at the back door. Father answered. For a moment there was muttering outside. Then, to my surprise, a black man in ragged and dirty clothes, smelling none too fresh, was shown in and the door shut quickly behind him.

'Mother, can we find a meal for Mr Herbertson? He's just passing by.'

'Oh no, Massa Burnett. I no interrup' yer fambly,' protested the man. He shuffled his feet, barely covered by the remnants of old boots. Toes poked out, soles were flapping and pieces of vine just managed to hold everything together. Truth was, he looked right uncomfortable to be in Mother's sparkling clean kitchen.

The girls looked up with interest and no sign of surprise. He was made as welcome as if he were Father's friend Mr Hicks from along the street. My mother reassured him. 'Feeding passing friends is never an inconvenience. We're delighted to have you here.'

As if it was normal for dirty men to appear unexpectedly at her dining table, she jumped up and began to dish out another meal. Sarah fetched cutlery, Ann filled a glass of water and Father pulled up another chair. I looked at Joseph with surprise. He gave a small shake of the head, as if to say explanations would come later.

I took a closer look at our guest as he hesitated, then shyly came further into the room.

'C'n I jus' wash up then, please, Massa?' Father showed him to the basin and towel in the corner of the kitchen.

As he limped to the table, I took a closer look. One shoulder was lower than the other. An angry red scar slashed his cheek and some of his teeth were missing. I tried not to stare.

Once we'd all finished eating, Father, Joseph and Mr Herbertson went downstairs. They came back a while later with our visitor wearing different clothes, much better boots and not smelling as ripe.

'Back directly, Mother,' said Father as the three of them went out into the yard.

'What happened to that poor man?' I blurted out as soon as they'd left. 'And how does he come to be Pa's friend?'

Mother didn't answer immediately. 'Girls, please wash up. Alfred, come with me.'

She took me into the parlor. As we sat down, she sighed. Pulled me into a hug. 'You've led a very sheltered life in peaceful Utica, Alf.' She paused while she chose her words carefully. 'I can't tell you anything about him. He's just passing through. We often have hungry people at our table these days.'

'How do you think he got that horrible scar on his face?'

'Many black people have very harsh lives. Almost everyone who's been a slave has been exposed to cruelty such as you'd never imagine.'

I looked at her, perplexed. 'Was that man a slave once?'

'Until very recently.' She pursed her lips. A shadow of distress crossed her normally calm face.

I thought back to Eli and Hetty, and Elijah on the Wetzel's canal boat with his slave stories that I never did hear.

'What kind of cruelty?'

'Mr Herbertson's latest injuries will have almost certainly been caused by a whip in the hands of a white man – his owner or overseer. Many whippings are because a slave moves too slowly, or answers back, or for some offence – often quite small and insignificant. Or stealing a morsel of food when they're hungry and not given enough to eat.

'If they're caught running away, the punishment is even more severe. I've heard of runaway slaves being hung from a tree for several days from sunrise to sunset through summer heat. When they're finally released, their tendons are cut so they can barely walk, let alone run. Or made to wear iron collars, or iron face masks that prevent them from opening their mouths. Unable to eat or drink for the duration of the punishment.'

My mouth dropped open. I struggled to absorb her words.

She continued, 'There's a high chance he has dreadful damage to his back too. I expect that's why he wasn't walking straight. A lashing with a cat o' nine tails is a terrible thing to observe. I don't want to fill your young head with the horror of it, but fifty or even a hundred strikes are not uncommon. Frequently more. Many die under the lash. It's murder.'

I looked at her in horror. 'That's terrible! Why doesn't someone stop it.'

'Slavery is a dreadful blot on our society. Our family hates that it's legal just across the river in Kentucky, less than a mile from where we sit. We do what we can to relieve some of the suffering of such people. But – and this is a very serious matter – you must never tell anyone about his visit. I don't wish to say any more on the matter. Please don't ask me why.'

No more surprise visitors turned up during my stay.

Abigail looked as shocked as I'd been when Mother shared the horrible details.

'Alf, the family secret *must* be something to do with helping the slaves, don't you think?'

Just then the back door opened and Joseph put his head out. He spotted the fork standing alone in the potato patch. 'Sakes alive. Where *is* that boy?' we heard him grumble.

Abigail said nothing. Just thrust the coin into my hand as she untied the cord. Pouff – she was gone again.

I waited until he'd gone back inside and scarpered back to the potato patch, hoping he'd think I'd been in the necessary.

Chapter 21

Abigail
Auckland February 2015

These forays back into Alf's time were becoming addictive. I couldn't wait to learn more. But it might be helpful if I wasn't so obviously different. I'd be less likely to cause problems for Alf – or myself. What if someone had come along when I was standing at his gate, or in the garden? And who knew what the location might be next time?

I spent ages trolling through Google images and YouTube clips. No wonder he looked sideways at Mum's nightie – his sisters probably went to bed in such garments, or used them for shifts underneath dresses. I had to find a day dress, probably stays, a stomacher, petticoats, a neck scarf, a cap or bonnet, and a cloth apron that covered the skirt and tied at the waist. But definitely no tightly laced corset! Even without that it would probably take me fifteen minutes to get ready for a visit.

Problem was, I had no idea where to get such things. Second-hand shops? Far too modern. Costume hire? Too expensive and I wanted something to keep. Although I earned money doing gardening for a couple of elderly neighbors, and occasional babysitting jobs, I'd be lucky if I had $100 available at the moment. Half my earnings went into the uni fund Mum and I had set up – it needed both our signatures to make a withdrawal.

Then I had a brainwave. One of Mum's best friends was wardrobe mistress for the local drama society. She was around at our place for wine and nibbles most Fridays.

I picked up the phone.

'Greta, it's Abi here. I'm involved with a history project that requires me to dress up. I need to look like a house-maid, shop assistant, or something similar, in the late 1830s in North America. I'm wondering, does your society have any old garments that would do the job?'

'For sure, Abi,' Greta replied. I made a silent fist of jubila-tion. 'I'd be glad to loan you some gear.'

'I'll need the outfit for a while. Is there anything I could buy? Doesn't have to be flash, just look as authentic as possible. No worries if it's old and shabby.'

Within a couple of days, I was equipped. Mum brought into the project story as well. They both assumed it was for school. Well, it might have been! I carefully didn't tell lies – but I kept my fingers crossed the subject wouldn't come up at the next Parent/Teacher meeting.

With the new gear hanging up in my wardrobe and Mum and Greta laughing over their wines, I stretched out on my bed to finish Alf's little book, in preparation for my next visit.

Chapter IX: Dreadful Discomforts and Amazing Adventures

The visit to Cincinnati over, Joseph and I began our journey home to Utica. The now-familiar discomforts of yet another packet's accommo-dations paled into insignificance in comparison with our reception at the northern end of the Ohio Erie Canal

Here's what my brother wrote in his Day Book:

'Arrived at Cleveland on Friday 11 o'clock in the morning. Waited and waited for a boat and walked about the town. Put our luggage into storage. Went to the Eagle Tavern, near the lake. Took tea. Had dry old tough beef, bitter cucumber, poor tea and rotten mutton. Horrible! Slept there on an old straw bed with the straw sticking out, for which I paid 4/- for me and Alfred. Got up at midnight, having heard a bell, to see if a boat had come. It was the *Dewitt Clinton* going up the lake to Chicago. Went to bed again, got up at 5am, walked to the point. Saw a boat coming in, woke Alfred and took our things on board.'

He was not exaggerating about that hotel. It was awful. The food upset our stomachs so much that we had to use the necessary more than once, rather than the chamber pot. And the bed! We tossed and turned all night on that prickly pallet, sharing it with an abundance of uninvited bedfellows — fleas and bed bugs. No wonder Joe was awake enough to hear ship bells and go checking boat arrivals in the middle of the night.

The accommodation on the steamer wasn't much better than the Eagle Tavern.

'Took a deck passage to Buffalo. Got turned out of our berth. Had to lie as we could — horrible set of passengers! Arrived exhausted at Buffalo about Sunday morning about 6 o'clock. Took breakfast at the Travelers' Home, Main St.'

We could have traveled straight home from Buffalo by packet via the Erie Canal, but only our bags went that way. Instead, Joseph had two treats in store for me. The first was the Niagara Falls.

'Took steamboat *Victory* for Niagara. Sailed down the Grand River. Arrived in sight of the rapids about 11 o'clock. Felt rather anxious. Landed at Chippawa, on the Canadian side, having been informed that the spectacle was better from there. Took stage down to Niagara.'

I was anxious too. The river current flows very fast as it gets closer to the Falls, and the Victory *was a much smaller vessel than the paddle steamer we'd just been on. We were both in hopes that the little vessel had no engine failure. It was a relief to disembark at Chippawa, upstream of the Falls. Any boat going over would be pounded to matchsticks in moments.*

Once the stage coach delivered us downstream of the Falls, we were ferried by a small excursion boat back to the American side, idling for some time so passengers could marvel at this most dramatic of sights. The mind-boggling volume of water, pouring like endless silk over the lip of the Falls, bombarded our senses. The air was full of spray and the booming of the water drowned out speech. We crowded up to the rails of the boat, in awe of nature's endless display of majesty and terrifying power. Although there were a few grumbles from unfit passengers as we climbed the steep steps to the top of the Niagara Escarpment after disembarking, no-one really minded. The view from the water was worth every puff and pant.

The second surprise Joseph had in store for me was a train ride. The new line between Niagara Falls and Lockport had just opened.

It went so fast! I'd never experienced anything like it. Sixteen miles an hour! It made the slow, smelly and mostly crowded canal packets look like slugs. How wonderful if trains had gone all the way to Cincinnati. We could have done the journey in a fraction of the time.

Joseph grinned at my ecstatic face as we started to move, at first with clanks and jerks, and then smoothly and at speed. Fields, trees and cows flashed by in seconds. I was so excited I could hardly get my words out. Being a train driver had to be at least as exciting as a paddle steamer pilot; my career ambitions would have to be re-examined.

When we finally reached home, Joseph enthused to Mary Anne about the prosperous and bustling big city of Cincinnati. I figured that, at some time in the future, we'd be packing up and heading west to join the rest of our family.

For me, my world had enlarged. Despite all the discomforts, I had fallen in love with the excitement of visiting new places. In a few short weeks I'd gone west from New York state to the far south of Ohio. I'd been inspired by a river-boat pilot. I'd crossed the border to Canada. I'd been struck to silence by the thunder-and-rainbow-making Niagara Falls. And I'd had my first experience of the power and speed of a train.

And so my destiny was laid before me — the wide world beckoned. I'd been bitten — not by a bed bug, but the travel bug. By one means or another, a traveler I would be.

The End

I smiled as I put down the book. I was looking forward to discovering what kind of traveler he became.

Chapter 22

Alfred
Utica December 1838

Joseph's health was a worry. In our harsh northern winters he would often get a deep chesty cough that turned into bronchial catarrh. Then he'd be forced to bed, too weak to work. Talk about removing to Cincinnati became more serious. He put the business on the market but the months passed with no buyer. Mary Anne began to fear for his life and the search for a buyer became more pressing.

For me, life continued in its usual way – school, assisting in the bakery and spending any spare time with Seamus and other friends. I kept my ears open for further clues to the family's mysterious secret, but nothing significant came my way. And I hadn't seen my future relative for ages – had I dreamed it all?

One winter's night, just about to enter the parlor with an armload of wood, I heard Mary Anne say, 'Are you sure you want to be involved with this, Joe? It sounds right dangerous.'

I pulled up in the hall, craning to hear Joseph's reply.

'I'm with Father in this matter, dearest. If good people ignore what's under their noses, evil will prevail. Though you need not fret. For now, it's just my name on a page. There's little I can do for the Committee from this distance. However, I'll put this away from prying eyes. No point in inviting trouble.'

I heard paper rustle, then the creak of his rocking chair as Joseph stood up. The lid of the writing desk creaked. More rustling. A drawer opened and was shut. Another creak and click as the desk lid was shut and I heard the key being turned. It clinked as it was hung back on the nail. He said, 'Say no more. Alf will be back in a moment.'

I tip-toed back to the other side of the hall. Then, stepping heavy, I stomped into the parlor with my basket of wood. My surrogate parents were sitting in their usual chairs as though nothing of remark had passed. Dang it! When would they trust me? I resolved to investigate at the next possible opportunity.

It only took until the next Saturday afternoon for intention and opportunity to meet. The shop was shut and brother and wife both out. Taking note of the way the papers were laid in the top drawer, I carefully thumbed through. Most of it was boring stuff like mortgage documents, but tucked in at the bottom was an envelope with *Confidential* written in my father's strong cursive scrawl. Any instruction about not poking my nose into other people's affairs flew out the window.

I pulled out a hand-written sheet of paper.

Constitution of the Cincinnati Committee of Vigilance

Constituted November 1838

Articles:

I   This association (Ass.) will be known and designated as The Cincinnati Com. of Vigilance

II   The Objects of this Ass. are to effect the protection and relief of all persons in this city state or union who are liable to be aggressed, kidnapped or reduced to slavery.

III To effect this we will render them all the aid & advantage in maintaining their title to Liberty which the law will afford & Justice & Honor dictate.

IV Any person, male or female may become members of the Ass. by submitting their names to the Committee & contributing their % to its funds.

V The officers of the Ass. shall be a Pres, V Pres, Treasurer, Corresponding and Recording Secretary, who with seven other members shall constitute an executive committee. All of whom shall be elected by vote or ballot at each annual meeting.

VI The Ex. Com. shall manage the Gen business of the Ass. & shall appoint three of their number to attend to all particular cases that may come before them.

VII This Ass. shall meet once a month at such time & place as the Ex. Com. shall designate.

VIIII The members of the Com. shall be a quorum at any meeting regularly called by the Pres, Sec, or Treas, to transact the ordinary business.

IX The minutes of all meetings & also all cases recognized by the Committee shall be regularly entered in a book kept for the purpose by the Sec.

X This Constitution may be altered or amended at an annual meeting by a rate of 2/3rds of members present, provided such alteration or aim be laid before the Ass. one month previous to such annual meeting.

<u>Exec. Com</u>.
Cornelius Burnett President
                   Vice President
J.L. Grainger   Corresponding Secretary
Horace C. Grosvenor   Recording Secretary
Royal Wellan   Treasurer
Samuel A. Alley
Joseph A. Burnett
Mark Robinson
A.W. Hicks
William O. Harris

None of this made sense to me. Given he didn't even live in Cincinnati, why was Joseph's name on the list? And what did *'liable to be aggressed, kidnapped or reduced to slavery'* or *'render them all the aid & advantage in maintaining their title to Liberty which the law will afford & Justice & Honor dictate'* mean?

Well, whatever it signified, it seemed they weren't just ranting about slavery. Would my family be in trouble if anyone of a different moral persuasion should find this document? The fact that the document was marked 'Confidential' and secreted away, suggested exactly that.

I carefully replaced everything and shut the drawer.

I was still standing by the desk, thinking about what I'd just read, when a sound I'd not heard for nigh on a year startled me. A bang. A female voice uttering impolite words.

I spun round. There was Abigail again, this time dressed far more appropriately.

'You're back! I'd given up on you!'

She looked surprised. 'It's only a couple of weeks since I last came. I told you time passes differently in my world. But never mind that. How are you, and what's news? Do you want us to go out to the tree house again?'

'It's cold out there and no leaves on the trees. Mary Anne is out at one of her committees and Joseph's gone to a musical rehearsal for our Christmas concert. We should be safe in my room for a while. But let me show you something I've just found.'

I quickly pulled out the Constitution and showed it to her.

She whistled in disbelief as she carefully scanned the page. I looked at her in bemusement. Well-brought up girls didn't whistle – she was like no girl I'd ever met.

'Wow!' she said. 'I've only just gone back to school and I've not had the first history class yet. I wish we'd already started – I might be more help. But my Great-Aunt Hanna told me a little more about slavery. If your Papa and his friends are helping to stop people being 'aggressed, kidnapped or reduced to slavery', whatever 'aggressed' means, it sounds scary and dangerous for everyone.'

We put the document away again and ran upstairs to converse in relative safety. Having seen her pull her vanishing act a couple of times, I now had confidence that she could disappear if discovery was imminent.

Chapter 23

Abigail
Auckland February 2015

When I arrived round at Aunt Hanna's place the day after seeing the Constitution, I found my aunt frowning at another page of crosshatch writing. She looked up as I walked in.

'Glad you've come, dear. I'm finding some good stuff. Cornelius is constantly urging his sons to join him. It seems that the other son, Thomas, was being encouraged to move too. Listen to this, from their father, in early 1839.'

She flicked back through a pile beside her, picked up a page and read: *If you're in more communication with Thomas, let me know if he will come or not. I wish he would. I know I could put him into a good business here. I had rather you would come – but I must say no more.*

'I think I've pieced it together,' she said, waving the crosshatched letter. 'Thomas must have moved to Cincinnati before Joseph. In this letter to Joseph from their mother, dated six months later, she's saying that Thomas, his wife Emma and their two small children have found lodgings only three blocks away from the rest of the family, on Fifth street between Elm and Plum.

'And listen to this: *I'm grateful to have Thomas here, aiding your father, but I do wish you would remove here too. I feel sure that you'll have better success at keeping your father to his work.* It sounds like Joseph is the son she relies on.'

I thought about what we'd learnt from Alf, one way or another. Chose my words carefully.

'What do you think Cornelius was doing, if his wife couldn't keep him at his work? I've found several mentions not to tell Alf things. What might the adults, including Thomas probably, be keeping from him? I'm thinking it has to be something to do with slavery. Have you seen any more mention of that?'

'We haven't read everything in every year. Let's look again at some of the other letters. I've become a bit bogged down with these hard-to-decipher ones. The answer might be right under our nose.'

I knew what I wanted to find – that Committee of Vigilance list I'd just seen in Joseph's parlor, nearly 180 years ago.

For the next half-hour we focused on careful reading of letters in the years before 1840. I went straight to late 1838, but I couldn't find what I wanted. Disappointed, I started on 1839. Still nothing.

'Is there anything left in the trunk, Aunt Hanna?'

'Take a look, dear, but I thought we'd pulled everything out.'

She was right. Nothing in the trunk. I glanced over the cluttered table. It was so like Aunt Hanna – when she was immersed in a project she let papers spread out on every available surface.

Over on the sideboard, I spotted a heap of documents of different sizes.

'What's in that pile?'

'Just an assortment of stuff. Not letters. I haven't had time yet to study them. Feel free to have a look.'

A yellowed old newspaper, the *Philanthropist*, was on top. It looked like heavy going. The type was small and the layout quite crowded – nothing like our modern newspapers. I dug down. More playbills. Larger envelopes. At first I thought I was out of luck, but then, to my delight, I spotted something familiar. Scrawled on a brown envelope in what I now knew was Cornelius's writing, I saw *Confidential,* pulled out a familiar sheet of paper and skimmed it. Yes!

'Take a look at this, Aunt Hanna.'

'Wow. This is an amazing piece of evidence,' she said. 'I'd guess they were helping runaway slaves. We know Joseph was still in Utica in 1838; maybe he and Mary Anne were doing their part up there, helping fugitives on the last few stages to Canada.'

We looked at each other with excitement, but then the text alert on my cell pinged. It was Mum.

'Oh damn. I want to know more, but I have to go. My cousins have just arrived. They're staying for the night, then Tui's having the weekend with me while her parents and brothers visit other family. I can't do any more here until she's gone home.'

I thought, but didn't say, that I also wouldn't be free to visit Alf.

Chapter 24

Abigail
Auckland February 2015

As we waved goodbye to Tui and her family, I looked up at the darkening sky. Lightning zipped across the clouds, followed a few seconds later by a deafening peal of thunder. Maybe now wasn't such a good time to bike round to Aunt Hanna's to continue our last discussion.

'I'd better get cracking if I don't want to get wet,' said Mum. 'I'm due at the movies with my book club friends in twenty minutes.'

What to do? Inspiration struck – the weather might be better wherever Alf was. As soon as Mum left, I struggled into my new traveling outfit and, with more confidence, slipped the coin and cord over my head.

Sure enough … a brief moment of blackness and whoosh, I was again back in time. It wasn't raining, but it looked as though it had been. The sky was heavy with black low-hung clouds.

As usual, I found myself sprawled unceremoniously on the ground. This time it was an unpaved and muddy road bordered by stone cottages, a few larger houses and some trees. It ran down to a swollen and dirty-brown river looking as though it was about to burst its banks. On the other side of the river was a range of high wooded hills. Judging by the rawness of the environment and the few buildings in sight, it appeared I'd landed in a frontier town.

Alf was coming towards me, but he looked a bit taller, broader, more filled out. He was looking down at a newspaper in his hands and almost walked into me.

'Beg pardon, Miss.' Then, in shock, 'Abigail! Is that you?' He spun around, scanning in front and behind to see if my arrival had been observed.

'It was, last time I looked,' I quipped as I scrambled up and tried to wipe off the worst of the mud from my new dress and apron. Bad plan – it just smeared more mud. I followed Alf's gaze. Down the street some people were walking away from us, but no-one seemed be looking our way.

'It's near on ten months since you last came,' said my surprised relative.

'Really! It's been just a few days in my world.'

The synchronizing of this time-travel was seriously screwing my head. But he couldn't help with that so instead I asked, 'What's the date now? Where are we? And what's happening?'

'It's late October, 1839.'

I did a quick calculation. 'You must be nearly fifteen now?'

'For sure – next month! And this is Portsmouth, Ohio. We're removing to Cincinnati.'

That explained the reduction in letters in 1840 – no need to write when they were living in the same city.

'Why are you moving?' I asked.

'Well, apart from my brother's poor health every winter, and our father's constant pressure to join him in the west, Mary Anne provided the final push. She's in circumstances again. I think I've told you their first three babies died at or very soon after birth. She's desperate for family support at her next lying-in and the baby's due in a few months.

'Their decision to move meant I was part of the baggage, of course.' He smiled. 'That suits me just fine – I've got the travel bug now.'

I laughed. 'That's how you finished the little book about your boyhood travels. So, fill me in. How's *this* travel experience been?'

'So far, not so much to report, except this is our second delay. First at Buffalo and now here.'

'What happened at Buffalo?'

'We'd planned to stay just one night in a lodging house near Lake Erie before heading west but the weather turned. During the night the winds increased to danger speed. We couldn't sleep; the windows rattled so much we thought they'd blow in. The scream and howl of the wind coming off the lake sounded like an angry giant trying to smash down the building. Come morning, enormous waves were lashing the foreshore. Water surged across the road to within a few feet of our wooden boarding house. All along the lake front we saw huge limbs of trees and all manner of other debris. Even a dead cow.

'By the end of the following day the wind dropped to a low bluster, but it took three more days before any vessels dared leave port.

'Thank goodness, our lake passage to Cleveland was uneventful, and once there, Joseph didn't take long to get passage on a packet.'

'You must be quite an expert on packet travel now, I imagine.' I laughed.

'I am! At first it was better than the first leg from Utica to Buffalo. I enjoyed seeing the growth of Cleveland as we wound our way along the Cuyahoga River; to the start of the Ohio Erie Canal system. And being a bit later in the season, we weren't as crowded as some of the packets I've been on; Mary Anne had plenty of room to work on her knitting and it wasn't as smelly and dirty. But we couldn't get out and walk much – rain again – and one of the passengers was a blow-hard. Nothing shut him up. I swear he'll be talking as they nail him in his coffin. We were right glad to reach Portsmouth.'

'So why are you here instead of continuing to Cincinnati?' I asked.

'Believe me, we're trying. All this rain has flooded the Ohio River,' he explained. 'We've been in Portsmouth three days already.'

'So that's why the muddy road,' I looked down at my embarrassingly dirty clothes.

'Yep. Everything's damp, our clothes are going moldy, and we're tired of traveling. Joseph's worrying about Mary Anne too – she's not feeling at all well. We just want to get to Cincinnati. He sent me down to the shipping agent for the second time today to see if there's any news of a departure.'

'And …?'

'Nope. The man in the shipping office sighed when he saw me walk in. He was ready with his answer before I even opened my mouth. "Still no, young fellow", he said and then added, "We don't want any of *our* boats going aground."

'I was about to ask what he meant when another customer came in and he shooed me away. As I left, a newsboy with a heap of *Portsmouth Tribune* at his feet was yelling, "*Ben Franklin* in trouble. Read all about it". I bought one for the family. I was just about to look at it.' Alf waved his paper.

Together we sat down on a handy rock to read the story. The pilot had misjudged the channel of the flooded river and the boat was now stranded in a cornfield, half a mile from the river bank.

As we laughed at the idea of a boat sailing through the fields, Alf glanced up. 'Here's trouble. My brother's walking this way. What do we do now? You can't disappear in front of him.'

I looked at the well-built whiskery young man coming towards us. 'Tell him you found me fallen on the ground – which is true. Let's say I twisted my ankle. Didn't you just promise to help me get home? As soon as we're out of sight, you can – but not in the way Joseph would expect!'

We had no more time to improve the plan.

'Alf, where have you been?' said his brother as he reached us, a concerned frown creasing his broad forehead.

'Sorry, Joe. After I'd been to the agent I came across this young lady with a twisted ankle. I've offered to help get her home, once she'd rested. We were just about to start. There's no rush, I'm afraid. No boats going today – they don't want more groundings like the one in the paper here.' He thrust the paper into his brother's hands.

Smart move that – Joseph was side-tracked by river news.

'A pleasure to make your acquaintance, Miss,' he said distractedly, glancing briefly at me, then down at the paper.

Alf offered me his arm. 'Shall we see if your ankle can take weight now, Miss?'

Inwardly giggling at this gentlemanly behavior, I tried to look like a damsel in distress, took his arm, pulled a pained face and stumbled as I stood up. Just as well Joseph wasn't taking too much notice – the newspaper had diverted his attention.

'See you back at the guest house soon, brother,' called Alf over his shoulder as we slowly headed for the nearest side-path. I looked back as we were about to turn the corner – Joseph was now sitting on the rock, immersed in the news. Once we were well out of sight, we did our now well-practiced transaction.

I landed back on the carpeted floor of my safe, warm bedroom at exactly the time I'd left it. But this time I'd brought something with me – the Portsmouth mud. My new garments went straight in the wash. And I was still none the wiser about runaway slaves.

Chapter 25

Alfred
Ohio River October 1839

When, the following day, we were finally allowed to travel, sure enough, down the river we were amused to see the once-proud *Ben Franklin* sitting forlornly among puddles and soggy cornstalks. I did hear later that she was dragged back to the river and refloated, good to serve again.

Later that day, *another* delay. A paddle-steamer coming up-river had hit a submerged log. It sank and the passengers had to be rescued by other vessels. Problem was, for a time no other boats could get past. It had gone down in a narrow part of the river, with wind-felled trees in the waterway on either side. By the time the obstructions and hidden snags were removed by one of Uncle Sam's Tooth Pullers and we were able to continue our passage down-river, some of our fellow passengers had become quite cranky. I didn't care. It was all adventure.

Some hours later, as we were cruising close to the Kentucky side of the river, I suddenly heard howling dogs and harsh shouts from the nearby undergrowth. Startled, I peered at the riverbank. What could be happening?

A young well-built black man and a fair-skinned mulatto woman, both with their clothing in tatters, burst through the dense undergrowth at the edge of the river. They saw our boat and reached out their arms. Desperately called for help. Right behind them a howling pack of hounds bounded out of the brush. In front of my disbelieving eyes, the dogs jumped. Dragged them down. Started to savage both of them. Screams rent the air. Moments later, three roughly dressed men pushed through behind the dogs. Stood on the riverbank, watching with satisfaction while their dogs growled, howled and mauled their prey.

Several other passengers were standing near me. We gasped in horror.

'Stop that! Call off your dogs,' shouted one of our fellow passengers, racing back to the stern of the boat as the engines carried us past the grisly scene.

One of the ruffians heard, laughed, and made a rude gesture as we slipped further downriver.

As we approached our final destination, we squashed onto the deck with our hand luggage, jostled by the other passengers. Not everyone was disembarking but it seemed that all were interested to view the city. For Mary Anne all was new; for Joseph and me, although the scene was familiar, it was surprising to see how many more buildings had sprung up in just over two years, not only along the waterfront but also back from the river. From the evidence in front of us, Father's assertions that Cincinnati was a coming place appeared to be true.

Black, brown and white men scurried like ants over boats, wharfs and wagons. Most had scraps of cloth tied around their foreheads to stop the sweat running into their eyes. Even from the river I could see black skins glistening like shiny coal. A number of the fair-skinned men were red-haired and slathered with freckles. In almost all cases, overseers directed the work. We could hear shouted instructions, liberally sprinkled with words I wasn't supposed to know.

As we nosed in to the landing, sliding into the only unoccupied spot at the dock, a gang of rough Europeans, following a swarthy character with a drooping black moustache, approached our boat. At the same time another ragtag group of equally tough-looking, ill-clad blacks arrived from the opposite direction. They started shouting abuse at each other. It appeared they were competing for the work of unloading our ship. I looked up at Joseph, standing next to me, for explanation.

'The white fellows sound like they're Irish navvies, Alf. I hear there's a lot of tension between them and the blacks. Each group blames the other for stealing their work.'

I watched, fascinated. Eventually the Irish gang lost out. Black and brown hands reached to grab the thick hawsers from our deck crew. In minutes our boat was secured. The gangplank was run out and the purser on our vessel stood by the head of it, like Noah with his Ark, ready to let his departing passengers file off in some semblance of order.

Eventually it was our turn. As the queue moved forward, I craned my neck around the side of a fat and fussing old woman carrying a canary in a cage. I peered into the crowd below. Yes, there was Father's white head of hair. And there was Mother, with a look of relief and a welcoming wave when she caught sight of us.

Our family was re-united again, but the incident of the runaways and the dogs stalked my dreams for weeks. Little did I suspect that far more dangerous and life-threatening events would make that incident seem small in comparison. I didn't have to leave home to experience them. Instead, they came to me – in ways no-one could predict.

PART TWO

Chapter 26

Alfred
Cincinnati October 1839

Father, apron dusty with flour, poked his head into the kitchen. He'd sent me up to get my breakfast fifteen minutes earlier and I was just finishing my bowl of porridge.

'Oh good, you're still here. We've got an errand for you. Ready for a walk?'

I hastily spooned up the last of the milk and jumped up, placing the bowl and spoon in the sudsy dish pan. In the family kitchen, dishes were women's work. In the bakery downstairs, I was now sharing that same chore with one of the apprentices.

It felt great to finally be a working man like my brothers. No more school rooms, chalk dust and grumpy masters. To achieve this wonderful status there'd been a short battle; this time the men of the family won. Mother was not pleased. It took Joseph and Thomas pointing out that they were also working by about the same age before she gave in.

'Now you're officially the junior member of Burnett & Sons, it's time to get off to your first delivery. Dr Beecher has an important function at Lane Seminary this afternoon and has need of four of our finest cakes. Mrs Beecher's maid is here to collect them, but they're too much for one person to carry.'

'Can I take the hand cart?' I'd seen it tucked in a corner, just outside the back door.

'No, sorry. We can't use the hand cart for cakes. The cobbles are too rough. Burnetts don't deliver damaged goods. Come with me.'

As we walked past the loaded coat pegs in the hallway he added, 'Take your jacket. You've a way to go and there's a cool breeze outdoors.'

I followed him downstairs to the bakery. He loaded two boxes into my arms and then, carrying the other two, led the way back to the store. Waiting for us was a petite servant girl. Stray blonde curls skittered out from the edge of her serviceable grey poke bonnet. Merry brown eyes crinkled in a friendly heart-shaped face as she smiled at me. A dark grey cotton dress with plain white collar was fastened demurely at her throat; a blue and white knitted shawl wrapped securely around her shoulders for warmth; and practical heavy boots poked out from the hem of her skirt. About my age, I surmised.

'Miss Purity, this is my youngest son, Alfred. He'll help you get these cakes to your mistress.'

'Thank you kindly, Mr Burnett,' she said sweetly. 'And how-de-do to you, Master Alfred. I do appreciate the assistance. It would take me most of the morning should I have to make two trips.'

'How far are we to go?' I asked in surprise.

Pushing a wayward curl off her rosy cheek she pulled a face. 'It takes me nigh on forty minutes to walk here and more to return up the hill with a load.'

We carefully adjusted our boxes then walked out of the store into the wide thoroughfare of Fifth street. Father was right; there certainly was a chill in the air. Winter was nipping at autumn's heels.

We paused just outside, waiting for a cluster of women to enter the market just a few steps from our door. Father was very proud of our prime location, for the big covered market between Vine and Walnut attracted a constant flow of customers.

As we stepped out, I remarked, 'Your mistress must like our cakes, to send you so far.'

'That is true. Your family makes delicious cakes, one of the reasons why she likes to buy at Burnetts.'

At first I thought she was going to tell me the other reasons, but that seemed to be the end of the topic. Instead, she looked at me curiously.

'I know your sisters, but I haven't seen you at the shop before. Why is that?'

'I just arrived here two days ago with my brother Joseph and my good-sister Mary Anne. Our mother always intended to return east to Utica, so I was left there with my brother in order that my schooling not be interrupted. But over three years have gone by, and Father's wishes and my brother's have now united to bring us here. So, here I am – a new resident of this fine city – at your service, Miss.' I made a mock bow, bringing a grin to her pretty face.

'Well, there's much worthy work to be done here, that is certain,' she replied. 'My employer, the Reverend Dr Lyman Beecher, don't completely agree with all aspects of your father's activities, but he has great respect for his steadfastness to the cause.'

I was surprised to hear praise of my father. Mother complained about his lack of focus so often that it was hard to see my father as an outsider might.

'What activities does he not agree with?'

She side-stepped the question. 'What do you know about Dr Beecher?'

'I'm sorry, but I can only report that I've heard the name. Pray do expand. There's much for me to learn.'

She nodded. 'He's President of Lane Theological Seminary, training Presbyterian ministers for the new territories opening in the west. He's also pastor of the Second Presbyterian Church.'

Now I had it. Only the night before I'd heard Father talk about him, and his son-in-law Professor Stowe. They were supportive of the end of slavery but tended to the colonization school of thought.

'Of course! My family speak of him with regard. But they hold different views about how to proceed with the abolition of slavery, I think?'

'Shush!' she hissed, clearly alarmed. 'You'll cause terrible trouble if you talk about it so loudly in public places like this.'

She quickly looked around. We were walking past another entrance to the market. Inside, we could see stall-holders standing behind their heavily-laden counters. Meat, poultry, fruit, vegetables and other victuals were laid out in colorful displays. Maids and matrons, baskets over arms, carefully inspected the produce and haggled with the vendors. Outside, carriages and wagons rattled along the cobblestones, and iron-shod horses' hooves struck occasional sparks on the road surface. A small group of men stood by a nearby building, sheltered from the breeze, talking with animation. The topic must have been contentious for their voices were strident. One was making a vigorous point with his pipe. Another waved his finger in a third one's fleshy face.

At first it seemed no-one was taking notice of us, but then I observed a couple of older lads with greasy hair and dirty clothes, slouching against a wall. They had marked our approach. As we approached, they straightened up.

'Morning, young Miss,' said one with exaggerated courtesy to Purity. 'Come to pass the time o' day wiv us, 'ave ya?' The other wiped his nose with his sleeve and leered at her.

'No thank you. I'm busy.' Purity drew herself up as tall as her short frame would allow, lifted her chin and marched briskly along. I increased my pace to match hers.

With a sneer, the talkative one replied, 'Don't be like that, Miss. We're much more interestin' than the whippersnapper wiv ya.' His companion, snaggle-toothed and ugly, sniggered. They stepped away from the wall they'd been leaning against. Moved closer. Bigger and taller than us, they carried an air of menace.

The spokesman looked more closely at Purity. 'I knows ya. You're a servant at that damn preacher's house – Dr High and Mighty Beecher. What's in those boxes yous're carryin'? Somefin' us'd fancy?'

I began to feel alarmed. I'd be in trouble if the cakes weren't delivered. No-one warned me that being an errand boy might have this kind of complication. And then, to my relief, a brawny apron-wrapped stall-holder walking past looked our way and frowned. He stepped over to where we'd been forced to halt, big hams of hands on hips, ready to use them if necessary. 'You two – leave these young 'uns alone and get about your business.'

Our would-be aggressors insolently sized him up and down, turned on their heels and sloped off, quickly disappearing between the stalls.

'Thank you, kind sir,' said Purity. 'I hate them boys. They often hassle me when I come to market.'

He frowned. 'It's my pleasure, young lady. They're scum. There's a bad element in this town, make no mistake. We stall-holders keep an eye out for such riff-raff. They frighten the young maids such as ye, here to do your rightful business. Always looking for trouble, they are. The sheriff should do more to keep such ruffians under control.'

I turned to Purity once we were clear of the market and there were fewer people around. 'Is Dr Beecher not popular in the town?'

'It's not him as such. There is great contention in this city regarding slavery and abolition. That's why I stopped you talking about it before. It's not safe. Many of the business people of this town are against abolition. They are especially angry against those who speak openly about freeing the poor slaves, whether immediately or over time. And that includes Dr Beecher – and your father.'

'Does Dr Beecher just talk about it, or is there something else?'

We stepped around a small pig poking into a pile of rubbish while she considered my question.

'I think it best I say no more on that matter. Ask your parents.'

Disappointed, I said nothing for a few minutes.

Soon the street began to rise. As we progressed, our road became steeper still. We were climbing through beautiful woods and mature beech trees up Montgomery Pike, one of the principal roads to Walnut Hills.

I cast about for topics I could safely discuss. The obvious one was right beside me.

'How long have you worked for Dr and Mrs Beecher?'

'Seven years now, since the family first arrived in Cincinnati. It was my good fortune they were looking for a skivvy just when my Da was seeking employment for me. They're good Christian people to work for. Kind to their servants.'

'You must have been quite young.'

'Indeed. I was but eight, going on nine. Old enough to be useful, my Ma said. She'd rather I'd remained at home another year to help her with the little ones, but it was hard times. The family needed my wages, plus that meant one less mouth to feed.'

'Do you often get out on errands?' I was hoping she might regularly be sent to our store.

'Once or twice a week. They only have two of us servants plus our cook, Zillah.

'Are any Beecher children still living at home?'

'Only a couple of lads now, though Miss Catherine, the oldest daughter, comes and goes. Of the adult children, only Mistress Harriet lives in Ohio full-time. She's wed to the Reverend Stowe and lives but a short step away. He's a lecturer at the seminary too. When she brings her twin girls and little Henry to see her father and step-mother, I'm tasked with looking after them.'

I chuckled. 'I can imagine what that's like! On Sunday I had to help look after my brother Thomas's two little ones. Do they come often?'

'Not really. Mistress Harriet is ever so busy with running her home and family. But sometimes, if Mistress Beecher can spare me, I get sent over to Mrs Stowe's to help with the children. She's a writer, you know. If I'm there to mind the babes it gives her an hour or so to get on with her compositions.'

'Doesn't Mrs Stowe have staff to help?'

'Yes, but not enough to do all the work. They're not wealthy. The other day I overheard her telling a friend that every cent had two possible homes. With a growing family and uncertain income from the seminary, it seems they need her earnings to help pay the bills. Until recently they only had Mina for all the work. Now they've also got Eliza, a young colored girl from Kentucky who's just started.'

'I've never met someone who's paid for their writing. What does Mrs Stowe write?'

'Quite a lot of short pieces for magazines and newspapers but some books too. I see them on the shelf in our library when I'm dusting. They seem not too hard to read. If I asked, I'm sure I'd be allowed to borrow them, but I have precious little time for reading. Do you read?'

'I do, when I'm not doing chores, or fishing or spending time with my friends. Mind you, now I've been allowed to leave school and go to work in the family business, spare time will be much reduced.'

The look she gave me was tinged with envy. 'Allowed to leave school, is it? I wish I'd been allowed to *have* schooling when I was a child. Do you not realize how fortunate you were?'

'Did you not attend school?' I asked.

Purity sighed as she stopped and rested her cake boxes briefly on a convenient rock wall. My arms were getting tired too and we were both puffing a little. It was a steady incline towards the top of the hill, though the tall trees cast welcome shade.

She didn't answer for a minute. Instead she turned to gaze out through the branches, their leaves just turning thirty shades of gold, red and brown, to the wide river far below. The undulating hills ringing the city and the neighboring Kentucky towns were laid out below us like a vivid painting.

'Indeed not. Book learning for girls is a tragic waste of money, says my father. He considers that girls only need to know how to run a household and raise their children. None of us girls learnt to read.'

As we picked up our boxes and continued up the hill I said, 'I thought you just said you could.'

'Only because of the Beechers. The family were greatly concerned when they realized I was unlettered. They all hold education in very high esteem. Miss Catherine, and Mistress Harriet before she married, took upon themselves the task of teaching me.'

I listened to her tale with interest. These Beecher people sounded like good folks. 'Isn't it passing strange that those who can't have schooling wish for it, and those that have it, ofttimes would just as rather not? I must admit, there's been many a time I've wished to be anywhere but a school room.'

'I assure you that's not the case in the Beecher family. Miss Catherine started a school for girls back in Hartford, Connecticut and Miss Harriet was a student there for a year. The next year, only aged fourteen, she began teaching at the school.'

I looked at her in surprise. 'That's very young to be a teacher.'

'They're an unusual family. Dr Beecher has the same high expectations of scholarship for his children as his first wife. I heard that Mistress Harriet was taught like a boy – subjects like logic, mathematics, science, history, literature, rhetoric and Latin. At fourteen she was far more learned than most other children her age – boys or girls.

'So the Beechers don't agree with your father about the value of educating girls?'

'Absolutely not! You should hear Miss Catherine on the subject. Recently they had a visitor from New York dining with them. I was waiting at table. I heard the gentleman quizzing her on her views of education for women. I near dropped the soup tureen at her reply.'

'Whatever did she say?'

'It was something like, "*Those who say women should not have the same education as men think it would make a woman unfeminine. As if nature had done her work so slightly that it could be so easily raveled and knit over*". I felt like cheering!'

The hill leveled off. Another ten minutes' walk and pleasant discourse brought us within sight of a large two-story white house on a corner lot. It was set back a distance from the street, with tall trees framing it. Mature forest crowded up to the back of the cleared yard. Early autumn leaf-fall had caused litter from the beech, oak and elm trees to blow out to the street, although the paths leading to and around the house were swept clean.

'We're almost here, thank you Alfred. Come you in for a glass of milk afore you head back to the store.'

She walked me round the back of the building and up the steps into a warm and tidy kitchen. The smell of hot biscuits tickled my nose. A buxom black woman was hands-deep in a bowl, washing dishes. A beaming smile lit up her round face when she saw us.

'This is Zillah. She's the queen of our kitchen. We all love her.'

Courtesies over, milk consumed and a biscuit in hand, I was soon on my way. The walk back to Fifth street was fast. I had plenty to reflect on as I strode downhill, back to the bustling center of the city. My quest for information, however, had not progressed.

Chapter 27

Abigail
Auckland February 2015

It was always hard going back to school after our long summer break. The warm waters and beautiful beaches beckoned while we sweltered in school uniforms and stuffy classrooms. During lunch break, the second day of term, I left my girlfriends swapping notes on boys, beaches, presents and parties and headed to the blissfully cool library.

Mrs Watene, shelving books, smiled as I entered. 'It's lovely to see you, Abi. Have you come to get on the roster?'

'Ahhh, yes.' I'd forgotten I had to register again to help out at lunchtimes. 'But I've got a particular request as well. Do we have any books – fiction or non-fiction – about early American history?'

'I'm sure we have something,' she replied. 'Can you narrow it down a bit?' With a grin, she added, 'You've got a few centuries and topics to pick from.'

I knew enough about our library to realize that asking for info about Cincinnati in 1840 was far too specific. We were on the other side of the world and this was a school library with limited resources. What topic would be general enough? Then it came to me.

'I'm keen to learn more about slavery and abolition in the mid-1800s and what it was like to live in America in those days.'

She considered for a minute. 'I can think of two books that'll give you some insight into the period.' She walked me over to the Biography section and handed me a book. On the cover a young black woman was waving a gun in one hand and gesturing to come on with the other.

'This one, about Harriet Tubman, was written for young readers – too easy for you really, but it gives a good basic coverage of the Underground Railroad.'

'Underground Railroad?'

'That's what they called the escape routes and safe houses used to get runaway slaves safely to Canada. Pretty much what the Resistance did in the Second World War, helping Allies escape from occupied Europe. It wasn't a real train line. Frustrated owners and slave catchers complained that escapees seemed to vanish, as though they'd gone underground and then a train, at that time the fastest form of transport, had whooshed them away. Harriet Tubman was a runaway slave who put herself into danger time and time again by returning south to rescue others. She was one of the most famous black conductors.'

'Conductors?'

'That's what they called the people who helped the runaways,' she explained.

Shivers prickled my skin, and it wasn't the air conditioning. Could this be what the adult Burnetts were keeping from Alf? My attention was pulled back as Mrs Watene continued.

'The other title I'd recommend, and you'll manage it fine, is *Uncle Tom's Cabin*,' she said as she led me to the fiction shelves and pulled out another book. 'It might take you a few pages to get used to the slower pace of writing, but persevere – you'll learn a lot. It was published in 1852. It's apparently a very accurate depiction of the horrors of slavery. Sold more copies world-wide in the 19th century than any other book except the Bible. Still being reprinted nearly 170 years later. Uncle Tom was a fictional character, but the things he experienced were common in the slave states. It had an enormous influence on the way ordinary Americans felt about slavery. So much so that it was banned in the south as being inflammatory.'

I took the book from her. The author was Harriet Beecher Stowe. Not a name I knew. Quickly I scanned the first page, an introduction by a modern expert. What! Right there in the first paragraph my eye caught the word Cincinnati. No way! I slowed down, read again. This was amazing – she lived there at the same time as Alf and his family! I just about hugged Mrs Watene.

Just then the bell rang to signal the end of lunch break. Books in hand, I reluctantly headed off to Biology with Mr Widomski.

Chapter 28

Alfred
Cincinnati October 1839

It was only a week after meeting Purity that I stumbled across the first real information about the family's secret activities.

That morning I was assisting Mother in the storeroom off the bakery as she checked supplies.

'We're getting low on nutmeg and cinnamon, Alfred,' she said. 'I'll just go along to the market to get more.'

As she bent to pick up a basket, she gave out instructions. 'Please go down to the cellar and see if your sharp young eyes can find another cask of molasses. I was sure we still had one more but I couldn't find it earlier.' She sighed. 'Maybe your father counted wrong when he checked the last deliveries. Thank goodness Joseph's running the business now. At last there'll be better attention to details.'

Joseph was Mother's favorite − he seemed to have the knack of steering a sensible course between our often-argumentative parents. And Father liked it too − he could now escape her watchful eye. He was always busy, but it seemed not many of the pies he had a finger in were those we baked in our ovens.

As I passed through the hot bakery to the cellar steps, Joseph's new apprentice, Martin, had his broad back to me as he pulled a heavy tray from the big oven. My eyes lit upon a wire rack of still-steaming and delectable-smelling sticky currant buns. The rich smell was too good to resist. Juggling a bun from hand to hand I slipped quickly through the half-open cellar door. I'd already been treated to the hard edge of Martin's wooden spoon on my knuckles. Retreat was a wise option.

At that precise moment no one in the house knew where I was. Glorious peace. Joseph was in the store, Thomas had the morning off and both parents were out. It was grand to stop for a moment. I stood there in the dark cellar, blowing on my still too-hot bun.

I'd barely taken the first bite when two sets of footsteps sounded on the floorboards above.

'Martin, hop up and mind the store for a moment, if you please.' It was Father's deep voice. 'Joseph and I have to check something in the cellar.'

'Righto, Mr Burnett.' I heard him run upstairs.

My bun and I just had time to wriggle out of sight behind the barrels of flour and dry goods. You'd think my brother would remember what it was like to be an ever-hungry youngster, but I knew from hard experience he had strong opinions about when and how much of the produce I was allowed to sample.

'Shut the door, Joseph,' I heard.

A lucifer was lit. They'd had the foresight to pick up the lantern I should have grabbed.

Then, to my surprise, I heard Father say, 'Some things it's better for the family and staff not to know details of, in case they're questioned by the sheriff.'

Soft light almost reached my hiding place. I tried to make myself as small as possible, pressing back against the rough brick wall. The barrels blocked their sight of me but I was merely a hands-reach away, listening intently to every word. I even stopped scoffing my bun lest they hear me swallow.

'I've received a note from Mr Grainger. We can expect a delivery tonight or tomorrow. The hardware will cross just upstream of the river Licking. I need you there, both nights if necessary. Let's pray there's no watchers on the Kentucky side or the crossing may not be possible.'

I listened with surprise. Whatever were they talking about? Hardware? Watchers? Crossings?

'I'll be there, Pa. One thing I do ask, however. Can you help keep Mary Anne occupied? Now she's so close to birthing she's more fearful than usual. But I can't just sit here and do nothing, much as I love my wife.'

'I'll do what I can, but I can't deny that it's dangerous.' Father sighed. 'Tell her the least you can, and I know you've already cautioned her to keep it a deep secret. You can be sure that many of our neighbors and customers would denounce us to the authorities should they discover our activities. And for the Lord's sake, don't tell young Alfred. He's such a light-hearted scamp. He'd think it naught but a game and want to be right in the action. He never thinks of consequences.'

Just in time, I swallowed the annoyed words bursting to escape.

'Now, since this is your first run, let me take you once more through the routine. When we shut up shop at the end of the day, you'll head off from here with the horse and cart I'll hire this afternoon from Gideon Langston's livery. Go to the woodcutter's yard I showed you last week. Load the cart two-thirds full but use the kindling boxes to create space in the middle for a package to slide in later. Leave horse and cart tethered around the back, out of sight. The woodcutter's one of us, so you'll get no questions from that quarter. Then I've got two other errands I'd like you to do while you fill in time. First is to drop round to Mr Salmon P. Chase's law office with some documents. You'll find him on East Third, between Sycamore and Main. He's working on a Committee matter for us. Then I've got some supplies for Mr Howell. He'll invite you to dine. Once it's well dark and people are off the streets, head back to the river.'

Slide a package in among the wood? One of us? How mysterious!

Father was still speaking. 'Once you're back at the river, take up position where you can see and hear but not be seen. When the delivery is ready, you'll hear two whippoorwill calls from across the river, in quick succession. You're to reply in kind if the coast is clear. If there's danger on your side, reply with your nighthawk call. Or they sometimes signal with a lantern, so take our shutter lantern just in case. Three quick flashes lets you know they're in position. If you reply with the same signal, that indicates 'safe to proceed'. A single longer flash from your side says 'don't come'.'

'It's good there's no moon tonight. One less thing to worry about.'

'That's right, son. But I stress, keep out of sight as much as possible. There could be spies on our side too. Once the cargo has landed, get it up the river bank and stowed as fast as you can. We'll have the back gate and kitchen door unlatched. If for some reason one of us can't meet you there, bring the delivery into the cellar before you tend to the horse. Mother will have placed food and dry clothes here.' I nearly yelped when he banged on the barrel I was squatting behind.

'Once the coast is clear and we know Jane and Alf are safely asleep, we can sort out the package and arrange passage to the next destination.'

Stunned, I remained squashed up behind the barrel until I heard their heavy boots above my head.

I took a deep breath. Once I was sure the coast was clear I scampered up those steps as fast as my cramped legs would take me. My mind was so engaged, the missing molasses went clean out of my mind. A growling from my annoyed mother was my reward.

The day slowly dragged to a close. Finally, Martin and I were directed to clear out the few remaining cakes from the display cabinet and take them to Mother for supper.

Armed with new knowledge, I kept a close eye on the actions of my parents, brother and sister-in-law. Sure enough, just before we shut the shop door, Father arrived with a horse and cart and tethered it in the back yard. As he came indoors he said to Joseph, 'Son, I do believe we need a bit more wood. Would you mind taking the rig out back along to the wood merchant. If you hurry you might find someone still at the yard. And then, since you're going past, you might just deliver a parcel around to Mr Howell. No hurry to return the horse. Gideon said to keep it 'til morning.'

Mother chipped in. 'Poor Mr Howell has been very lonely since his wife died. He'll probably invite you to stay for supper, if you can spare the time. He always likes to converse with folks newly arrived from upstate New York. The other day he fair drove me to distraction, quizzing me for the latest news back in Utica.'

'Is that suitable with you, Mary Anne?' she added, suddenly remembering to defer to her daughter-in-law.

'Certainly, Mother Sarah,' said Mary Anne, looking less than happy.

The evening dragged on and on – I swear every hour was the length of two.

Supper time came. Rattle of plates. Clang of spoon against Mother's black stew pot. The family favorite – meat dumplings. No Joseph.

I was fair driven to distraction. 'Alfred, do this. Alfred, don't do that.' Nothing I did met with anyone's approval. I had thought to take a nonchalant wander down to the river as soon as supper was cleared and my tasks complete. Foolish me! Pigs would fly sooner than I be left to my own devices. The girls and Mother kept me so driven with chores that I was a prisoner in my own home.

I began to suspect that little sister Jane and I were the only ones not in on this dark secret, whatever it could be. Even Sarah and Ann seemed unsettled. That made the mystery even deeper. My family was so law-abiding. It was I who had the reputation for mischief, though my misdemeanors were mostly trivial. What on earth could they be up to? And if it was something my older sisters knew about, why couldn't I be told? That thought really rankled – I could understand why Jane wasn't included – after all, she was only ten, and a girl.

At last Papa took pity on me. He knocked his pipe out against the hearth and popped it back on the carved pipe rack beside the mantelpiece.

'Women, leave the lad alone,' he growled through his bushy beard. 'Alfred, come with me into the parlor where we'll get peace. I want to show you the plans for our new display cabinets. You're showing a good eye for layout and design – let's see what you think of them.'

Eventually it was bed time. I tugged my night-shirt on over the top of my day clothes, ready for quick removal, hopped into bed and pulled up the blanket. At least there was one small mercy – my room overlooked the back yard and access lane, rather than fronting on to busy Fifth street. A cold breeze chilled my room but I left the window ajar in order to hear every little noise from the back of the house.

Nearly an hour later, cart wheels rumbled in the lane. Jumping up, I peered cautiously through the half-open curtains. Nothing to see yet. I started to pull off my night-shirt, ready to sneak down.

Whoops. Footsteps coming up the creaky stairs.

I dashed back to bed. Slid under the covers. Hoped that whoever it was didn't come too close. With a tiny click, the door opened.

Breathe deep, breathe slow. Listen like a fox.

A tiny whisper. 'Alfred.'

Had I been asleep I would not have heard it. My devious old lady.

Again. 'Alfred, are you awake?'

A pause, then the door was carefully and quietly shut. The loose board three steps down the stairs gave its creeerk. I listened intently. No, she hadn't gone far – just to the next landing.

Silence for a couple of minutes. She was running the same check on Jane, no doubt sound asleep in the girls' big bedroom. The stairs creaked again. Footsteps receded. I breathed with relief. Safe – for now.

I tip-toed back to the window and peered out into the yard. It was very dark. I could just make out Joseph's shape in the yard below. He had already led the horse as close to the house as possible. He strode to the back of the cart. Stopped. Looked around the yard. Up at the house windows. I shrank back, praying that he'd not seen me.

The back door opened and a narrow spill of light fell into the yard. Quickly it shut again. Father was out there with him. I strained my ears but no words of their low mumble could I discern. Together they pulled out some of the wood neatly stacked at the back of the cart. Unusually quiet, they placed it beside the back door as if ready for the women in the morning.

And then, the moment I'd been waiting for. It appeared that something big was being pulled out over the tailgate of the cart by my father and brother. I leaned out as far as I dared but couldn't quite see what was going on. Then the back door re-opened, this time with only a tiny glimmer of light showing. Someone inside had dimmed the lamp in the kitchen. It appeared that two figures stepped inside, but in barely a second the door was shut again. I rubbed my eyes. What had I seen? Joseph was still in the yard, leading the horse to our shed.

I whistled quietly under my breath. The mystery deepened.

Joseph came out of the shed, secured the wooden bar in the frame, and rinsed his hands under the pump. Why was he so slow! A fellow could bake a loaf of bread in the time he was taking.

Finally, the back door opened and closed one more time. My brother was inside at last. I waited a few minutes more, but the yard seemed empty now. It was time for the next stage of my plan. Carefully – tip-toe to the door. Cautiously – inch the door open. Pray – please don't squeak.

Thank goodness my room was two floors up or perchance they'd have heard my footsteps. Like a tail-twitching cat after a bird, I eased my way to the top of the stairwell.

Right then my adventure finished before it had fully begun. Sitting on the bottom stair was my sister Sarah, reading a book by candlelight.

Chapter 29

Alfred
Cincinnati October 1839

The next morning I woke to the sound of drizzle on the tiles above my head. Normally I loved my cozy new bedroom, an attic room with white wooden floor boards, decorated with my rag mat from Utica. The little dormer window, with cotton curtains to keep out the drafts, gave me a birds' eye view over the roofs of Cincinnati as well as down into our yard. But this time the room and its virtues was the last thing on my mind. I hated being excluded.

I bounded down the stairs, pretending nothing was wrong. A searching sweep of the crowded kitchen – nothing out of place. Not a sign of unfamiliar or illegal activities could I see.

Sarah was laying the last platters and spoons on the oak table. She gave me a hard look. 'Did you sleep well?'

'Oh, most soundly, sister. Didn't hear a thing once my head hit the pillow.' It was my secret as to when the pillow was finally embraced. I could play at their game. If they didn't want to share their silly little secrets, I'd go and find my own.

Porridge eaten, before my mother could even begin issuing orders, I surprised her with, 'What errands would you like me to run this morning?' I'd go stir-crazy if I couldn't get out of the house soon.

Half an hour later, wearing my waxed cloth raincoat and with Mother's wicker basket in one hand, I was in the Fifth street market, looking for carrots, parsnips and two chickens. My mood brightened when I spotted Purity, also with a basket.

'Well, hello! I didn't think you came downtown on a Tuesday?' I'd made it my business to learn her regular market days. She gave me a cheeky grin as she took a bunch of onions from the stall holder.

'You can't be up with all my activities, Master Alfred,' she teased. We bantered for a few minutes, then she explained. 'Family have just arrived unexpectedly so I've been sent for extra supplies. Dr Beecher's third son Henry is enjoying a small vacation before he takes up a new pulpit. His father is very proud of his son's popularity as a preacher. I'd love to chat but Zillah will not be pleased if I dally.'

With a bouncy wave she headed off. I stood there watching her go, my heart doing a little tap-dance. Lost in hopeful dreams, I didn't hear my name being called.

'Hey, Alf. Are you deaf?'

I looked around with a smile, my thoughts still on the trim figure disappearing swiftly through the crowd. There was Patrick, an apprentice from just along Fifth street, hopping excitedly from foot to foot. His employer, Mr Hicks, a bonnet and shoe merchant, was a close friend of our family. Their premises were just the other side of the market, between Walnut and Main. I knew Mr Hicks' name was on that mysterious Constitution, but cautious questioning of Patrick had added nothing to the puzzle.

His freckles were only a slight shade lighter than his russet hair, which normally stuck out at all angles from under his scruffy old cap. Today it was plastered down, drips of rain falling off the end of his nose.

'What's doing?' I asked.

'There be a right feisty stoush going on down the Public Landin'. The Irish rivermen are 'avin' a go at some darkies. Me Da reckons the blacks bin stealin' their business.'

Mother's chickens and vegetables forgotten, I was out of the market as fast as a rat down a sewer. With an occasional slip on the wet cobbles, we ran the four blocks down to the river, splashing through puddles and dodging passers-by, the wicker basket banging at my side.

Clearly others had heard the news – as we got closer to the river other men and lads joined us, intent on a bit of fun.

We couldn't get up close to the action. Too many fellows, most of them shouting and yelling, were already crowding around the brawlers. We made for a vantage point up the bank. Men on moored vessels were watching too. About fifty men were going for it – punching, throwing, hitting with sticks. About a third of them were black men and the rest were white. All were roughly dressed. Some bowler-hatted fellows with notebooks and pencils hustled around the fringes of the action, taking bets on the outcome.

I was yelling and shouting with the rest when suddenly I was hauled backwards by my wet coat collar.

'Hey, stop that,' I squawked.

'No, you stop. You get back to work IMMEDIATELY.' It was brother Thomas, sent to find me. Picking up Mother's basket, fortunately still intact, I slunk off like a kicked puppy.

Alfred
Cincinnati November 1839

It wasn't long before I made two friends.

The first time Ralph came into the store was one afternoon on his way home, hoping for something to fill the hole in his belly. He was apprenticed to brothers-in-law Mr Proctor and Mr Gamble in their soap and candle-making factory on Main street.

When he put his hand in his pocket to pay for two sultana buns, all he found was a hole. I'd already set the buns on the counter and he was almost licking his lips in anticipation. Instant disappointment took up residence on his square and open face.

'Tarnation! I put a penny there at noon.' I took pity on him. Gave him the buns for free. I'm sure Pa would have done the same. I found out later his landlady was very stingy with the meals; poor Ralph was ever hungry.

He got into the habit of calling in to our store pretty near every night on his way home. When a bun or loaf of bread was like to be thrown out as too stale, it became a regular habit to save it for Ralph. This small kindness paid off in a most unexpected way, as I will tell in due time.

And Will, soon to play a very significant role in my life, was introduced because of my sister Ann's romancing. Will was apprenticed to my future brother-in-law, Samuel Alley.

We had received a note from Mother, shortly before leaving Utica, saying that Ann, only sixteen, was to wed. There hadn't been time for much back-and-forth about the coming event before we headed west, so I was not surprised as, about to step into the kitchen shortly after our arrival, I'd heard Mary Anne asking for more information.

'Mother Burnett,' she said. 'What line of work is Ann's intended in?'

Mother had sighed. 'He's a printer. Got his own press. I hope Ann knows what she's letting herself in for. She's so young. And I'm none too sure the publications he prints will provide a secure source of income, if previous events are anything to go by.'

All ears, I stopped just inside the door as Mary Anne asked, 'What events do you mean?'

My mother glanced up. Spotting me, she changed the topic. I heard no further explanation.

Whatever Mother's concerns, it didn't seem a bother to Father. He'd given his permission and, judging by the number of times I saw he and Samuel with heads together, it seemed they did a lot of business together.

Mother's remarks made me curious about my future brother-in-law but there was seldom opportunity to learn anything of significance. If I entered the room when Samuel was in conversation with other members of the family, the subject was almost always changed. This made me really cranky. Now I was fifteen, it was high time they realized I was an adult.

So, it was to Will that I turned for information. I was minding the store late one morning, a couple of weeks after the mystery event with the firewood, when an opportunity presented itself. Will had called in to collect a document Father wanted printed.

'Exactly what kind of publications does Samuel print?' I asked while he waited for Father to fetch the paper, his inky hands crossed behind his back and well away from our polished wooden countertop and sparkling glass display containers,

'Books, pamphlets, and such. Anything someone wants printed, really. But our bread and butter is the weekly newspaper for the Ohio State Anti-Slavery Society, the *Philanthropist*. It comes out every Wednesday.'

'I've seen copies of that around here. My father says it's the only one that gives the true story about the evils of slavery.'

'He's right. There are many people in this place who don't like us telling the truth. I didn't realize how dangerous the job would be when I started working for Samuel. In some places it isn't safe to say where I work. I've even had stones thrown at me, and been hit with sticks.'

'What! Surely not!' I started to worry about *my* safety, if this was true.

'Yep. And that's just for starters. Right from the early days of the paper, before Samuel took over and I began my apprenticeship, there were threats and even riots against the printing press and the people involved. More than once, in fact.'

I looked at Will with awe. Here was I, learning to be a lowly confectioner and pastry cook while my new friend lived a life of danger.

Then Father returned, a sheet of paper in hand. This conversation would have to wait for another time. How it rubbed like a pebble in my shoe to practice patience.

The next opportunity came the following Wednesday. The night before, Samuel had asked Pa if I could be spared for the morning to help Will deliver papers out to Lane Seminary and other subscribers in Walnut Hills. Normally they used a horse and cart, but the horse was needed for something else that morning – no-one explained what. We loaded the heavy papers in our hand-cart and taking a handle each, headed for the hill.

This time I knew not to ask sensitive questions while in the busy streets. However, once we were safely away from listening ears and starting to rise up the hill, I grabbed my chance.

'Hey Will, those riots you were telling me about the other day … I still don't understand why anyone would riot against a newspaper office. It's only putting ink on paper.'

He looked sideways at me. 'As far as the critics are concerned, our paper is a rabble-rouser.' He added, 'I imagine you've not been here long enough to know, but many of the most respectable and wealthy residents of this town passionately hate abolitionists.'

I looked at him in surprise. Purity had hinted at this, but here was a more specific source of information.

'Are you an abolitionist too, Will?'

'Absolutely. I wouldn't have chosen to work for Samuel if I didn't believe in freedom for all men. I *hate* slavery and everything it stands for.'

I looked at him with something akin to hero worship. It was rather flattering to have an older boy talk so openly to me. 'So, these riots – can you tell me more?'

He collected his thoughts. 'The background goes like this. Near on three and a half years ago, July 1836, was a dire month for the paper. At the time it was edited by James Birney and printed by Samuel's predecessor, Achilles Pugh. On 12th July a mob broke into the printery, damaged it, and disabled the press by carting pieces away. The next day a slanderous handbill, supporting the lawlessness, was plastered on walls and buildings all round the city. The writers thought to revile, threaten and deter Mr Birney. Instead, he turned the tables on them. He shared the poster in the next issue of the paper, as soon as they got the press working again, adding his own editorial comment. By telling his readers about the intimidation, subscriptions to the paper and support for the cause of abolition dramatically increased. He had the last laugh!'

We both chuckled. 'Why do you think subscriptions increased?' I asked.

'I think it brought other abolitionist supporters, people who hate bullies and cruelty, out of the woodwork. Attack a man's right to free speech in this country and you strike at the heart of what so many Americans hold dear.'

'Did Mr Pugh continue to print the paper?'

'Yes, but only for a short time. Two weeks later an even bigger and more violent mob broke in again and completely destroyed the press. He had a family to support; he gave up soon after.'

'But surely the officials of the city stop such mob behavior?'

'Far from it. The pro-slavery *Republican* of July 21st advised their readers to *"eschew the society of James G. Birney and avoid him as you would a viper"*. Not one word of criticism of the mob or the encouragers of violence did they print. Many leading citizens and a goodly number of senior city officials are quite happy when mobs attack abolitionists.'

My jaw dropped. 'Surely not!'

'I'll name you a few – you'll be shocked. There's the Mayor, Samuel Davies, for starts. Pays lip service to law and order but is remarkably tardy at sending officers to quell riots. Another is William Burke. He's the Postmaster and also a Methodist minister, can you believe! Then there's Robert Buchanan, the President of the Bank of Cincinnati. Oh, and there's also someone of the same name as you – Burnet but spelt differently. Believe me, he's no friend to your family. Judge Jacob Burnet is a wealthy lawyer, a former Senator and Judge of the state's Supreme Court. He's even had his friends at other papers put statements in their publications to say he has no relationship to your family, much less any affinity on the subject of abolitionism. He *really* hates your father. Calls him a scurrilous and trouble-making Britisher who should return from whence he came.'

'But I don't understand. Why would such people be against abolition? There's no owning of slaves in Ohio, I'm told.'

'It hits their pockets. It did three years ago, and it does today. The same people, and many others whose pockets are filled by trading with the south, hate the fact that Kentuckians are increasingly reluctant to come to Cincinnati for business and pleasure. Thing is, they can bring their slaves but once a slave is on free soil, if they're not runaways, they're technically free. People from south of the river, who like to travel with their enslaved valets and maids, fear their attendants will be tempted away.'

'I don't get this. You mean that an escapee who makes it across the river isn't considered free but someone who's come with permission is, even if they're with their owner?'

'Basically, yes. The bottom line is the issue of permission. The point of law, which clever lawyers like our friend Salmon P. Chase have won cases on, is that Ohio is a free state. Therefore, anyone who lawfully enters the state cannot be a slave because our state forbids slavery.

'There is another law, however, that says that no person anywhere, in any state including free ones, is allowed to aid and abet a runaway slave. I know it seems contradictory to the law about permission that I first explained. I'm learning that there are many contradictions in the law. Seems it often comes down to a matter of interpretation and how clever the lawyers are.'

I scratched my head. 'It's amazing to me that anyone can make sense of such complications.'

'That's why Mr Birney was so influential with his editorials,' was Will's response. 'He's great with words, and interpretation of the law.'

'I *think* I understand.'

Will grinned. 'It does take a lot of getting your head round it. Mr Birney used to be a lawyer and a state senator for Kentucky. He gave it all up to work for the end of bondage. He really does understand both sides of the situation, for he's the son of a wealthy slave-owning family in Kentucky. And our current editor, Dr Gamaliel Bailey Jr, is just as skilful with his content.'

'The thing is, a runaway is property – the lawful property of a southern owner. The slave has no rights. If he or she runs away, they're essentially stealing themselves from their owners. So, anyone assisting a runaway, as do the members of the Underground Railroad, is breaking the law.'

'Underground Railroad?'

'Haven't you heard that term yet? That's what people have started calling the escape network.'

I tucked that nugget of gold away for further investigation, but we were drawing near the Beecher house. I looked around, hoping to see Purity. Distracted, I didn't hear what he said next.

'Hey, Alf, are you listening?'

'Sorry.' No pretty maid was sweeping the preacher's sidewalk or shaking mats. I turned back to Will. 'I am now.'

'I've had a thought. Do you want to read about the riots? That'll give you more understanding. We've got back copies of the paper since it began. I'm sure Samuel won't mind me showing you what was written when Mr Birney was still the editor.'

I jumped at the chance.

A few hours later we were back at Samuel's noisy printery. The smell of ink and other fluids I couldn't identify permeated the room. A tall wooden flat-bed press took up a large amount of the room. Nearby was a work bench, with boxes of metal type – many repeats of the letters of the alphabet, Will explained.

Samuel, draped in a scratched and stained leather apron, gave us a wave as he operated the heavy platen. Sheets of paper were pinned up drying. With Samuel's permission, Will went to the storage shelves at the back of the room, pulled out a big cardboard-covered folio and flipped quickly to the relevant pages.

'Look there,' he pointed. I skimmed the reproduced handbill.

'The citizens of Cincinnati … satisfied that the business of the place is receiving a vital stab from the wicked and misguided operations of the abolitionists, are resolved to arrest their course. The destruction of their Press on the night of the 12th may be taken as a warning. … Citizens engaged in the unholy cause of annoying our southern neighbor .. are appealed to, to pause before they bring things to a crisis.

'If an attempt is made to re-establish their press, it will be viewed as an act of defiance to an already outraged community, and on their heads be the results … Every kind of expostulation and remonstrance has been resorted to in vain … longer patience would be criminal. The plan is matured to eradicate an evil which every citizen feels is undermining his business and property.'

A further handbill, dated 17th July, had also been reproduced. It offered one hundred dollars reward for *'the delivery of one James G. Birney, a fugitive from justice. … Birney, in all his associations and feelings, is black, although his external appearance is white. The above reward will be paid and no questions asked, by Old Kentucky.'*

My heart swelling with indignation at such injustice, I almost cheered when I read Mr Birney's editorial response.

'Must we trample on the liberty of white men here because they have trampled on the liberty of black men at the south? Must we forge chains for the mind here, because they have forged them for the body there? Must we extinguish the right to speak, the right to print in the north, that we may be in unison with the south? No, never.'

As I helped Will put away the heavy folder, I thought of all the odd and unexplained things that I'd seen, both here and in Utica. Mary Anne taking Joseph's old clothes down to the Negro settlement. The letters and documents I'd found in Joseph's desk. The conversations that stopped when I walked into a room. The mysterious load of wood a few weeks ago.

Like untangling a snarled fishing line, the random and unexplained pieces of the puzzle, hints, allusions and clues, all slipped into place. A clear picture emerged from the fuzzy background. Of course! I'd known for some time that the family hated slavery. But finally, I saw it. Not only did they hate and abhor it, but, in every way they could, they were trying to destroy it. They were deliberately, proudly, breaking the law. Helping slaves escape from bondage. Members of the Underground Railroad.

It was time for a showdown.

Chapter 31

Alfred
Cincinnati November 1839

It was dinner time on Sunday – family night for the Burnett clan. Thomas and Emma always came for dinner on Sundays and Samuel had started coming too, even though he and Ann were still a few weeks from being wed. Thomas and Emma's little ones had eaten earlier and their eleven-year-old Aunt Jane, who'd eaten with them, was putting them to bed. She'd practiced on so many dolls, having real babies very much suited her.

Perfect opportunity. I'd decided it was best to hit everyone with my request in one go. I waited until Mother and Sarah had finished dishing out the food, grace had been said and everyone was eating. There came a momentary pause in the conversation.

'Pa, is this family helping slaves get away to Canada?'

Some had forks loaded, half-way to their mouths. Others were chewing. Everyone froze. Father spluttered. Nearly lost a mouthful of pork pie.

'What makes you ask that?' he hedged.

'You all think you're so good at keeping secrets. Well, I'm not stupid – and I'm not a child any more. I've known for ages that you're all up to something. I just didn't know quite what, but I've finally worked it out.' I couldn't say it was Will's information that had tipped me off. I didn't want him in trouble with his employer, sitting at our table.

'I want to be included. I hate being ignored and pretended to.'

Raised eyebrows, a momentary silence, and then everyone started talking at once. The outcome? To my delight, I walked away from the dinner table with a part to play. From now on I was to be a lookout for danger when runaways were crossing the river, and the messenger boy to let other safe houses know a delivery was coming. However, I wasn't included without a very serious caution.

'Alfred, I need you to understand something,' said Father. 'This is not a game. Many lives and livelihoods are at stake here. If you forget yourself, if you speak carelessly, or in the hearing of the wrong people, it will have terrible repercussions, not only for slaves recaptured, but also for us and all the other brave people who make up the network of safe houses. Can we really trust you not to act impulsively?'

'I promise, Pa. I'm responsible now.'

Mother and Joseph raised their eyebrows.

That night, I went to bed so excited I couldn't sleep. Eventually I gave up chasing elusive dreams and wandered downstairs to find a snack.

I opened the kitchen door to find my father seated at our well-scrubbed wooden table. Across from him was a black man of middle years, shoveling food in as if he hadn't seen a decent meal in days.

As I entered the room, the visitor dropped his spoon. Jumped to his feet. Gazed at me in terror. His head swiveled on his skinny neck, seeking the door. My father hastily reassured him. 'Sit, friend, sit. 'Tis only our son Alfred. He's about to start assisting us in our activities. He'll not betray you.'

The frightened man reluctantly sank to his seat again, visibly shaking. I felt bad for giving him such a scare.

A heap of Joseph's old clothes sat on the dresser. Sarah, stopped in mid-act by my unannounced arrival, had been pouring a bucket of cold water into the copper hip bath waiting in front of the wood stove. The old screen, used to afford a bather privacy, was waiting in the corner. On top of the wood range, our big pan – the one we mostly used to heat up bathing and washing water – was steaming and bubbling in its familiar and companionable way. The rich aroma of chowder tickled my nose. The hissing oil lamp, hanging from its hook in the ceiling, cast warm light and soft shadows over the familiar yet unfamiliar scene.

Mary Anne, big with child, rocked back and forth in the rocking chair as she knitted baby clothes – I did hope for her and Joseph that this one survived more than a few months. Ann quietly stitched a pretty garment, no doubt for her trousseau.

'Alf, your timing is excellent. Mr Thompson was about to tell us what happened,' said Father. He turned to our visitor. 'I apologize, Mr Thompson, for the interruption.'

The man picked up his spoon again and finished the last few mouthfuls of my mother's excellent corn chowder.

'My people bin slaves for three generation on a fair-size farm south o' Lexington, Kentucky. Until two week back we figure we lucky. Our owners good people. From gen'ration to gen'ration we bin treated pretty fine.

'Two weeks ago, our Marse thrown from a new horse. He break his neck. Dead. They shot de horse. And now Marse's brother inherit our estate. He a bad man, wid a wife mean as a 'gator. You'd cross the street to pass her by. He ride up de day afer de funeral. Demand to see de Missus. He prance in, tryin' to look solemn, but in truth, more like de cat what got de cream. I seed him comin' an' get a bad, bad feelin'. I head down to kitchen gardens to get a mess o' vegables for ma wife. She bin cook at da Big House for nigh on ten year, and I bin a house slave since I knee-high to a grasshopper.

'De Missus walk into de parlor like a lamb to slaughter – she got no idea what comin'.

'I's out in the kitchen gardens when I hear terrible wailin'. I race back to de kitchen and find my Bertha standin', apron over her head, keenin' like someone bin taken by de Lord.

'Oh Amos,' she cry as she clap eyes on me, wailin' even louder, if dat be possible, 'bad times is on us. We're losing Miz Cecile now, and de new Marse gwin sell you south. Say we got more bucks dan he need on dis place.'

'Our kind mistress, Miz Cecile, run into de kitchen a moment ahine me, fit to be tied. She as upset as Bertha. My sweet chilluns, playin' outside wid some new-born kittens, hear their mother's cries, an' come runnin'.

'De kitchen a jumble of grief-stricken people. I see de new Marse ride away, a smirk of devilish satisfaction on 'is face.

'De new Marse's nasty wife, she want Miz Cecile's beautiful home for many year. Her husband don' provide so sweet a place – he done wasted his inheritance from his father at de gamin' table. We figure he desperate for more funds. He an evil man. This nex' inheritance be gone in a few year, like de last, I be bound.

'Miz Cecile gonna be bundled off to live in a poky lil house in Lexington, away from all things famil'ar an' nice. Away from her home, de only one she knowd all her married life. She bin treated not much better 'n us. And me, I to be sold as soon as de new Marse take over – nex' week.

'So, with de help of Miz Cecile, we plan my 'scape. She done give me a note of permission to be off de plantation. An' here I is.'

He wiped his eyes with his linsey-woolsey sleeve. 'I fear I never see my wife an' chilluns again. But, Lord willing, once I gets to Canada an' find a place, I go back an' help dem 'scape.'

He reached for bread to wipe his bowl clean.

'May I serve you some more, Mr Thompson?' politely enquired Mother.

Chapter 32

Alfred
Cincinnati December 1839

It was beyond wonderful to be fully involved in the family doings. I sensed it was also a relief for the others; now they could speak freely inside our walls, except when Jane was around. And she was not an inquisitive child. Biddable, obedient – these were the kind of words you'd use to describe Jane. Oddly enough, they weren't words anyone seemed inclined to apply to me.

A week after my induction into the family's exciting activities I was sent to deliver a message and a big parcel of clothes to Mr Hopkins, a wealthy but secret supporter. He lived a little out of town, in the wooded and upmarket district of Mt Auburn. Father stressed the importance of what I was to say and I'd repeated it several times to prove I was word perfect. Nothing could be put to paper, lest I be intercepted.

Before heading to Mr Hopkins' place, I had to drop off some papers to one of the shipping agents down at the Public Landing. From there I decided to take the less direct way, along the riverbank for a short while, before heading for the hills. Thinking about the importance of my errand, I didn't immediately notice a girl sitting on a log beside the well-trodden path.

'Hey, Alf. I'm sure glad to see you!'

Startled out of my reverie, I stopped in shock. Was I imagining things?

'Abigail, you're back!'

Since our arrival I'd occasionally wondered if she would come again. But recent events had crowded my thoughts to such a degree that, right then, she was the last person I expected to see.

'Sure am! Hell, it's cold.'

I ignored her profanity and focused on her appearance. She'd got the seasons wrong. It was a bone-chilling day and she had just a light shawl over the cotton dress and apron I'd seen last time. No overcoat or mittens and her nose was red with cold. As before, my coin dangled conspicuously around her neck.

She pulled her shawl closer and shivered as she looked around at the bare-leaved trees and the low-hung wintery sun peeking through iron-grey clouds. I plonked down beside her.

'I'm a working man now,' I told her with some pride.

'You are? How did that happen?'

'Father is an irresistible force when he becomes determined on a course of action. And my brothers agreed. Mama was cross but the men of the family got their way this time.'

'So you're all settled in Cincinnati now? How long is it since we last met?'

'Only a couple of months,' I replied. 'It's late December 1839 and I'm on an errand for my parents.'

She gestured to the rain-swollen waters flowing swiftly beside us. 'Is this the famous Ohio River that was flooded when you were at Portsmouth?'

'It most decidedly is. But,' I noticed her fingers were blue, 'you're cold. Walk with me; that will help warm you up.'

As I stood, I picked up the parcel and was reminded of the contents. I'd watched my mother wrap them up. 'There's clothing in here you can borrow, as long as you give it back before we get to Mr Hopkins' place.'

After checking that no-one was coming along the path, I carefully untied the string and folded back the brown paper. Inside were two coats, not new but still with good wear in them, plus four scarves, some woolen hats and several pairs of mittens and socks. I now understood why my mother and sisters were always busy with their knitting needles of an evening, and why I seldom saw their handiwork worn by any of the family.

Abigail was delighted. In no time she had wrapped up warm. We carefully re-tied the parcel and began to walk along the river path together.

'So where are we going? You said it was an errand for your parents, but this isn't cakes or bread.'

I hesitated. 'I can't take you right to where I'm headed, but we can talk while we walk. It's a good forty minutes still. Time enough to catch up on some of the news. You'll never believe … Oh, I mustn't talk about it.'

She gave me a hard stare. 'You can't leave it there! I'm not exactly a security risk, you know. I'm not planning to stand on street corners and tell the world who I am and where I'm from, let alone your little secrets.'

'Well, maybe not, but who knows what might happen while you're here. You might be apprehended and interrogated.'

I added, 'And it's not a *little* secret. It's life and death.' I was parroting my father now.

She bounced with glee. 'Oh, are you talking about slaves and stuff? Like, helping them escape? Are they conductors on the Underground Railroad?'

I was shocked. 'Shh! Don't say that out loud!' I swiftly looked both ways. No-one else was visible on the path, thankfully. 'How could you possibly know that?'

Abigail tapped the side of her nose. Looked annoyingly smug. 'Some advantages of being from your future.' Then relented when she noticed my worry and confusion.

'I'm reading up about your time period. My school librarian found me two books. The first one is about Harriet Tubman, a really brave runaway slave from Maryland. Once she got free, she went back south many times to help others also escape to Canada. Have you heard of her?'

I shook my head.

She paused, then, 'Of course you haven't. Silly me. Right now, she's still a young girl, about our age, living on a plantation. And I'm about to start the second book. *Uncle Tom's Cabin* by Harriet Beecher Stowe. It says in the foreword that she lives here now.'

'She does too! I know about her – my friend Purity works for her parents! She told me Mrs Stowe's a writer.'

Abigail's mouth dropped open. 'That is *amazing*!' She looked at me with new respect. 'It's a bit odd, this time-travel thing, don't you agree? She might write about stuff you and your family are involved with. But the book won't be published until 1852. And it's a novel, so maybe you guys won't get a starring role.'

I got goosebumps.

She continued. 'And something else. Aunt Hanna and I found that constitution you showed me. It was in the tin trunk, along with the other stuff. She guessed the bit about 'rendering aid and advantage in maintaining their title to liberty' probably meant the Committee of Vigilance were helping them escape. I've learnt a lot about the Underground Railroad since we last met. Is that really what your family have been keeping from you?'

I still hesitated to answer.

She just about danced on the spot with frustration. 'Come on, Alf. Don't hold out on me. Are they?'

Again I looked around – really frightened. 'You MUST NOT say this kind of thing out loud. You could get us killed or thrown in prison, talking like that.' My father's warnings reverberated in my head.

'No! Surely you're exaggerating!'

'I'm not! My father, just this morning, reminded me of Mr Lovejoy. He was an abolitionist newspaper editor and publisher in Illinois. In his paper he regularly condemned the evils of slavery. Four times his press was destroyed. The fourth time he was shot and killed by an anti-abolition mob as he tried to put out a fire they'd started. And that's just one example.

'Our family lives daily with this kind of threat, for my father is very vocal on his views on slavery. He's passionate about protecting the slaves and anyone else, black or white, who helps them to freedom. So, it's not safe to admit to direct involvement. Enemies are always trying to catch us out.'

She thought on that for a moment. 'Well, judging by what you're not allowed to say, at least they've let you into the secret.'

I sighed and relented, talking very quietly. She laughed out loud when I described lobbing my bomb into the middle of last week's dinner conversation. Then nearly cried as I told her the tragic story of Mr Thompson, the runaway in our kitchen. From there we moved on to other topics – working in the bakery, the Beechers and Stowes, Will, and what he'd shared about the *Philanthropist* and the riots.

Too quickly, we drew nigh to Mr Hopkins' residence. It was tucked in amongst many trees and set back off the road, out of sight of neighbors. According to my father, his big home, numerous sheds and secret hiding spots made him a godsend to the cause.

I stopped near the gate.

'I'm sorry, Abigail, but you can come no further. I must be alone when I speak with Mr Hopkins, and I'll have to get back that warm coat. It's needed by others.'

Reluctantly she took off the coat, scarf and mittens, folded them and helped me re-tie the parcel.

'Thanks for the loan, Alf.' She shivered. 'I might as well go home now, back to summer. And here's the coin. Keep it safe, great-great-great uncle, or whatever you are.'

With a chuckle at my startled face, she disappeared.

Chapter 33

Alfred
Cincinnati December 1839

I quickly got to know our key contacts. They were family too – united not by blood or color, but a shared belief in the rightness of our common cause. We hated the laws that encouraged such extreme cruelty.

Mr Henry Boyd was one such – an ex-slave who'd bought his freedom years before. He sheltered many runaways in his home or workshop, readying them for the next part of their journey. My father and Mr Boyd first met in 1836, when Father was preparing to open his new store. He had engaged Mr Boyd's company to build a new counter for the store, and also to make a gold-etched sign; it hung above the door, proudly informing passers-by that here was *Burnett's Wedding Cake Manufactory, Fancy Cake Store, Wholesale & Retail Confectionary*.

From then on, Pa and Mr Boyd became close friends. By the time I met him, he had a successful furniture manufactory with sometimes up to 50 employees. A man's skill with wood was the important thing to Mr Boyd; black, brown and white men worked side by side in his workshop. His main stock-in-trade was very high-quality beds, including bug-proof ones, according to the advertisements in the papers. I had no idea what they might be! His quality workmanship and business acumen had made him one of the wealthiest black men in the city and well-respected in many quarters.

Another of my regular stopping points was the boarding establishment of Dumas House in McAllister street. Free black lodgers came and went at all hours, so it was reasonably easy to hide a runaway there for a day or two. However, its obvious advantages also made it an obvious target. Slave catchers and bounty hunters sometimes illegally forced their way in – unannounced and with no search warrant.

I was nearly at Dumas House one morning with a message when I noticed a crowd gathered outside. I could hear shouting from the middle of the melee. People were being shoved out of the way. Two roughly-clad bearded men emerged from the house, carrying whips. Between them they dragged a pretty caramel-colored girl, I guessed about seventeen, out onto the footpath. Two other scary-looking white men were beside them, holding four snarling, slavering bloodhounds on chains. All of the men carried or were wearing guns.

The girl was crying. Struggling. Through her sobs, she screamed, 'No. No. I's free. You can't take me.' But her wrists were chained together. They ignored her pleas.

In the crowd, some tried to stop the men but no-one could get close for fear of the dogs. Others yelled the same thing, that she was a free woman. The foul-faced men took no notice. Other spectators looked smug, as though they approved.

I took to my heels and ran for home. Bursting into the bakery, I nearly knocked a tray of hot cakes out of Martin's hands.

Joseph looked up from decorating a pound cake. 'Land sakes, boy. Watch …'

'It's not right!' I blurted out.

'Calm down, lad. What's not right?'

I was close to tears as I told my story. Joseph, ever quick-thinking, said, 'Quick. Run to Mr Chase's office. If he can get help before they cross the river, he might be able to stop them.'

I took to my heels again. Mr Chase was just unlocking his office door. As soon as he'd unraveled my story he headed fast for the Sheriff's office, a determined look on his face. I wouldn't want to be on the receiving end of his wrath.

Sadly, on this occasion he was unable to get aid for the young woman before she was dragged across the river in a waiting boat.

'What will happen to her?' I asked Joseph that evening. Mr Chase had called into the shop with an update later in the day.

He scowled. 'She'll almost certainly be on her way south down the river by now. Kidnappers take their victims well away from their homes. Probably to the slave markets of Natchez or New Orleans.'

'How can they do that? The people at the house said she was free.'

'If there's enough kidnappers, and they've got guns, whips and dogs, it's a brave person who'll defy them. They often force their way in, especially into places like Dumas House. They say they're searching for a runaway, even though they're supposed to have a search warrant to hunt for a particular person. More often than not, they're just being opportunists, on the lookout for anyone they can nab.'

'Can't they be stopped?'

'All of us in the network keep our ears to the ground. Do all we can to thwart their evil ways. Some we win. But today wasn't one of them, sadly.'

He saw my crest-fallen face. 'You couldn't have done anything else, Alf. We need to know *before* they get their hands on someone. It's very difficult to extract a victim in the situation you saw today. We're so close to the river that kidnappers can escape to Kentucky while we're still marshalling support. We have to be seen to work inside the law, and it takes time to activate the Sheriff or other law enforcement officers.'

❀ ❀

And so my involvement progressed. Within a couple of months, I was a regular part of the network and known to many of the residents of Bucktown, just a few streets away. It was here that many of the free blacks lived and worked.

Many runaways went straight to Bucktown or were taken there. Other times we were the first stop. It was not uncommon to hear a knock on our back door, accessed by the service lane. With many colored men employed on and around the river, it was easy for a riverman to quietly whisper directions to a safe house. Sometimes we fetched them from the riverbank, alerted by messengers. Other times white abolitionists or our black friends brought them to us, if they suspected their homes were under surveillance.

Some slaves planned their escape for a long time. Others ran when they found they were about to be sold, or an unexpected opportunity arose. Either way, if they'd travelled more than a day or so, they were almost always in pretty poor shape by the time they reached the river. The regular routine when a delivery was received, no matter whose home they first sheltered in, was food, clothes and doctoring. Their clothes were often ripped and inadequate, especially in winter. All the stations kept spare clothing, and keeping up these supplies was a very important role for all the abolitionist womenfolk.

Many fugitives needed doctoring. Because so many started ill-shod or with no shoes, after running through deeply wooded forests, rocky streams and rough fields, it was common for them to arrive with blisters, cut feet and twisted ankles. In winter, frostbite and hypothermia. And far too commonly, grievous injuries from vicious overseers or owners.

The other thing that very few runaways had was money. Much help for this came from invisible sources – wealthy and prominent businessmen, under deep cover. By pretending to be against our aims they were of immense help to the cause.

A runaway's elation once he or she got across their River Jordan to the Promised Land was a sight to see. It was the first time most of them had ever set foot in a free state. But they were still a long way from safety. Bounty hunters earned very good money when they returned a runaway to an angry and vengeful owner, so Cincinnati could only be a staging post. With the aid of a widely diverse network and with as much haste as was safe, we moved them north, from station to station, all the way to Canada.

The conductors were as diverse as those they aided. It was not uncommon for a hard-drinking and swearing riverman to deliver a 'parcel' to a gentle Quaker grandmother. Or a sophisticated city lawyer or doctor might be the escort of terrified and tattered people, conveying them into the hands of a rough tobacco-chewing and whisky-breath backwoods man living in a primitive dirt-floored cabin.

However, not all runaways had to be shipped out under cover of darkness. Thomas walked into the bakery one afternoon with a big grin, back from luncheon with his family.

'I heard a good one just now from Mr Chase. You know how skilled slaves are sometimes hired out to other people. Well, a beautiful high yellow girl with very light skin, slave to a family in Virginia, was particularly skilled at needlework and often hired out to make fine garments for other people. She wasn't allowed to keep any of the money her owner made from the hiring.'

I interrupted. 'Do you mean that some owners *do* let their slaves keep some of their earnings?'

'Exactly,' answered Father, who was making chocolate. 'That's how Mr Boyd was able to purchase his freedom. He was lucky to have a decent master and, with a natural talent with wood, was often employed to make furniture for others.'

'Let me finish my story,' said Thomas, frowning at Father and me. 'The wealthy woman who'd hired the seamstress hated the institution of slavery, so hatched up a plan to help her escape. The young woman was married to a man on an adjoining plantation. He had a much darker complexion. The girl dressed in fine clothes given by her temporary employer, pretended that her husband was her slave, and with money also given by the kind lady, took a ship from Norfolk to New York. They thought they were discovered when a friend of her owner sat down near them, but she was dressed so fine the fellow had no idea.'

We laughed. Surrounded as we were with so much risk and opposition, it was good to hear success stories.

'I've heard another variation on that,' added Joseph. 'Sometimes a runaway with a very light skin is dressed in fine clothes and, accompanied by a white person, travels north to Canada by normal transport. People see what they expect to see – in this case, two white people.'

'Those are the lucky ones,' said Father. 'What about the people with a tiny drop of Negro blood who get sold at slave auctions. They're often as white as the people bidding for them. Any light-skinned beautiful girl is in high danger of being bought by a house of ill repute, or sold to service the carnal desires of her new owner. The injustice of it makes my blood boil.'

We knew about Father's boiling blood – it was the reason we were all engaged in this dangerous game of subterfuge. It didn't matter how they came, or through whose agency. No matter the color of our skin, we all worked together for the greater good. The main thing was not to compromise each other. Mind you, Father didn't seem to care if he compromised himself. He was fearless in his outspokenness, despite my mother's pleas for him to be less audacious.

What we white abolitionists were deeply mindful of was to avoid stirring up trouble for the black community. Even though their leaders were well regarded in some quarters, and the likes of Henry Boyd the furniture maker, Gideon Langston, both a livery owner and a barber, and William

Watson, also a barber, provided quality services to the white population, many whites resented colored success and were always on the lookout for ways to make trouble. It didn't take much tinder to start a racial fire, and anyone with a dark skin was seen as fair game by the thugs of the town.

Mind you, just breathe and some would take exception, as an occasional perusal of the various newspapers showed. The editors of the *Enquirer* made no secret of their opinions: '*We were overrun with Negroes. They took the inside of the pavement upon all occasions – swelled and swaggered, and obtruded their miscreated visages, like Milton's devils, where they had no business.*'

A few days later, Father read out something else from the same source: '*The city is overrun with free blacks, laboring, when they do labor, in competition with white citizens, and when they do not, subsisting by plunder…*' It made him so angry that, if he'd been a kettle, steam would have billowed out of him. He only reduced to a simmer when he read a more open-minded correspondent's observation, that intolerant people had '*a disposition to be more angry with their [*colored people's*] virtues than with their vices. More than one Cincinnatian was angered simply by respectable and responsible black behavior.*'

Such arrogant bigotry and unjust discrimination simply made us all more determined.

Chapter 34

Alfred
Cincinnati 1st January 1840

Apart from store and errand time, I could normally be found suds-deep in dish water, greasing pans, or any other dogs-body duties my parents and older siblings threw my way. When I complained about all the menial work, Thomas put me in my place. 'You're only just fifteen, Alf. Every artisan has to start at the bottom.'

On the family front, it was in many ways satisfying that we three Burnett brothers had finally rejoined our parents and sisters. Now, when Father disappeared off on his private matters, we were well able to keep business running satisfactorily. For this alone, Mother was grateful. It meant she could rely on her sons to keep food on the table and a roof over our heads. There was even talk of opening other Burnett enterprises around town.

The new year started with a bang, but the fireworks were not of an incendiary nature. As we shut up the store on the last day of 1839, I spotted Mother and Ann helping Mary Anne upstairs.

'What's up with Mary Anne?' I asked Sarah, who was putting the left-over biscuits into a tin to keep them fresh for the morrow.

'I think the baby's coming.'

I knew what this meant. The house would be in upheaval for the duration, Joseph would pace anxiously, women would rush up and down stairs and we fellows would shift for ourselves. At least this time there were other female family members to assist, as well as the midwife. I knew the drill

– I'd been a concerned bystander three times before. Then I remembered something else.

'But tomorrow it's Ann's wedding.'

Sarah replied tartly, 'I don't think this little one consulted the family's social calendar. Babies set their own schedule.'

Ann came down, looking a mite upset. Sarah looked at her enquiringly. They muttered quietly, backs to me. Ann shrugged her shoulders and disappeared back upstairs, carefully carrying a jug of hot water. We always had water simmering on the stove.

No-one slept much that night but by early morning we all rejoiced – a healthy baby girl arrived and was immediately named after her mother, as was the custom. Ann and Mother were probably even more delighted than Mary Anne and Joseph – the rest of the day, with Ann's wedding to Samuel, could proceed as planned.

Soon after, our parents and my sisters Jane and Sarah found elsewhere to reside and Joseph took over the house on Fifth street. Just as in Utica, it made sense for me to continue living with him and Mary Anne. This time it was proximity to work instead of school that dictated my abode. I was happy for that arrangement. Although it was good to be united as a family, it was a tad restricting to have my mother again looking over my shoulder. I think she'd forgotten I was no longer nine, always up to mischief or needing supervision. Plus, I didn't want her disapproving eye watching my attempts to be more than a friend to Purity. I'd overheard her muttering to Mary Anne about someone being too immature to think of walking out.

Being the youngest son was a frustrating inheritance at times.

Chapter 35

Alfred
Cincinnati 1840

Purity came running into the store, nearly tripping over the doorstep in her haste. Her bonnet was trailing, her cloak flapping. I'd never seen her so disheveled.

'Alf, we need your family's help,' she panted. 'The catchers are after Mrs Stowe's new maid.'

I looked at her in shock. I'd met petite Eliza with her mop of tight black curls and merry eyes when she'd come into the store once with Purity. She'd been like a butterfly, flitting around in delight, oohing and aahing at the candy displays and delicious cakes.

'What do you mean? I thought she was free.'

'So did everyone. She says that her Kentucky mistress brought her into Ohio some months ago and gave her liberty to stay here. So, by our state laws, she's free.'

'Why would the mistress have done that?'

'She's a northern lady. Hates slavery. Decided to give Eliza her freedom. Now, all this time later, the husband has come seeking her. I was over at Mrs Stowe's this morning to help with the children when Eliza ran in, frightened near out of her wits. She'd been doing errands near the Findlay street market when who should come out a tavern door but her old master. He recognized her. Shouted out, "That's my slave. Stop her."'

'She got away, but she's beside herself with terror. He'll be hunting all over for her. Mrs Stowe is desperate for help. Says that all it needs is a corrupt lawman and Eliza'll be dragged back, no matter the justice of the matter. The Stowes have kept out of the business of aiding runaways until now and don't know where it's safe to send her. Her husband can drive Eliza but they need a guide. You were the first people we thought of.'

I ran downstairs to the bakery, where Joseph was deftly adding pink roses to an ornate wedding cake. We were well regarded in the town for producing beautiful multi-tiered creations.

'Of course I'll help,' he responded, as soon as I'd blurted out Purity's message. He put down his icing bag, thinking quickly.

'Give her this message for Mrs Stowe. If they can provide a horse and vehicle, I'll be at her father's house on dusk. It doesn't have close neighbors like the Stowe place. Get Eliza there and I'll guide them to old John Van Zandt. He's within driving distance at Glendale. He'll send her on through the network to the north.'

Professor Stowe was waiting anxiously when Joseph arrived at the Beecher house, with a horse already in the shafts of the seminary's small wagon. His brother-in-law, Henry Ward Beecher, visiting from his new parish in Indianapolis, joined them. As soon as it was quite dark they hustled the terrified girl out, wrapped up in a dark cloak of Mrs Stowe's, and helped her lie down in the back of the wagon.

'What sacks of produce can we put around her?' Joseph asked. 'We can't just jog out of town with a black girl visible to anyone who bothers to look. Someone would report us for sure.' A hurried consultation, some scurrying round, and in short order Eliza was hidden in a cave made of artfully positioned sacks of potatoes.

Joseph didn't arrive home until many hours later.

As was common after a delivery, Father worked the early shift so Joseph could sleep in. By the time we stopped for a break the next day, Joseph had emerged. We sat round the kitchen table with cups of tea and hot biscuits, keen to hear of his rescue mission.

'It was as well I went with them, for the two preachers knew neither Van Zandt's farm, nor the safer back roads, and with no moon it was hard to see the road once we were north of Walnut Hills and the lighted houses. We only showed the lamp light when we really had to, for we didn't want to draw attention. They would've probably taken a wrong turning if I'd not been with them. Or landed in a ditch or overturned on a sharp corner. That back way is right tricky.

'We'd been on the back road about an hour when we heard a trotting horse coming up behind. I managed to persuade the two reverends to keep their pistols out of sight until we knew if danger was approaching. I hissed a warning to the lass not to move.

'The rider pulled up alongside. Slowed his horse to our jog-along walking pace. His face was hidden under a wide-brimmed hat. A pistol in his holster.

"Good evening, gen'lemen," he said. "Out late the night?" Clouds of strong liquor wafted our way.

'I felt my fellow slave-runners tense. Then he said, "Where might ye be heading? Not many properties down this 'ere road."

'I couldn't tell if he was friend or foe. He didn't have a whip wrapped around the saddle horn or on his back, and no hounds ran at his heels, but informers don't advertise their affiliations.

"'I think we took a wrong turn," I told him, doing my best to keep my voice relaxed and conversational. "I trust we're now in the right direction to get back to the north road." I could sense the waves of terror coming off my reverends. Hoped the chatty horseman was too liquored up to notice.

'He leaned forward. Nearly fell off his horse as he peered curiously down into the back of the wagon. "Not hidin' a runaway in there, are ye?" Chortled as if it was the best of jokes.

'I felt an indrawn breath from Stowe, sitting next to me. Nudged him to keep his mouth shut. Laughed in response and replied, "Don't be foolish, man." Turned the tables on the interrogator. "And where are you headed?"

'He pulled himself back upright in his saddle. Rubbed his forehead as if trying to remember. "Ah yes. 'Ome to me nagging wife, the fussy old battle-ax. She'll be after giving me wot for agin. 'Snot fair. A man should be able to 'ave a wee drap wiv 'is buddies wivout gettin' grief when 'e gets 'ome."'

We chuckled at the thought of the man's reception from an annoyed wife, who'd probably had dinner cooked for hours. Father even looked a bit sympathetic to the man's plight. He'd caught the sharp end of Mother's tongue on a good many occasion, but his tardiness was due to distractions, not hard liquor.

Joseph continued, 'With that, our unwanted companion kicked his horse back into a trot and took off into the dark ahead of us. Stowe and Beecher could barely talk for the next few minutes. Sat there shaking. It was just our luck to get a drunk, nosey and unpredictable passer-by. Until then, I don't think they'd really appreciated what it feels like to operate outside the law. It's a fine line we run between helping fugitives and becoming fugitives ourselves.

'It took another hour after the scare to get the sixteen miles to the Van Zandt farm. Our two worthy fellows breathed easier once we were on the way home with only potatoes. I do admire John Van Zandt. He never turns a hair whenever I turn up with fugitives. Makes them welcome and sets them quickly at ease. He's a wonderful friend to all.'

Chapter 36

Alfred
Cincinnati 1840

Fishing was a very good smoke screen. No-one takes much notice of a young boy or two heading to the river with fishing poles and hopeful buckets. Even Mother didn't complain about me spending time at my favorite pastime when I was acting as lookout.

But – it was fishing that contributed to a conflagration of grief and pain. To my eternal shame, it was my hot temper and wayward tongue that ignited the fire.

After the family entrusted me with their life-threatening secret I was constantly on the alert, concerned that a careless word might slip my tongue. I became good at exercising caution, or so I thought.

One clear but chilly Saturday afternoon, Will and I headed off to fish. Samuel didn't usually need him in the printery on a Saturday and I'd finished my chores in the bakery. With poles over shoulders, we headed towards the cleaner water near Mt Adams.

We'd just turned into a narrow street, clear of the main thoroughfare, when five ruffians blocked our way, about the age of Will and a lot heavier than both of us. In the previous months I'd seen them several times in the market, being chased away by irate stall-holders. Until now I'd always managed to give them a wide berth. They had the same air of menace as the two who'd accosted Purity and me on my first delivery.

'Where d'ya think yous're goin'?' their ferret-faced leader demanded. He stood square and strong, surrounded by his intimidating henchmen. They glowered at us threateningly.

I tried to bluff my way out. They responded with curses and accusations, moving aggressively closer. Will and I spun around, desperate to get away. At that moment, around the corner behind us and half-blocking the street, came a top-hatted gentleman on a fine chestnut mare. He reined in, stopping to observe the scene. Would he help us? I looked up hopefully but he didn't intervene. I realized he was one of the pro-slavery city dignitaries Will had warned me of.

Ferret Face came stomping up to me. I reeled from his filthy breath as he leaned forward, shouting into my face.

'Yous're the scum o' this city. Go back where ya come from, ya skinny mongrel.'

I'd never even exchanged words with him before.

'What're you talking about? You don't even know me,' I yelled back, wiping off his noxious spittle with my sleeve.

Will stood firm beside me, shifting his fishing rod to his left hand, ready to fight if needs must.

The Ferret scornfully screwed up his ugly mug. 'Oh, we knows who youse are, a'right. An' yur whole sodding family. Damned nigger lovers. Youse and yur kind 're trash, makin' life 'ard fur honest citizens wiff all yer talk 'bout freedom fur slaves. You should mind yur own damn business. As for you,' turning to Will, 'it's time we larned you a lesson too. Workin' for that trouble-making abolitionist paper. Yu're as bad.'

He clenched his fist, as though about to take a swing at one of us. Stopped in mid-swing when I stepped forward instead of ducking his blow. I'd had enough. Shouted at him, my fists also at the ready.

'Cowards! You're not worth a fart in a whirlwind! My father has more bravery in his little finger than you lot. You're so pathetic that you only attack in a group. He's prepared to stand up and be counted for the causes he believes in. He doesn't go round attacking innocent people.'

The leader of the gang glanced sideways at his henchmen and grinned nastily. 'Oh yeah? Should us take the word of a brat like you? Prove it, why don'cha.'

I saw red. All the cautionary advice of my family slipped away, like dead rats down the city's stinking drains. I forgot the man on the horse.

'He doesn't just talk. He helps ...' I flung my hand over my mouth, horrified.

'Yeah, helps who?'

'Nothing,' I mumbled, wishing the earth would open up and swallow me.

The man on the horse moved his steed a couple of steps closer. Pushed past our attackers. Leaned forward. Rapped me on the shoulder with his crop.

'What's your name, boy?'

'Alfred Burnett, sir.' I hung my head in shame, but my mother's teachings about lies would not allow me to offer another name.

He snorted with disgust. 'Another of that damned British abolitionist family. You people are destroying the commerce of this fine city. I can guess what you were just about to say. You'll not get away with this any longer. We're watching you all – closely.'

He threw some coins to the ruffians who'd ambushed us and quickly turned his horse, flicking the reins as he urged it to a trot. While they scrabbled for their reward, Will and I took to our heels.

'Damn, damn, damn! This is a bad day's work, Alf,' gasped Will as we made for home and safety.

'Please don't tell Samuel,' I pleaded as we ran. 'Please. My father would skin me.'

Two days later a riverman, on his way home to Bucktown, called in with the tip-off that a husband and wife from Louisville were hoping to cross the river that night.

Thomas and I were put in charge of collection. At the end of the day's work, Thomas took a cart and horse down to a supportive dry goods importer's yard. It was upstream of the junction of the Miami Canal and the river, conveniently tucked in amongst commercial premises and with no nearby homes. Once the owner had let us in, he followed his workers homeward, with instructions that a firm pull on the gate would lock it when we left.

Thomas's job was to stay with the horse, ready to load our 'guests' and then head north to a safe house some miles away. A storage shed gave cover to him and the horse while we waited. On the tray of the cart, laid on their sides and tied down to stop them rolling as the horse jogged along, were five big barrels of molasses, if you believed the labels or even the smell. However, the middle two barrels were empty.

As usual, my job was to fish, with eyes and ears open for the signal that fugitives were coming, or alerting all parties to danger.

For some time the fish just swam on by, laughing at my puny attempts to lure them onto my hook. The last of the light left the sky. The night got darker and early stars began to show. A chill wind whistled off the river.

I pulled my muffler closer and tucked it into my jacket, trying not to think about the warm fire back home in our parlor. It was cold and lonely. Nobody passed by. I could hear no bird calls above the movement of the river. Our shutter lantern, flame hidden behind the closed flap, sat ready by my fishing tackle, but no lantern on the other side gave the three-flicker signal.

What was that? Yes! A nibble on my line. Then a tug. At last! Hallelujah! I began to reel it in. It was heavy. All my attention went to landing my struggling catch. With a final tug and a flick, there on the bank at my feet was a big catfish. It was a beauty.

A quiet splash of oars drew my eyes. While I'd been otherwise engaged, a rowboat had approached from the other shore. I could just see the silhouette outlined against the lights of dwellings on the other shore. Someone in the rear spoke softly, the rower turned his head to check, then angled his boat to where I stood. It slid quietly up against the riverbank. A young black couple scrambled clumsily out.

The chap on the oars was one of our regular friends from Newport, just across the water on the Kentucky side. He recognized me. In a low voice, he asked, 'Did you not see or hear our signals? Had to take a chance – people were approaching.'

'No. I heard nothing.' I didn't want to admit that my attention had been distracted.

He gave me a hard look. Glanced down at my prize on the bank. Said nothing. He pushed his skiff off and, with a couple of strokes, was back in the current and pulling strongly for the southern shore.

I picked up my fish and gear, turned to the new arrivals and said, 'My name is Alf. We've a wagon ready to take you to safety. Please follow me.'

In the faint glimmer of light reflecting off the water I could see their clothes were threadbare and torn. Bare feet. Cuts and scratches all over what was visible of their bodies. They looked as if they'd gone many miles through rough country.

The woman bent over, clutching her side as if in pain. I reached out to assist her.

Suddenly – a rustle in the nearby bushes. A swarthy vicious-faced man burst out, cowhide whip in hand, a rope looped over his shoulder.

'Gotcha, ya black bastard,' he shouted harshly, cracking his whip round the ankle of the man. Grabbed his arm.

The woman screamed. The strongly-built young man fought back. He couldn't break away.

'Run, Tabitha. Run,' he yelled, punching, fighting, frantically trying to untangle from the whip. The slave catcher could barely hold him.

I dropped my pole, fish and lantern. Grabbed her hand. Dragged her, crying, up the bank.

'Stop, brat. I was warned about ya. Come back wi' that bitch. She's mine,' roared the angry catcher, delayed by the struggling husband.

Thomas, hearing the noise, ran out of his hiding place, pulling the horse by the reins. He almost collided with us in the gateway. Together we half-carried the poor woman to the back of the cart, shushing her wails of distress. If we were to get her away, we didn't want anyone poking their nose in.

'Please keep quiet, Ma'am. Don't let your husband's sacrifice be in vain,' Thomas begged as we helped her crawl into one of the empty barrels. 'He would want you to keep going.'

Her heart-breaking cries reduced to sniffles and low moans. I pulled the lid shut. Anyone looking closely would have noticed air holes drilled in the lid, but at night we hoped it would pass muster. I lept off the tray and ran to pull the gates shut as soon as the cart passed through.

Thomas flicked the reins, gave the horse a giddy-up and disappeared down the road at a tidy but unobtrusive clip. Behind us, coming slowly up from the river with as much delay as the struggling husband could manage, came captor and captive, the slave catcher yelling and cursing.

My fish and gear were left, forgotten, on the bank. I ran for home, trying to hold back my sobs. A few minutes later, slowing down to avoid unwanted attention, I turned into a dark side street, seeking a short-cut home. Then stopped.

Ahead was a group of youths, silhouetted by a lantern on the ground. They were passing a bottle around. Oh no.

Ferret-face and his cronies. I held my breath. Flattened back against the wall. Had they seen me?

My blood ran cold as I heard one say, 'Wonder if the catcher got those no-count Burnett boys red-handed? Should us go an' give 'im a hand, ya reckon, lads?'

'Yeah, good plan. I'll give those bastards wot for if I catch 'em,' said another. 'An' the darkies they're stealin'.'

Their evil laughs chilled me. Someone bent and picked up the lantern. They started to move – in my direction.

Terrified, I slid backwards round the corner.

And then – nearly fell as I bumped into someone.

Chapter 37

Alfred
Cincinnati 1840

As I got my balance back, I looked at the person I'd almost knocked off their feet. In the faint light from a distant gas street lamp, I realized with horror that I was looking at Abigail.

'What are you *doing* here?' I whispered. 'Terrible timing!'

She looked at me in surprise. 'Nice welcome, I don't think!'

'Shh. Quick. Run.' I grabbed her hand and darted back the way I'd come, hoping she could keep up. Desperate for a hiding spot, I dived into an alley close by, pulling her with me. We fell into a pile of stinking rubbish.

'Shit,' I heard from my unwanted associate.

'Quiet!' I hissed.

In the distance we could hear the swearing slave catcher, uttering oaths. Then a crack of his whip. A scream of agony. As the thugs turned into the street we'd just ducked out of, they heard it too.

'Quick, lads. They've caught 'em. Let's go,' yelled one of the gang. Evil laughs. Raucous shouts. Curses.

I shuddered. Cringed back further, pulling Abi further into the muck with me.

The thud of feet – right past our hiding place.

I waited a few seconds, listening hard. No more footsteps. Waited another minute.

'What the hell … ?' Abi demanded, as we finally scrambled to our feet, trying to wipe muck off herself.

I so didn't want to tell her, but there was no dodging the awful truth. I cried again as the story spilled out. She looked horrified.

'Oh Alf, that's awful.' I winced.

We had to get out of there. At any time, our enemies could come back. And it was dangerous for Abi too. I didn't want to think what they might do if she was caught in my company.

We started running together, heading toward the main part of town. And then I stopped. Banged my forehead with my hand. 'I've lost my mind! What am I doing? I can't take you home, Abi. We're getting close to the street lights. If we go any further you'll be seen. It's too dangerous to be with me.'

Thank goodness she was quick on the uptake. No further discussion was had. Our usual transaction took place and she vanished. I clutched the coin tightly – still warm from her skin – as I took to my heels again. It was the only warm thing in my devastated world.

Abigail

I landed back in my bedroom, shaken to the core.

Suddenly it was a game no longer. This time I'd seen the violence. Heard the threats and screams. Felt the menace in the air. Rolled in the stinking garbage in the alley. It was no longer just an exciting, fun but surreal escapade. An adventure in living history. Now – it was real. People's lives were at stake. Life or death for the runaways. Terrible risks for Alf and his family. And, if I'd not got away, danger for me too.

I felt helpless. If I went back too soon, what added complications would I create for Alf? What danger would I walk into? I didn't know what to do.

It took ages to get to sleep that night. Awful nightmares. Alf caught. Whipped. Beaten and bloody. Runaways screaming. Running, running, running. Dogs barking at my heels. Falling.

The only good thing was that I'd gone when Mum was out. Even my fertile brain would have struggled to explain the rotten vegetable stink on me and my clothes.

Chapter 38

Alfred
Cincinnati 1840

Father took me into the parlor. Shut the door. Craggy face stern. Bushy eyebrows almost meeting in a deep frown.

He sat down heavily in the big armchair by the fire. I was not invited to sit.

He remained silent for what seemed like an eternity. I stood, fearful, tear marks still on my cheeks, my shoulders hunched. I almost hoped for a whipping, to get it over with. Anything would be better than this silence.

Eventually he spoke.

'Alfred, I'm beyond disappointed. We've all told you, this is not a game. With your inattention, you've destroyed the lives of those poor people. Almost certainly that man will never see his wife again. He'll be whipped within an inch of his life – literally. If he survives that, he'll almost certainly be sold south. Few come back from there. The conditions for field hands on those big plantations are hell. You're going to have to live with the consequences of this bad night's work for the rest of your life, but at least you have a life. Thanks to your inattention, you've taken something beyond precious – that man's freedom.'

The distraught faces of the runaways haunted me for days. The struggle on the riverbank consumed my sleep. Their cries of anguish were in my dreams, still echoing as I woke. Always running, never getting away. Vicious dogs pouncing. Slavering jaws biting. Fugitives falling. Whips breaking dark skin. Blood pouring down backs. Cruel-faced men grabbing. Screaming. Agony. In other dreams, I was being chased.

It was a relief to wake up but the days were not much better. I didn't want to talk to anyone. And it seemed that no-one wanted to talk to me. My family walked around with grim faces. I was left out of conversations. Not given lookout duties. Not sent anywhere with messages.

Purity, enquiring for me in the store a week after the botched escape, found me sitting forlornly on the wooden bench in our wintery garden, blindly staring at Joseph's cabbages. She sat quietly down beside me, putting her small hand on mine.

'How are you, Alf?' She spoke gently. Not in her usual light-hearted way.

'I've done a terrible thing. I don't know how to tell you.' I didn't want to look at her. How could I ever expect her to like me now, even as a friend. I couldn't be relied upon for something as simple as being a lookout.

Sighing, she put her arm around my shoulders. Pulled me in for a hug. 'I know what happened.'

Her compassion warmed a small corner of my heavy heart. We sat silently for a moment or two. Finally I spoke.

'How did you hear?'

'The family sent me out to talk to you. They're worried about you.'

'I thought they hated me for what I did? Didn't want to include me in the work anymore.'

'You're being too hard on yourself. Of course they're upset, but they want their happy Alf back. They know you'll learn from this. It was a tragedy, but what you do from now on is what matters. Don't let this mistake stop you from helping others.'

I brushed away the tears that sneaked down my cheeks. 'How can anyone trust me?'

'Alf, you're one of the good ones.' She looked up, gave my hand a pat, and stood up, looking over my shoulder.

I sat up. Turned to see Mother coming towards us.

She took Purity's place on the bench. Now it was Mother's turn to give me a rare hug. At her touch, I dissolved into body-shaking sobs. She just sat, holding me tight while I wept.

Once my crying slowed, she said, 'If you weren't upset, son, I'd wonder about your maturity. And know this. We all make mistakes and errors of judgement.'

Another pause while I tried to get myself together. Eventually I sat up, sniffling. Went to wipe my face with my sleeve.

Mother passed me a handkerchief. 'Son, the cause is in dire need of courageous people, prepared to put their lives on the line to help. We're all in agreement; it's time for you to get back out there – if you want to.'

Bit by bit, I was re-incorporated into the network, a far more cautious and careful youth.

Chapter 39

Alfred
Cincinnati 1840

On the surface, the rest of the year proceeded smoothly. Our business flourished and expanded, thanks in large part to Joseph taking it over from Father. He was a far better businessman than our father and I learnt a lot from watching him. Thomas was his trusty lieutenant in the bakehouse and we took on more men. As well as myself and 19-year-old apprentice Martin Erickson, we now had two journeymen, Mr Leveridge and Mr Lewis. Sarah had the main responsibility for the store and enlisted help from Mother and me when needed.

However, under cover of night, we Burnetts lived a perilous life. Every day we danced on a knife-edge. More and more fugitives came our way, as the word spread in the neighboring Kentucky towns of Newport and Covington that Cornelius Burnett and his family were one of the gateways to freedom. At any time, as I now knew much too well, a random moment of inattention or a careless word spoken in the hearing of the wrong people could have runaways recaptured, us thrown into prison, or worse. However, apart from unsuccessful surprise visits by slave catchers trying to intimidate us into giving information, we reached the end of the year with no significant trouble.

There was a price to pay, however. Samuel came in one day, clutching a paper and looking very grave.

'Where's your Papa, Alf?'

'I think he's in the bakery. Do you want me to fetch him?'

Samuel nodded. Sighed. 'Ask him to meet me in the parlor, if you don't mind.'

That sounded serious. I scarpered off to find my parent.

'What's up, Samuel? Nothing wrong with Ann, I trust?' Father asked as he stepped into the parlor. The door was shut.

I stood outside, close to the door.

'Look what I've just been handed by one of our friends across the river,' I heard Samuel say.

There was silence for a minute. I leaned up against the wood, craning to hear. At that precise moment, I heard Sarah greet my mother as she walked into the shop. Foiled again!

How I wanted to know what was on that paper! But soon enough, the secret was no secret. On the Kentucky side, pro-slavery men had placed a bounty on Papa's head. He was worth a lot of money – dead.

The whole family came to dinner that night so we could discuss the situation.

Mother spoke firmly. 'Cornelius, you must not go into Kentucky – for ANY reason. And be very careful when you go anywhere near the Landing. It will only take a small gang to kidnap you and take you across the river.'

At first he blustered. He hated being told what he could and couldn't do. Wanted to show the bullies what he thought of their threats. But eventually commonsense ruled.

Mary Anne and Emma were looking alarmed. Had a quiet confabulation at the end of the table. Emma spoke for them both. 'Samuel, do you think they're after our husbands?'

'I heard nothing about the rest of the family,' he replied. 'I know it's unfair, Cornelius, but the anti-abolitionists are blaming you particularly for the disappearance of so many slaves. Maybe you should tone down some of your public comments for a while?'

Father's face went dark with anger. 'They'll never muzzle me, the worthless scum.' Then his face lightened. 'There's a good side to this. While they're ranting at me, it takes atten-tion off everyone else. The rest of you can get on quietly helping our persecuted brethren to safety.'

Joseph spoke up. 'I don't think your theory is entirely correct, Father. I think they take particular note of anything any Burnett does. Our name is out there every time you rush into print or put posters around town, complaining about yet another travesty of justice.'

Father shrugged. 'It's mostly only the *Philanthropist* that publishes my letters to the editor. The other papers usually ignore my pleas for justice for the black man.'

'Or they criticize you, and we're brought into the public eye again,' Thomas reminded him. 'What about that latest comment in the *Daily Gazette*, *"This man is represented to us as a mischievous and swaggering Englishman, oftener in trouble than half the other abolitionists in the city together"?'*

But nothing any of us said could muzzle Father. We brothers believed that he thrived on the adverse publicity. Took a contrary pride in the notoriety that was fueled by his outspoken ways. Nothing daunted him; the greater the controversy the louder he spoke.

The day after Samuel's warning, Dr Gamaliel Bailey, the editor of the *Philanthropist*, came to call. He and Father sat down for a coffee in the parlor but left the door open. I was able to usefully engage my ears while I tidied shelves in the shop.

'I've been informed of the threat on your life, Cornelius. You're in good company! Both Mr Birney and I are on their hit list as well. Samuel tells me you've wisely agreed not to cross the river. A very good decision, if I may add my two bits. I know we don't always agree on how to go about an issue, but we're all committed to the same righteous cause. Neither of us back down, do we!'

I heard Father laugh. 'You take the more diplomatic way, Gamaliel. I admire your skill with words and your knowledge of the law. I know I'm a blunt instrument in comparison; I'm a baker, not a wordsmith. But I will not stay quiet when face-to-face with such evil.'

Chapter 40

Alfred
Cincinnati 1840

A quiet knock on the door one evening brought the Olsens to us. Dirty, exhausted, covered in scratches, limping and their clothes in tatters. As always, unless a posse was on the heels of our visitors, we quickly dished out food for them. Mary Anne always had extra food ready.

Mr Olsen had a deep and jagged scar on his lower leg, showing through ragged trousers, and two fingers on one hand were missing. I tried not to look as I served them, but my eyes kept drifting to his wounds.

'Alf, help me here please,' said Mary Anne, putting down a pile of clothing she'd just collected from her emergency supplies. Once she had me away from the table she hissed, 'It's impolite to stare.'

Mr Olsen heard her. 'I don' mind, Ma'am. We glad to tell our tale – the more people know how we treated, de better. Many white people don' know de truth of dis matter.' His wife, who'd said nary a word since she'd staggered into our kitchen, nodded in agreement.

Mary Anne looked embarrassed at having been heard. *I* was embarrassed at getting a ticking off!

'That's generous of you, Mr Olsen, but please finish your meal first,' she replied.

He didn't need two tellings. By the way they ate it had been some time since food had passed their lips. Finally he put down his knife and fork, thanked Mary Anne for the meal, then turned to me.

'You still want to know 'bout my scars, young massa?'

'Only if you don't mind,' I replied, feeling awkward now. 'But please don't call any of us 'massa'. Once you get to Canada, hopefully you'll never have to call anyone that ever again. I'm just Alf.'

He cracked a slight smile. 'Ain't that the Lord's truth, young …Alf. I Daniel an' dis my wife Rebecca.'

I sat down at the table with him while he settled back in his chair. Rebecca got up to help Mary Anne clear the table and wash their dishes.

'So, you ever see a big plantation?'

I shook my head. We'd seen a good many grass pastures and fields with crops on our travels between our old home and Cincinnati, but we'd had no reason to go south, where the big plantations were found. Now there was a price on Father's head, even less reason.

''Tis like dis,' Daniel explained. 'De plantations need lots o' workers. We from South Carolina. Not so long ways from us, dey grow indigo an' rice. But on our planation, baccy. 'Tis baccy done dis to me. Well, de harvestin' of it.' His wife nodded.

I looked at him, surprised.

'Harvest time be terrible punishin'. De wors' time o' de year. Den, us all work from afore sun-up to way past dark. No time to cook our food, mostly too exhausted to eat anyways, no time to rest, never nuff sleep. Always hurry, hurry, hurry. Whipped by de overseer if us don' keep movin'. Powerful hard work. We cut de crop wiv machetes, load de wagons, den drive de load into de curin' barn. In de barn, peoples spear de stalks of baccy onto sharp sticks, hang em up to dry. When dey dry, bring down de sticks an' pack de dry leaves in big heavy barrels, ready for market. Accidents happen when peoples exhausted an' hungry.'

'Don't they give you *any* rests through the day?' I asked, trying to imagine their life.

'Nope. Not at harvest. The overseer jus' crack his whip. Say, "Time to rest when de crop is in". But really, he lie.' He scowled. 'God's truth, der's nebber a *good* rest time, not any time o' year. Always more work dey want.'

He held up his hand. 'Dese missing fingers – accident wiv machete. De leg – a stake fall from up high when I in de barn hangin' up de baccy. An' you don' see my back. Many whippin's.'

Baby Mary had been lying asleep in her cradle while her mother attended to our guests. Just then she gave a snuffle. Chubby little fists started to wave. Rebecca's eyes turned to the baby and she spoke for the first time.

'How old yo bebe, Mam?'

Mary Anne smiled at her. 'Just six months. She'll need feeding in a minute. Would you like to hold her while I finish wiping down the bench?'

Rebecca didn't need two askings. In a flash she was at the cradle and picking up my niece. The strain on her face eased. She cooed to Mary, jiggling her on her knee. With her back to me, I could see raised weals of skin through the rips on her sack garment.

Jacob smiled sadly at the scene. 'We don' have no bebes. My wife bin treated so cruel, she can't carry dem to birth now. Her was carryin' our secon' one when de overseer decide she workin' too slow. Whipped her so bad she lost the bebe. No others since den.'

Mary Anne shivered with sympathy. 'It was your second one she was carrying?' She hesitated tactfully.

Rebecca answered. 'Our first bebe boy a beautiful chile. Age three, Massa sol' him to a rich woman in Charlotte, North Carolina, for her page boy. I still cry for my Eli.' She added simply, 'My heart broke.'

At the name, Mary Anne and I looked at each other in surprise. 'Were you ever told the name of his owner?' I asked.

'Yes, young sir. She were sister to one of our neighbors. Miz Gerard. My chile gone to Jesus now. She took 'im to New York state for a visit to friens. Dey drownded in a 'splosion on de river. Mistress an' her slaves. My boy.' She wiped away a tear tracking down her brown cheek.

Every now and then the family still talked about our part in the rescue of Eli, back in 1834. I now knew that the people who'd opened their arms to him, and Hetty, must have also been part of the Underground Railroad.

'How old would he be now, if he were still alive?' my good-sister asked.

Rebecca and Daniel looked at each other. 'Eleven year, near 'nuf.'

Mary Anne and I could barely wipe the grins off our faces. 'You're never going to believe this, but we're pretty sure we met Eli,' she said. 'God willing, he's alive and well in Canada somewhere.'

Rebecca looked at us in disbelief. 'How you know dat?'

As we described Eli and his mistress, and the disaster that we'd witnessed, she and Daniel became more and more excited. They were still exclaiming over the story as I led them downstairs.

'Hold the lantern, please Rebecca,' I asked as I gestured for Daniel to help me shift a couple of barrels. I removed a brick that hid the handle to a door, cunningly disguised as the cellar wall. Behind the false wall that Father had Mr Boyd erect at the same time as he made our shop counter, was a small room – our short-term hiding place for when we couldn't quickly move our 'parcels' on to the next conductor. It was most cleverly constructed. Quite impossible to spot if you didn't know about the secret latch. Even I had to be shown it, and I don't miss much!

Inside the windowless room was a pile of sleeping mats and blankets, water, a bucket with a lid for toilet needs, and food. A pipe poked up through the wall; it brought fresh air in from a camouflaged vent in our back yard. Daniel took Rebecca's hand as she hesitated in the doorway.

'My wife not so good 'bout small spaces,' he explained. 'But we 'preciate yo' help. She be fine. We talk 'bout Eli.' She gave us a tight smile and stepped inside. I shut the door and pushed the barrels back.

Chapter 41

Abigail
Auckland February 2015

A week had passed since Alf and I had run from the gang of thugs. It was killing me not to know if he was okay, but things were busy at school, the teachers were piling on the homework, and Mum hadn't been well, so I was needed at home. Were they excuses?

To be honest, I was scared.

I'd nearly finished *Uncle Tom's Cabin*. It was gripping, but the stories of unimaginable cruelty beat a pattern of grief in my brain. Generous-hearted Uncle Tom, hard-case Topsy, saintly little Eva and the evil Simon Legree kept me company as I cycled to and from school. At times I wanted to shake Uncle Tom. To tell him to hit back. Run away. Stop turning the other cheek. Other characters had me chuckling with delight, like Mrs Bird, as she cleverly turned her husband's apathy to compassion. But my favorite character was Eliza. I cheered as she crossed the cracking ice floes on the Ohio River with her baby, with the slave catchers left on the southern bank, unable to follow.

Where did Mrs Stowe get her ideas, I wondered? No wonder the die-hards in the southern states who enjoyed their comfortable lives, and didn't want any challenge to the status quo, had the book banned!

I looked her up on Google. Wow – what a lot of information. There was even a Harriet Beecher Stowe House in Cincinnati. Did Alf ever go there, I wondered? I couldn't wait to go back and ask.

Chapter 42

Alfred
Cincinnati 1841

I became a regular visitor at the Beecher house to see Purity, sometimes using deliveries as an excuse to ascend the hill, other times confident enough of my welcome to just call in if I had reason to be in the neighborhood – or sometimes with no reason. Purity had become a good and trustworthy friend. I could tell she liked me, but when I invited her to walk out with me on her Sundays off, she rarely accepted. Why, I could not discover. Perhaps she had another admirer? But when I tried to discover if I had a rival for her affections she just laughed and changed the subject.

One warm spring day I was enjoying a glass of thirst-quenching lemonade in their kitchen when I heard a deep voice in the hallway.

I sprang to my feet as her employer and a slight clean-shaven man with a firm chin, expressive eyes and white hair almost touching his collar, walked into the kitchen.

'Don't get up, Alfred, thank you. Nice to see you,' said Dr Beecher. He turned to Purity, who'd been resting her feet for a few minutes while we chatted. Nonetheless, I remained standing. I was keen to stay on the good side of Dr Beecher.

'Purity, would you please bring tea into the library for us?' He paused and then, to my surprise, added, 'Alfred, do you know who this gentleman is?'

'No sir, I'm sorry.' I looked hard at the man standing quietly beside Dr Beecher. He was of medium height, with a kindly air of calm confidence. I instinctively knew he was a man of significance, but not in a worldly way. By this time I'd met or seen many of the influential men of the town, some of them very full of their own importance. I was sure I'd not seen this one. He was not a fellow you would easily forget.

'It's a wee step to Ripley, so I daresay that's why. This is the Reverend Rankin. John, this young fellow is Cornelius Burnett's youngest son, Alfred.'

I stuttered with excitement as I said hello. This man was a star! He, his wife Jean, and their thirteen children were famous, or infamous, depending on who was talking. In the parlor window of their hill-top home in the quiet village of Ripley, about fifty miles upriver, was an always-burning lamp, shining across the river to the deeply-wooded shores of Kentucky. It shone its beacon of hope to a steady stream of runaways who swam, were rowed by friends, crossed the ice in winter, or waded if the river was exceptionally low, to the northern side.

Only a few weeks earlier Martin had come in to work with a grand story.

'Did you hear the latest about the Rankin family?'

This was sure to be good. We'd all paused.

'A posse of gun-toting angry men, with dogs yapping and sniffing around, came riding up the hill to his front door two mornings ago. It was just on day-break. Tried to force their way in. Said their dogs had tailed a runaway couple to the bottom of the Rankin steps. Knew they were there. Reverend Rankin stood at the door with his gun in hand, refusing them entry. Meanwhile, just before the posse reached the top of the hill, two of his sons had saddled up and, with a fugitive mounted behind each boy, got them safely away north through the trees to the next station.'

We'd gone back to our tasks with a will. Every successful escape gave us even more determination to fight on.

And now, here I was – meeting my hero!

The great man extended his hand. 'I hear good things of the activities of your father and your family. You all do a fine job in the Lord's work. Does your father ever take the steamer to Portsmouth? If so, and if he could spare the time to break his journey, it would be a pleasure to exchange ideas and experiences.'

After a few more pleasantries the two men departed to the library. I sank back onto my seat with awe.

Purity laughed at my stunned expression.

'Does he come here often?' I wanted to know.

As she bustled around, shifting the kettle to the hot part of the stove and preparing the tea tray, she replied, 'His oldest son, Adam, just finished his studies here at Lane Seminary in June so we've seen a bit of him during the last four years. Even though Dr Beecher doesn't actively aid the runaways in the same way, he and Reverend Rankin have many common beliefs.'

'Do you ever hear him talk much about the runaways, and how their family gets them away?'

'Not much from him. He's very discreet about what he says when I'm in the room. But I recently heard Mistress Stowe telling her father a grand tale. She and her husband heard it from the Reverend Rankin when he was paying them a visit. Wait while I take this into the library, and I'll tell you what I know.'

I settled down in anticipation.

In a couple of minutes, Purity was back. She knew that I loved her stories. She poured another lemonade for us both and sat down again, laughing at my eager face.

'It happened early in the spring – last year or the year before. The river had been iced up for at least a week but the temperatures were starting to lift. One night a woman, carrying a small child of about two, arrived in great distress at the Rankin home. She'd struggled up their steep hill, arriving wet through and exhausted.

'She belonged to a farmer of Dover, Kentucky, not far downriver from Ripley and only ten miles from the river. He'd fallen upon hard times. By chance, she overheard him telling his wife that the child would need to be sold. Terrified, she ran.

'When she reached the river she was lucky to find an old Scotchman. Reverend Rankin described him as *"an intemperate and wicked man, but he had not sinned away all his humanity"*. Anyway, his heart must have been in the right place, for, on the night in question, he fed them and gave them shelter for a short time in his humble cabin. He also warned her that the river was now impassable. No boats were running and the ice was breaking.

'As they talked, the runaway kept her ear tuned for any sounds of pursuit. She knew bounty hunters would be on her heels as soon as her owners realized she was missing. And then, above the sound of the crackling fire, they heard the distant baying of hounds.

'Boat or no boat, the river was her only option. The old man ripped a rail off his wooden fence to give her support should she fall through the ice, then helped her down a narrow path to the riverbank. She prayed the little one would make no noise.

'Pointing to the beacon of light shining from high up across the river, he said, *"A good man lives in that house on the hill beyond the river; cross over and go to that house; go right in, and you'll be safe there."*

'She reached the river bank and stood there, desperate, trying to decide what to do. Due to the narrowing of the river at that point, the ice floes had packed tight, turning into a dangerous and unstable raft – reaching right across to the Ohio side.

'Suddenly, a shout rose up behind her. The dogs howled. She was discovered. She hesitated no longer. It was try, or die with her child. Nothing was going to take her baby from her but death. She ran into the water, jumped on a piece of bad ice and stumbled as the ice cracked. She leapt for the nearest floe. It cracked. She jumped to the next one. And the next.

And the next. From time to time she slipped. Sometimes she had to throw her child onto the floe in front, using the rail to get herself out of the icy water. She lost her shoes. Her bleeding feet left a trail of red across the ice. But she made it to the other side. The pursuers stood on the southern shore, cursing and swearing, their hounds baying in frustration.

'She staggered the last few feet through the freezing water to the northern shore, shivering, exhausted and distraught. As she collapsed on the river bank, another slave catcher patrolling the northern bank found her. He'd heard the sounds of pursuit. However, this time the courage of the young mother touched his heart.

'He extended his hand to help her up the bank. Said, *"Any woman who could cross that river carrying her baby has won her freedom"*. Cautioning her to silence and as much speed as she could muster, he helped her to the outskirts of Ripley village and pointed to the steep steps at the bottom of Rankin's hill. He said, *"No nigger was ever caught that got to his house. The door will be unlocked. They will help you."*

'Pulling on her last reserves, she climbed up to the Rankin house. As the man on the river had said, the doors were not locked. Mrs Rankin found her warm clothes and Reverend Rankin roused two of his sons and asked them to guide her to the next safe house before day broke.

'Before morning the ice had broken up and the river was impassable. Had she not dropped a piece of the child's clothing on the Ohio side of the river, her pursuers would never have known that she'd survived. By spring she was safe in Canada with her little child.'

I sat agog as the saga unfolded. Purity was good at telling a tale.

Chapter 43

Alfred
Cincinnati 1841

A few weeks after she'd told me the story of the young woman and baby, Purity came in for the Beechers' weekend supplies. My heart did a little leap of delight. Sarah and I, wrapped in our canvas aprons, were both busy with customers. I tried to speed up my dithery old matron, but even a circus parade outside our door wouldn't have moved her faster. Sarah finished with two customers and was greeting Purity with a smile while I still counted change. The best I could manage was a quick hello before I got stuck with a couple of young lads, each with a penny to spend, too much time and too much choice. How I wished them gone, but Joseph's edict, 'the customer comes first', had been well drummed in.

The two girls chatted as Purity's order was filled, and I was about to ask Purity to wait, for I hoped the next Sunday she might agree to a walk after church, when the door opened again. Bringing a blast of crisp spring air with him, my friend Will entered. Usually he went straight through to find Father, on an errand for Samuel. This time, unfortunately, it appeared that he'd come to buy a cake for his landlady.

Purity glanced up to see who was standing beside her, then took another look. I suppose a girl would think he was handsome, if your tastes run to tall, broad-shouldered, red-haired older fellows of at least twenty. To me, he was just Will. She kept sneaking looks at him under the rim of her bonnet.

The door opened again and three more people were blown in, squashing everyone up. In the shuffle to keep places in the queue, Will accidently bumped Purity, who dropped her reticule.

'Oh, I'm so sorry, Miss,' he said and, quick as a flash, bent down to retrieve it. Their hands touched and they both blushed. He looked at her as though he'd found the pot of gold at the end of the rainbow. The smile of thanks she gave him pierced my heart. She'd never looked so admiringly at me.

This was not good. Was I to lose the girl I wanted for girlfriend? They began to chat while Will was served next, also by Sarah. Then, to my dismay, Purity waved me a nonchalant goodbye and walked out of the shop with my *former* friend, chatting animatedly. I was still busy with the rush of people.

It would seem Mother had no need to worry about my affairs of the heart.

Chapter 44

Alfred
Cincinnati 1841

One windy and overcast Saturday morning I was sent with a message for Mr Boyd. On reaching his office on the corner of Broadway and Eighth I found he wasn't there.

'He went to Watson the barber's a while ago,' said the studious-looking man with ink-stained fingers, seated at a paper-loaded desk. 'If you run down there now you should find him.'

I knew Mr Watson. Father had taken me to his shop, on the corner of Third and Walnut, for a haircut and introduction soon after I joined the network. Back down town I went.

A number of the better barbers in the city were free blacks, with Mr Watson being one of the best. His salon was well patronized by the upper class of Cincinnati society, and an occasional wealthy black man was tolerated by his white customers. The place was buzzing. A long row of chairs sat at the side of the room for customers waiting their turn. Occupying them were four men I didn't know; two I took for German, judging by their speech. Three barbers' chairs were occupied with draped customers and Mr Watson and his employees were busy with clippers, razors and pomade. An energetic light-skinned boy of about eleven was sweeping the well-scrubbed floor boards with a flourish, humming a little tune.

Mr Boyd was one of the draped and lathered customers; Mr Watson was deftly shaving him with a cut-throat razor. They both spotted me in the mirror as I walked in, full of importance about my errand. Without thinking of the watching men, I made straight towards them. Quick as a flash, Mr Watson headed me off at the pass.

He said to the curly-headed boy with the broom, 'John, here's young Alf. Probably come to see if you'd like to go fishing. Take him out the back and give him a drink of water while you have your chat. He looks like he could do with it.'

As I hesitated, wondering what was going on, Mr Boyd caught my eye in the mirror. He gave the tiniest shake of his head but showed no obvious sign of recognition. I opened my mouth to protest. Then realized, in the nick of time, that I was being warned not to speak.

The youngster was quick-thinking. He showed no surprise as he leaned his broom up and beckoned me to follow. The back room was both a store room and a tiny kitchen. Given my still-beardless state, most of the items stacked on the shelves I had yet to learn the use for.

Speaking softly so the men in the other room couldn't hear, he said, 'Whatever you were about to say, I think William wants you to tell me.'

I stuttered for a moment. 'But I don't know you.'

'That's easy to fix. I'm John Langston. I work here when I'm not in school. I've seen you at your store a couple of times when I've gone past.' He leaned forward. Whispered. 'I know your family are friends to our people.'

With Father's cautions now well and truly brought to the fore with this unexpected diversion, I was still stumbling for direction when I heard Mr Watson say loudly, 'Excuse me, Henry. I don't think John can reach the water jug.'

Next moment, razor still in hand, he was there beside us.

He whispered in my ear. 'Alf, have you got a message for one of us?'

I nodded.

'You can't say anything here. Sheriff Doty is waiting his turn out there.' I gulped. How close I'd been to making another dreadful mistake. 'I'll send John over to your store shortly to get the message. You can trust him.'

Then, in a louder voice, 'Here it is boys, up on the shelf', and bustled back to his chair and rather anxious customer.

John arrived at the store about thirty minutes later. I'd taken over counter duties until he turned up, with Sarah primed to step into the store when needed.

When he entered I was serving a tired-looking and harassed mother, her two small children plastering their sticky fingers all over the glass jars on the counter. They couldn't make their mind up between sugarplums or peppermint drops so I borrowed Mr Watson's quick-thinking excuse about fishing.

'Hold there, John, I'll be with you in a moment,' and called Sarah, in the room just behind. 'Can you take over, sister? John's come over to talk about going fishing.'

Lifting the counter, I beckoned him to come through. Sarah caught his wistful peep at the barrel of rainbow-stripped candy sticks. 'Here, John.' Handed him one.

No words were spoken until I'd steered him past the wide staircase and into the kitchen, well away from any listening ears in the store. He looked around the spacious and comfortable room, the shelves loaded with Mary Anne's serving dishes and dinner platters. On the oak table was a basket of vegetables fresh from the market. Checked curtains framed the tall windows.

'You've got a nice home, Alf. It reminds me a bit of my old home with the Gooches, back in Chillicothe.'

'That's on the Ohio Erie Canal, isn't it?'

'The canal's the easiest way to get there, although it's only a hundred miles as the crow flies.'

'We came down that way from New York state. My favorite parts of the journey were the paddle steamers. What about you?'

From that moment we didn't stop talking. He loved paddle steamers as much as me. And fishing.

'So why are you in Cincinnati?' I finally asked.

'To get me some better learning than I could have at Chillicothe. I'm told that my father had a great love of education.'

'You sound like you don't know much about your father. How come?'

'My parents both passed away when I was but four. I remember them some, but luckily our father had arranged for Colonel Gooch to stand as guardian. He and his family took me in. Made me part of their family.'

I looked at him in surprise. From what I'd learnt already about life for black people, I hadn't heard of colored soldiers, let alone a colonel.

'Is the Gooch family Negro?'

He laughed. 'No indeed. They were good friends of my father, who emigrated from England to Virginia. My mother was one of his slaves. I miss her still, but now I only have a picture of her. I've heard people say it was her mixed Indian and colored blood made her so beautiful. My father freed her but the law wouldn't let them marry. So my sister, my two brothers and I are all free. Apart from not being allowed to give us his name, in every other way we were his family. He left us very well provided for.'

'So will you stay in Cincinnati now for all your schooling?' I asked. I knew there were several schools for Negro children, mostly run by their churches.

'No. I expect to be here only a couple of years. When I was but a tiny child, my Papa enrolled me in Oberlin College's preparatory school, up north near Lake Erie. My big brothers Gideon and Charles have both done some schooling there.'

He added, rather proudly, 'They were amongst the first boys of color to go to Oberlin.' Then frowned. 'It's not easy being different from your fellows. They had a hard time from some. The white boys weren't used to being schooled with colored folk. I hope things are better by the time I go there.'

'Is your brother Gideon Langston, the barber who also owns the livery stables?'

'Indeed. He's a very good businessman. I hoped to live with him when I came to Cincinnati but he says that, being a single man, that would not be right. So, I'm living with Mr Woodson's family just now.'

I knew the carpenter and community leader Mr Woodson – he was well-respected by my father – but it was Gideon Langston I'd heard most about.

'My father often talks about your brother. Just yesterday morning, when we were preparing the day's bread, I heard him tell Joseph that he'd be popping out to see Gideon Langston for transport that night.'

John smiled. 'Did you know that some of Gideon's carts and wagons are kept only for the use of friends such as you.'

I was curious. 'No. Why would that be?'

'It's a secret.' He tapped the side of his nose. 'See if you can guess.'

I reflected for a moment. 'Would it be that Gideon doesn't want his other customers looking too closely at their construction?'

John's wide grin told me I was right. 'Deep seats, false bottoms, wider than necessary sides. Mr Boyd constructs them.'

'So that's why your brother almost always has a conveyance available when we need it?'

'Indeed. He stores them in a separate shed. And have you heard about the coffins?' John asked. 'Mr Boyd makes those too. Puts air holes in them. A friendly undertaker uses them to get people away from prying eyes. Good trick, don't you think?'

We laughed. It felt good to be part of such exciting clandestine activities, tricking the wicked people of the town.

One thing puzzled me. 'If your brother is a barber as well, why are you working for Mr Watson?'

'That's simple. The Woodson family are good to me, but they don't have a lot of room and it's possible I might remove to Mr Watson's home. I'm working for him to see if we rub along together well enough for that move. He's got plenty of space in his big house for another young 'un, so I'm told.'

'And do you? Get along with him, I mean?'

'For sure. He's very kind. And he lets me keep all my tips from the clients. Says I need to save for my future. I work for him all day Saturday, in either his barber shop or his bathhouse. They're open until midnight that day.'

Sarah came through from the front. 'Brother, when are you taking over the store? I've got to make lunch, you know.'

I looked up at the clock on the mantelpiece. Where had that twenty minutes gone!

A few minutes later, John left with our message for Mr Boyd as well as an arrangement to go fishing that evening. It was the first of many such excursions, for we became fast friends. It was good to have someone to fish with, for Will was no longer available for such outings. I tried not to think about what he and Purity might be doing – it gave me the glums.

There was one upside; I enjoyed having a younger boy look up to me, in the same way I'd once regarded Will. It was the beginning of a life-long friendship.

Chapter 45

Alfred
Cincinnati June 1841

Father came rushing into the house, waving the *Philanthropist*.

'Listen to what the Ohio Supreme Court just ruled!'

We all gathered around as his normally firm voice shook with excitement.

The bringing of slaves into this state, even with the view of passing through it to settle in another slave state, of itself makes such colored persons free, and any claim of right or attempt to carry them into a slave state in order to retain them as slaves, is an offence against the laws of Ohio, which any citizen has a right to prevent, even by such force as is necessary to rescue them from such illegal custody of any person in whose possession they might be found.

The bit about a slave being technically free if they were brought into the state by their owner was not new; Mr Chase and other lawyers of abolitionist sympathies had used it for some years, defending both runaways and abolitionists brought before a sheriff or judge. But this new legislation tightened loopholes and put more power in the hands of the abolitionists. A ruling in our favor by the state's Supreme Court was a serious matter.

We could almost feel the shockwaves from our near neighbors in Kentucky, well-used as they were to bringing their body servants with them into our town for both commerce and social engagements. They were up in arms – and they weren't the only ones. Many Ohioans, the ones who made money from the slave owners, were equally incensed. Misguided people, they blamed the abolitionists living in their midst for causing the problem in the first place. Seemed to overlook the fact that the very institution of slavery was the root cause of the problem.

But it wasn't all to the benefit of the slaves. Another law allowed a slave owner, or his representative, to come into Ohio to take back his property – if he could prove said two-legged property belonged to him. This increased the already vicious industry of slave catchers and kidnappers. No person of color was safe. Nor were any known abolitionists. That included us. The only saving grace of the ruling was that a householder could refuse admittance to anyone chasing runaways if they could not show a permit. Also, they had to procure a writ issued by an Ohio law enforcement officer before they could take any captives out of the state.

It didn't take long for us to feel the effects of the Supreme Court ruling.

Chapter 46

Alfred
Cincinnati June 24th 1841

Early evening Thursday 24th, a hesitant knock sounded on our back door. I opened it to find an anxious young light-skinned Negro boy, about my age, standing in the yard. Unusually, he was neatly dressed, his clothes in good repair.

'Is this Burnetts' house?'

As was our normal way, I quickly ushered him into the kitchen. It was not a good idea to leave potential trouble standing in sight of random passers-by, even though the lane was not a busy thoroughfare.

The aroma of sizzling pork and roast vegetables filled the room. Mary Anne was about to dish out dinner. Little Mary was sitting in her high chair, banging a spoon impatiently. I'd been laying the table.

Politely our visitor introduced himself. 'Evening, young sir. I'm George Williams. My old Massa, Mr William McClusky, told me to come to you. Says your family will help me.'

We seated him down. 'Have you eaten?' asked Mary Anne, looking at him with concern. She'd spotted his involuntary swallow when he saw the food on the table.

He hesitated, but the delicious aroma was too much. 'I don't want to be a trouble but some vittles be mighty nice, thank you Mam.'

'No trouble at all, George. I always cook extra. Lay another place, please Alf,' she instructed as she prepared to dish out. 'And call Joseph for dinner.'

As he tucked appreciatively into his heaped plate of food, George told us his tale of misfortune. He'd been a valet for

Mr McClusky of Maysville, Kentucky, not far from Ripley, but the week before things turned very bad.

'Massa William and his wife were good to me. When I was a nipper I played with their children and my mama was cook for the Big House. Mistress McClusky taught me to read at the same time as she taught her own children. She didn't care about the law. She also taught me to speak well.

'When I was ten, Massa William had me trained up to be his valet. My grandpa had done for him 'til then, but he'd become terrible crippled with swollen joints. We got on very well, the Massa and me. I enjoyed the work. He took me with him on all his trips.

'But the Massa has one weakness – cards. I was attending him at Covington last week when he got into a card game with a bad bunch. I'll not bother you with the details but in a moment of weakness, his money all gone to a nasty character, name of John McCalla, he was challenged to gamble me. McCalla won. I was watching the play. I'm sure he's a cheat but no-one could catch him at it. He's scum. Started abusing me right then.

'Massa William was horrified at what he'd done but there was nothing for it. He tried to hide his tears when he signed the papers. He came to McCalla's house a day ago. Asked my new master if he could take me to see my dying grandmother at Newport. I don't have a grandmother alive but I played along. I began to suspect what Massa William was up to. To the surprise of both of us, McCalla reluctantly agreed.

'And so we climbed into the McClusky buggy and headed off. As soon as we were out of sight, Massa William changed direction and, leaving the buggy at a livery stable, we caught a ferry to the city.

'He gave me a note saying I was in Ohio with his permission. He's staying at a hotel here for a few days on business. Directed me to come to you for help to get out of town. We figure that McCalla will soon realize I'm not coming back and be hot on my tail.'

We listened in amazement. This was a new one!

Joseph listened quietly. I could see his mind ticking over as to how to help George.

'I've already got a trip with a big party tonight and unfortunately, there's no room in the wagon for another. You'll have to stay here until tomorrow night. You can sleep in our hideout in the cellar and, if it's safe, we'll get you upstairs for breakfast. The law enforcers aren't allowed in without a warrant, so if anyone comes looking for you, one of us can get you back downstairs while someone else checks their papers.

The next morning, 8 o'clock and the first baking had come out of the ovens. Joseph had arisen and we were sitting having breakfast, George included. Suddenly, with no warning, three armed men burst into our kitchen.

Chapter 47

Abigail
Auckland February 2015

One Friday evening Aunt Hanna rang me. 'Abigail, I know you'd want to see what I've just found. I thought it was just a liner for the second trunk, but it's probably the most dramatic item we've found so far.'

This sounded important.

'I'll be round tomorrow morning,' I replied, and was – straight after breakfast. Mum was surprised I was up so early on a Saturday.

Aunt Hanna looked excited. Picked up a page of old news print. 'Read this!' she said, thrusting the paper at me.

It was ripped out of the *Philanthropist*.

30th June, 1841

A Mob in Cincinnati

One of those scenes of violence of which slavery is so prolific a source took place in Cincinnati last Friday morning, 25th June 1841. …

Thursday eve, a colored man came to the house of Mr J Burnett on 5th st., near Vine, stating that he was from Kentucky, and that his master had given him a pass to come to Cincinnati. He remained at Mr Burnett's till Friday morning.

Friday morning, while C. Burnett, his son Joseph and daughter-in-law, Mr Lewis (a man who was at work there) and two young apprentices, were at breakfast, the colored man sitting in the room, three persons entered quickly through the store, and rushed in, as if in search of someone. J. Burnett rose and demanded their business, but received no answer. C. Burnett, suspecting that they intended to seize the black man, in order to direct attention from him, cried out 'Go ahead', *pointing to the yard. One of them, happening to see the Negro sitting in the corner, called out, when another turning his head exclaimed,* 'That is my boy! Seize him!'

No warrant was shown by any of the individuals – no permission was asked or given to search the premises – no words spoken as to their business, til this moment.

Confusion immediately arose – they were ordered to quit the premises but rushed upon the Negro. Mr Burnett, his son, and Mr Lewis interfered at once, and attempted to put them out of the house. C. Burnett seizing one, got his head under his arm, and had him completely at his mercy, but declared that he did not strike him. He drew him towards the door, put him out and immediately received from him a severe blow in the face. J. Burnett grappled the person (named McCalla) claiming the Negro. A scuffle followed. The wife of J. Burnett, a delicate woman, laid hold of his shoulder to put him away, but was struck two or three times by McCalla across the neck and shoulders with a knotted stick – her cape was torn by him, and he pushed her with considerable force across the room. Her husband fell upon him with redoubled vigor – was thrown down. While prostrate, McCalla drew a pistol, pointed it at his breast, pulled the trigger, but it missed fire. Leveridge, a journeyman, who had been downstairs and had run up on hearing the noise, here interfered and pulled McCalla off. J. Burnett then flogged McCalla severely and drove him out of the shop.

Meanwhile, the Negro having been dragged away by a fourth man who came in, the fracas ended.

The disturbance attracted a crowd to the door, who became greatly incensed when they saw the bleeding face of McCalla, heard it reported that the Burnetts had been harboring Negroes, and resisted the peace-officer in his attempt to arrest a runaway. Besides, the Burnetts are Englishmen, and this was used to aggravate the irritation already awakened.

The report spread over the city. A great number of low characters, and half-grown boys, and respectable citizens, assembled about the store. Threats of violence were freely uttered. Sheriff Avery ... appeared on the ground and commanded the peace. The crowd seemed disposed to disperse, and the Sheriff, telling Mr Burnett to protect his own rights, departed under the conviction that no further disturbances would take place.

On his departure the crowd again closed up and beset the door – the street and market place began to be thronged – and violent menaces were openly made.

C. Burnett, standing in the door, bade them on their peril enter the premises, threatening to shoot the first man who should attempt it.

Sometime before noon, a very large stone was thrown with violence into the store, which C. Burnett immediately seized, and standing on the pavement, held up, appealing to it as proof of the cowardice of the mob. This greatly irritated the mobocrats. In accordance with the advice of friends, the windows were then closed, and doors shut; but one of the shutters was soon removed by the mob, and a few stones thrown, breaking the glass. They next let down the awning, when Mr C. Burnett went to the door to prevent them, still bearing in his hand the large stone, which he intended to preserve but which some say he designed to use as a missile. The stone was immediately wrenched from him, and he was knocked down. His sons Joseph, Thomas, Alfred and Mr Lewis ran to his assistance, but were at once assailed by the mob and most of them knocked down. A fight ensued, and they defended themselves as well as they could against such numbers, until at last they reached the house and closed the door.

The leading fact that the mob commenced the assault can be established by the testimony of several persons who were lookers on.

T. Burnett was very much hurt, and Alfred Burnett, a lad of fifteen, received a severe cut in his head. The rest were considerably bruised.

The wife of T. Burnett, hearing that her husband was dying, ran over in great haste to the scene of violence, but before she could obtain entrance into the house, was roughly used, and cursed by the mob.

C. Burnett, his three sons and Leverage, Lewis, and Erickson, an apprentice, were arrested in the afternoon, and carried before Esq. Doty – a mob, greatly excited, following.

The parties arrested admitted nothing but thought it best they should be committed till the excitement was allayed. Esq. Doty accordingly, as they declined giving bail, which was demanded to the amount of $3000, committed them to prison.

While the prisoners were on their way to jail, it required a strong force to protect them. An attempt was made to lynch them, but the determined spirit of the constables prevented it.

Saturday night an abortive attempt was made to set up another mob, the object being not only to destroy the property of Burnett but pull down the press of the Philanthropist.

A few remarks, and we conclude. … The attack on Burnett was in part owing to the number of southerners now congregating in Cincinnati; their hostility to the late decision of our Supreme Court; the bitter denunciation of this decision by the Cincinnati Enquirer, *a democratic paper, and its calls upon the people virtually to annul it – and to the indignation awakened by the decision among some of our steamboat captains, hotel keepers and merchants. …*

The captain of a steamboat remarked on 5th st., while the mob was on foot, that he would give five dollars to anyone who would drive Burnett from Cincinnati. A pork merchant standing by, said, he would give another, and there was not a merchant in Cincinnati that would not give his five. The keeper of one of our principal hotels complained that his business had fallen off sadly … And another steamboat captain was incensed because it 'had been already $100 out of his pocket.' …

Let it be understood, that so long as the constable failed to show his warrant, Burnett had the legal right to use any amount of force necessary to drive him from his premises: and let it further be remembered, that while the press is striving to irritate the prejudice of the community, by calling Mr Burnett an 'Englishman', he is a naturalized citizen, and a better American than the patriotic lovers of Slavery and Lynch-law.

I looked up at Aunt Hanna, horrified. I had to remind myself that for her, it was just fascinating history but for me, this was scarily current. So Alf hadn't been joking when we met on the river path two visits ago!

'This is dreadful!' I blurted out. 'Are there any more articles? What happened to them?'

'I've not found anything so far, dear,' she replied. 'But we can take comfort from the fact that there are many letters written after 1841, so presumably all turned out well.'

Her bland remark did nothing to reduce my worry. Not for the first time, I wished I could control when I arrived. But, even if I got there before the 25th June, should I give him warning? From every time-travel story I'd ever read or watched, it seemed that you couldn't change the past. But maybe, just maybe, this time I could think of something to help reduce some of the danger coming at them.

I had to try. Saying I had homework waiting, I headed home. Mum had gone out for coffee with an old school friend, thank goodness.

A worrying thought struck me. What if I arrived in the middle of the attack? Or at the prison? Or what if I couldn't reach Alf? Would I be stuck there if I couldn't give him the coin?

'Suck it up. Stop being a wimp,' I growled at myself. Got into my traveling clothes and slung the coin around my neck. Sure enough, everything went black.

Chapter 48

Alfred
Cincinnati, July 1841

I was out in the back yard, resentfully rebuilding our big wood pile. Those of the mob who'd found our back entrance had used wood as missiles to break any windows they could reach. They'd also smashed the pile, throwing it all over the yard. It angered me to remember how many hours I'd spent stacking it under the eaves of the house, once the woodshed was full. If any of those wastrels had been within reach as I worked, they'd have got firewood – right where it hurt.

They hadn't stopped at pulling down the wood pile either. Joseph, who loved his garden, shed tears when he saw his vegetables destroyed. Tomatoes, beans, sweet corn about to form cobs, lettuces, carrots – all deliberately trampled on. We'd be eating market-bought vegetables for a long time.

Mary Anne still hadn't recovered. The nasty bruises on her neck and shoulders from McCalla's stick healed reasonably quickly. However, her state of mind was another matter. Whenever a loud noise happened outside, she jumped in fright. She was in dread of another screaming and vicious mob coming at us. And she hated to put little Mary down. Even though we'd swept up the shards of glass, she was scared the baby would find a sharp slither in joints of the wooden floor. She went around in a permanent state of anxiety, a worried frown on her normally tranquil face.

It was the awning that upset Father the most. He'd saved for weeks, when he first set up shop, to afford the colorful arch of canvas giving shade to passers-by and keeping sun off the delectable treats in our display window. The mob had turned the struts into spears and shredded the canvas into unrecognizable strips. We'd ordered a new one, but still waited on its completion.

I caught a movement out of the corner of my eye. I swung round, a piece of wood in my hand. In my present mood, I was just itching to take my anger out on someone. But when I saw who was standing just inside the yard, I threw down the wood, a smile on my face.

Abi ran to me. Gave me an unexpected but welcome hug.

'Alf, I've been so worried. Are you okay?' She looked around. 'What a mess! Did the mob do this?'

I looked at her in amazement. 'Do you know about the riot?'

'Yep. Aunt Hanna found an article ripped out of the *Philanthropist*. As soon as I read it I had to come.' She peered at the still-red scar on my head. 'It said you'd had a bad cut on the head. Does it still hurt? How long since it happened?'

'It was last week, but just give me a couple of minutes and I can tell you more. I've got to check if our new awning is ready; if you come with me we'll find somewhere to talk that won't raise questions.' I looked up at the windows, hoping no-one was looking out.

Abi sat down on the chopping block, conveniently behind the woodshed and out of sight of the back door.

Very soon, hands washed, jacket on, and Joseph informed of my destination, Abi and I headed down the lane. Five minutes later, in a small park a couple of streets away, we sat down on the grass, sheltering from the hot sun under a leafy poplar tree.

I began …

Chapter 49

Alfred
Cincinnati June 25th 1841

At first all the mob did was shout and yell abuse. We tried to ignore them, leaving the door open for customers, but only a few hardy souls braved the aggression of the circling pack.

Sheriff Avery's intervention was completely ineffectual. The mob only pretended to obey. As soon as the Sheriff's back was turned, back they came. If anything, having heard him instruct Father to manage his own protection, it gave them confidence to escalate their attack.

Incensed, Father went to the door and shouted at the crowd. 'You're cowards, the lot of you. Is this how you treat honest citizens? Leave us alone. Just try coming in here and I'll shoot you.'

They jeered, laughed and hooted with derision. Just abused him the more.

Our neighbor, Mr Hicks, had been keeping an eye on things from the side. If a mob got out of control his premises were also at risk, though few knew he was also an abolitionist. He came rushing over and pulled Father inside the shop.

'Cornelius, for God's sake, don't incite them. Get your shutters up and shut the door.'

Father just snarled at his friend. 'Those bullies aren't going to stop me doing an honest day's work.' Refused to close the shop. Foolish Father.

Poor Joseph had the worst of it. On one hand he was trying to keep Father from taking on the mob, with Thomas itching to get into the fray as well. At the same time he was very worried about Mary Anne and Mary. We were just thankful the little one had been upstairs in her cot when the slave catchers burst in. I hate to think what might have happened if a toddler had been underfoot. We'd heard her cries as the struggle in the kitchen escalated but her poor mother could do nothing until the intruders had been forcibly ejected, dragging poor George with them.

Reluctantly, Joseph made a decision. 'Mary Anne, you must take Mary and go, right now, to Emma's.'

'What if the mob breaks in, Joseph? I'm that frightened for you all. I want to help,' replied Mary Anne.

He was normally very gentle with his wife's requests, but this time he put his foot down.

'I know you do, dearest, but there's no question about it. I can't be worrying about you both as well as trying to keep the hot-heads in this family under control.' He looked pointedly at our father. 'You'll help most by being safe. And look at the bairn. She's right upset with all the shouting and noise.'

Just then, another barrage of small stones hit the front windows. That decided her. Grabbing a bag, she threw together a few necessaries. I was delegated to escort her out the back door and down the service lane to Emma's. Thank goodness the mob hadn't come round to the backyard at that stage.

Semi-running, with me carrying Mary pickaback, solid wee lass that she was, in only a little over five minutes we were pounding on Emma's front door. A neighbor had given her the news and we found her all of a dither, not knowing what to do. She couldn't leave two small children and knew she couldn't take them with her.

As the two sisters-in-law exchanged news, I ran quickly back home, arriving just in time to see a really big rock come hurtling through the front door.

Father was so incensed that he went out to face the mob again, holding up the rock so all could see what he was so upset about. All hell broke loose.

We brothers pulled him back in and ran to close the shutters, locking the door as we re-entered.

However, once they couldn't see our faces, the cowards became bolder. First one of the shutters was ripped away, then the sound we dreaded to hear – a loud crack as yet another rock hit the display window we were so proud of. I can still hear the sound of smashing glass. We had to jump to avoid both incoming rocks and the dangerous splinters of glass.

Next, to our indignation, through the broken window we saw a bold rascal taking a run at our expensive striped awning. He reached up and started to swing from the arms. We heard the crack as it broke away from its fixings. A roar of approval came as men and boys at the front of the crowd yanked it down. Trampled on it. Threw broken pieces of the frame back to their mates to use as weapons.

The sight of destruction incited the mob to even more violence. Louder shouts. They egged each other to climb through, but no-one was quite that bold – yet.

Father, ever careless of his safety, could not be contained. He ran for the door with one of the missiles. The paper kindly suggested he just happened to have it in his hand, but I know he was looking to defend his property.

This was a very bad move, for by now the mob was uncontrollable. Like a swarm of angry wasps, they pounced on Father. It took all of us to extract our father from the mêlée, taking numerous injuries as we did. Our apprentices and Joseph were knocked down. Stones hit both me and Thomas on the head. Thomas took the worst of it – for a few minutes he was knocked unconscious.

With great difficulty we managed to extricate ourselves, dragging Thomas with us, and regrouped inside, doing our best to stem blood, much of it from my head. Thank goodness Thomas soon came round, just a bit groggy for a while. But, if possible, it got worse.

About twenty minutes later we heard a woman's scream, more shouts, and then a pounding on the door and someone crying, 'Let me in. Let me in.' Peeking through the broken window, Joseph, to his horror, saw Emma, disheveled, her clothes twisted, bonnet ripped and hanging by a thread, with ugly faces crowding round, jeering and poking at her.

Swiftly we unlocked and, throwing ourselves against the men who tried to follow her, we managed to force the door shut again. Emma fell into the room, looking wildly around the room, crying, 'Where's Thomas? Is he dead?'

Then she saw him, by now sitting propped against a wall.

'Oh Thomas, they said you were dead!'

Soon after this, we heard loud noises at the back of the house. A detachment of blood-lust mobsters, foiled at the front door, had gone looking for the back alley. Thank goodness our kitchen door was of stout oak, with an iron bar on the inside as well as a padlock. And we could only be grateful that the mobocrats didn't take an axe to either of our doors.

At one point I was sent upstairs to see if law enforcers were coming to help. Nothing. All I could see was a steady flow of more spectators. Instead of relief, many of the increasing flood of men and boys joined the gangs and started pulling up loose cobbles, or ran around searching for stones and debris. Anything not fastened down was ammunition against us. At the back of the crowd, standing well clear, I spotted some of our friends, looking horrified but powerless to intervene against such a dangerous mob.

The noise was awful. The thud of missiles hitting the walls was a never-ending background to the shouts, yells and abuse. Soon broken glass littered the floor in nearly every room in the house. Ugly laughter, shouts, howls – we were under siege on all sides by a pack of ravening wolves.

We were terrified. Afraid for our lives. Praying that the law would come and save us. Sometimes close to despair. Several hours went by with no hoped-for relief.

But Burnetts don't crumple easily. Once Thomas was back on his feet, he grabbed one of our double-barreled guns and wanted to get to a window to start shooting. Thank goodness Joseph prevented him. It would have been the death warrant for the lot of us. However, we determined that we would give no quarter, should they force entry. Joseph prepared the two guns, two brace of pistols, the axe, the cleaver and the irons we used for candy. We could have injured a great many and probably killed some before they got us.

Finally, a squad of soldiers and constabulary approached. The mob reluctantly stepped back, still shouting, waving fists and missiles, as the relief party banged on our door. We opened it with thankfulness. That rapidly changed when, to our amazement and disbelief, the burly leader, armed with a gun, said, 'Men, I'm taking you into custody.'

The mobsters cheered and mocked us.

At first it seemed most unfair that we were the ones arrested. Why didn't they arrest the leaders of the mob? We'd just been defending our home, as any red-blooded man would do. But one of the constables said quietly to Joseph as they began to take us out of our home, 'Sorry about this, Mr Burnett, but it's for your safety.' He then delegated a couple of his men to escort Emma back to her house. We found out later that Mary Anne had been beside herself with worry, fearing the worst with Emma away so long.

We were greeted with howls of derision as the constabulary ushered us out the door. Sharp stones were thrown at us. The special constables, sworn in for the occasion, had their work cut out to protect us. Frightening mobsters with angry hateful faces ran alongside, trying to pull us out of the clutches of the arresting officers. They particularly focused on Father and Thomas, probably because my father and brother shouted defiantly back. Thomas can be as hot-headed as Father at times. Father was kicked viciously in the spine by one of the mob, who leapt in while the constable guarding him was distracted.

Later, we realized the comment about our safety was not said in jest. Had we started ten minutes later, we would probably never have reached the Court House alive; several hundred Kentuckians came across the river, determined to lynch us.

Once we were sentenced and warders had escorted us out of the raucous courtroom to a dark, windowless and dingy cell, a strange lethargy descended on us all. Our nerves had been at stretch all day, never knowing where the next threat would come from. For the moment we were safe. We sat where we could, rubbing our bruises and retying bandages that had been applied earlier in the day.

Joseph and Thomas were worried about their wives. 'I do hope Mary Anne doesn't try to go home tonight,' was Joseph's concern.

'I saw Mr Hicks and Mr Grainger at the back of the crowd when we were marched off. I'm sure they'll look after the girls,' Father reassured them.

Many hours passed. With no outside light we could only guess at the time. Exhausted and sore, we took turns to doze on the two smelly straw pallets thrown in the corner. The rest of us squeezed onto an old scratched wooden bench or sat on the floor. No-one had told us how long we'd be incarcerated.

And then, lantern light flickered along the corridor. A surly-looking warder put down his lantern when he reached the iron grille and shuffled through a bunch of big keys.

'Righto, you lot. Yer lucky ya got friends in high places. You young uns is free t' go. A gen'leman paid yer bail.'

'What do you mean, the younger ones?' demanded Father.

'You and yer oldest son stay 'ere.'

'Why?'

'Not for me to say,' was the unhelpful response.

He pushed the door open, counted us through, then clanged it behind us, leaving Joseph and Father behind. Thomas, limping from his injuries, our workers and I were hustled out to the wooden-paneled foyer. There was Mr Chase, sitting on a hard-bottomed chair and looking at his pocket watch. A look of relief crossed his face as he caught sight of us.

In answer to our anxious questions he explained that both he and Squire Doty felt that Father and Joseph's presence back at the house that night would just aggravate the mob again.

'We should be able to get them out tomorrow,' he explained. 'Thomas, you'll need to take Alfred to your place tonight, or to your mother. He must not go home. Joseph's wife and baby are now with Mrs Burnett senior, safely away from trouble. You lads,' addressing our workers, 'had best head straight to your lodgings, but take a different road from the Burnetts. If you go out in a group, you're liable to attract more unwelcome attention.

'I've had some very stern words with Sheriff Avery and Squire Doty, threatening them with a law suit regarding dereliction of duty. The mob should never have been allowed to develop and remain for so many hours. I suspect the ruffians will make another attempt tonight to damage your property. If the law officers don't monitor the situation closely this time and quickly disperse any further illegal gatherings, they'll be hearing from me in court.'

His assessment of the situation was accurate.

The *Gazette* reported: *Immediately after supper time, boys and half-grown men began to collect about the house of Burnett, and by 8 o'clock several hundred persons were present. Very decided manifestations of a determination to break into the house, for the purpose of destroying whatever might be therein, soon showed themselves.*

Squire Doty addressed the crowd and besought them to disperse. Very little regard was paid to him, and about 9 pm an attack was made upon the door. Being upon the alert, he was at this point in an instant, and succeeded in suspending operations for a few minutes, til Mr Avery, the Sheriff, who had been sent for, arrived upon the ground, and addressed the throng from one of the side benches of the market house. This had the effect of drawing the crowd away from the door, along with the Sheriff's assurances that Burnett and his associates were in jail and would be held to a strict accountability for any violations of law of which they had been guilty.

The crowd soon afterwards began to disperse, in obedience to his appeals to their sense of duty and propriety, and at this time there are not more than a hundred persons present, and these such as are thoughtless enough to remain to satisfy their curiosity.

Clearly the writer of that column had never had one hundred 'curious' people crowded around his front door. Neighbors told us later that shouts, catcalls and occasional rocks at our windows and roof went on well into the small hours.

Father and Joseph were released at 11 o'clock Saturday morning and that night we returned to our home, hoping against hope that we wouldn't have to deal with such frightening events again.

I finished the story for Abigail with, 'It was the most chilling experience of my life. I hope to never go through such a thing again. Now, I must get back. They'll be sending out a search party if I'm too long, for we're all on tenterhooks these days.'

Reluctantly, Abi gave me hold of the coin and we parted in our usual way.

Little did we know that even worse was to come.

Chapter 50

Abigail
Auckland February 2015

Summer term had just begun and it was a stinking hot day. I was trying to stay alert in history class. I'd drawn the short straw with the teacher this year. Instead of cool Mr Woodyard, who kept us entertained and absorbed as he brought history alive, I'd ended up with fussy old Miss Galloway. She was a stickler for facts and figures, droned on like an irritating fly, and didn't like being contradicted.

'Right, class. This term we'll study the American Civil War. It began in April 1861 and didn't finish until four years later, in April 1865. Does anyone know what caused it?' she asked.

I waited to see who would contribute. Pushing her glasses firmly into place on her pert nose, Sally Longford, one of the nerdy girls in the class, put up her hand.

'Yes, Sally.'

'The South wanted to be self-ruling and independent of the North. The North wanted them to all be one Union.'

'Excellent. Was there any particular issue that caused the division?'

'I think it was slavery, Miss.'

'It was certainly a contributing factor. Can you tell us more?'

'I don't know much more, Miss, but I think the northern states didn't want the newer states like Texas and California to allow slavery,' Sally replied.

'Excellent.' Miss Galloway beamed. 'The northerners were against slavery. Wanted it abolished. There were a number of other complex reasons for the war as well, including distribution of wealth and political influence. We'll dig into that a bit more. Does anyone else want to add something?

I couldn't hold back. 'Miss, many northerners were *not* against slavery. For a long time, abolition, or at least immediate abolition, was very unpopular in the north.'

Miss Galloway looked surprised. 'I'm not sure that's correct, Abigail.'

'Miss, I've been learning about it over the holidays. I know I'm right, at least up until the early 1840s.'

Her mouth screwed up. She was displeased. My friends and I called it her chook-bum face. She hated being challenged. Hated even more being shown up.

'Well, young lady, it's important to be able to substantiate claims. Bring your evidence to school and let us have a look at it.'

Did I have evidence! I couldn't wait to get to school the next day with the newspaper clipping. I wished I could say I'd been at the scene of the violence, but that was a step too far!

Chapter 51

Alfred
Cincinnati August 29th 1841

The ordeal of 25th June took a heavy toll on the whole family, but especially Mary Anne and Joseph. They began to talk about returning to England. It wasn't the gun fired at Joseph point-blank that worried him, and Mary Anne was surprisingly philosophical about her bruising and sore shoulders. It was their precious little girl they feared for. What might have happened to little Mary, had she been downstairs at the time of the forced entry? And later, in those hours of terror with the mob baying and howling, what if a random stone had hit her?

After the attack on us and our premises, we exercised more caution. We knew the slave owners and their depraved henchmen were watching us. However, runaways kept coming so of course we kept helping them.

The morning of Sunday 29th August began just after 4 o'clock. I was woken by a loud knock on the kitchen door. Coming to, I heard Joseph and Mary Anne's voices in the room below. Next was the thump of Joseph's heavy tread as he stumbled downstairs, half-awake. I extracted myself from my rumpled sheet, tangled during the hot humid night, and pushed my attic window further open to see who was below. Inky night was lightening to a soft grey. The air was still. Birds twittered and stirred. Another scorching day was on its way.

Below stood Mr Grosvenor, one of our many conductor friends, with an anxious-looking black man and two exhausted children. Joseph was opening the door as my window creaked. He looked up and silently signaled me to come down.

We'd developed the nightly habit of always leaving our clothes ready to swiftly throw on. In this line of work you never knew what was coming round the corner. I was down in the kitchen within minutes. The barefoot little boys, dressed only in threadbare cotton garments, perched shyly on chairs. Their frightened brown eyes were glued to the heaped plate of biscuits Joseph had just placed in front of them.

'Boys, please eat up.' They didn't need two tellings.

'Brother, this is Mr Benjamin Wallace and his children. We need to get them hidden for the day, as fast as we can. Our secret room isn't safe just now – too many are watching us. I think Mr Hopkins' place will be best this time.' As he talked, he swiftly threw more food into an old bag the fugitives could carry with them.

The family had been running for two days from a Kentucky plantation. A visiting relative of the owner had forced himself on their mother. She'd fought against him with all her might, and in the struggle, managed to bite off part of his ear. Their owner was incensed at her lack of willingness to oblige his visitor. The next time a slave trader crossed his path, she was sold south.

There was no warning. One minute she was in the bosom of her family; the next she was chained to a coffle of other poor unfortunates and dragged off, screaming for her children. Benjamin came home from an errand to the next-door farm, expecting his dinner, only to find his children distraught and his wife gone. Devastated, he marched up to the Big House, demanding to know what had happened. Angry words were exchanged. The owner threatened him with a riding crop and a promise to sell the rest of the family for his insolence. Small wonder they ran.

Within ten minutes we were silently slipping through back alleys. Mr Hopkins' place was close enough that we should be able to get there before day fully broke. In his wooded lot on Mt Auburn he'd recently built a well-hidden tree house that runaways could sleep in during the day, protected from the elements and away from his buildings should the catchers come unannounced.

That night Joseph and two other conductors, Mr Grainger and Thomas Howells, headed out of town driving two of Gideon Langston's wagons. Stowed away were Mr Wallace and his boys plus a man and wife from Georgia.

Joseph had been gone about thirty minutes when three tobacco-chewing and rough-talking slave catchers came banging on our door, demanding entrance. We had great satisfaction in innocently knowing nothing. They snarled as we turned them away at the door. You'd think the message that a search warrant was required before they could enter would have got through by now. But again, these fellows carried no authority to enter. I stood beside Mary Anne as she answered the door, one of our shotguns visible in my arms. We had become accustomed to defending our rights.

Just as well we did have that mindset, for five days later we faced a far greater peril.

Chapter 52

Alfred
Cincinnati August 31st – September 3rd, 1841

In a hot summer the Ohio River got very low, sometimes to the point that only the shallowest boats could travel. It put pressure on everyone, but especially those whose livelihoods depended on the flow of goods and people up and down the river. As so often happens in times of hardship, those who suffer the most are the poor people, with no influence and no financial reserves. In our city that was most of the blacks – and the Irish. Add heat, humidity and drought. Then stir in anger, bubbling away as a result of the Supreme Court ruling reinforcing the freedom of any slave on Ohio soil, and all the ingredients for conflagration were to hand.

The summer was on its way out, but rain was very patchy. By the end of August things had become very volatile. Raised voices could be heard on every corner. Tempers rose like the temperatures. Fights erupted. When men are desperate for pennies to feed their families, the thought that someone else might get work they were counting on is sometimes enough to trigger a fight. Brawls, such as the one I'd witnessed in the first days of my arrival, were commonplace. Just walking around town, I felt a sense of deep unease. An undercurrent of aggression spread, fog-like but invisible. And there were strangers in town: slave catchers, kidnappers looking for unwary free blacks, itinerant riverside workers with nothing to do, trouble-makers looking for fights.

Like smoke from a smoldering pile of ashes, corruption, crime, dissension and distrust seeped through the city.

Burglaries were on the rise. More beggars solicited on the streets. And people were afraid. All it needed was a small incident to spark the ever-present anger and hate into a raging fire.

On the evening of Tuesday 31st August, the match was struck.

Several well-dressed young black men, walking quietly down the road, were attacked by a group of uncouth Irish youths. With yells and crude taunts, the assailants began scooping up handfuls of gravel from the street and pelting their targets. Not surprisingly, the black men retaliated. Others joined in and a fight was soon in full flourish.

The fight escalated, as fights have a habit of doing. Wednesday night the quarrel was renewed. Sometime after midnight a party of fired-up men, armed with clubs and other weapons, attacked Dumas House. The attackers claimed they were after a runaway. This time the inhabitants repelled them; our black friends were tired of being victimized.

Other families in homes nearby were caught up in the escalating violence. An engagement took place and several were wounded. Strangely, neither city officials nor police seemed to receive a report of the violent street disturbance. Or – not a report they acted on, at any rate. I couldn't help wondering – were they conveniently letting the mob do their dirty work?

Thursday 2nd September brought a continuation of the troubles. The *Enquirer* reported that in another incident initiated by white agitators, some said Irish, a white man was stabbed by a Negro. His life was in danger. This took place at the Lower Market, only five minutes' walk from our shop. Tension worsened throughout the city. Sides were taken. Violence and destruction stalked the streets.

❁ ❁

Friday 3rd September started hot, and got hotter, in both temperature and tempers. The flames reached us.

We were busier than usual all day. I was called up from downstairs to help in the shop.

'I'm all of a dither,' said one housewife to her friend as she bought double her normal supplies. 'What if the violence comes our way? I want to get out of the city but my man says no mobsters will frighten him out of his home. It's all well and good for him, but what about the children?'

Another woman joined in the conversation. 'My husband doesn't want to leave his shop. Says that if it's empty the rioters will break in and help themselves. I'm right skeered.'

And so it went, all day. No-one knew what to do for the best. Conflicting rumors flew round the city like an out-of-control forest fire.

Late in the afternoon I was in our store, tidying up the last few items in the cabinet. At that precise moment the store was empty. With a bang, the door slammed open. My friend Ralph fell into the store.

'Alf,' he gasped. 'The mob – they're coming. To kill you all.'

I yelled urgently for Joseph and Thomas, who came running up the stairs from the bakery. Hearing the panic in my voice, Mary Anne came dashing at the same time.

Ralph panted as he told his frightening story.

'I was down at the Public Landing, doing a delivery of candles and soap for Mr Proctor. A big gang of rough-looking strangers were nearby, talking and cursing. In the middle of them were some of those louts that hassle us, Alf. I heard someone say 'Burnett' so I ducked behind a wagon to listen. Once I'd heard their plans, as I turned to come and warn you, I tripped and they spotted me. Chased me. Had to run for my life.'

Mary Anne looked frightened. 'What are they going to do?'

'They're coming after you. Maybe tonight. Or tomorrow. Plan is to destroy your store. Run you out of town. They're even talking about killing any of you they find, but especially your father.'

Mary Anne and I gasped in horror. Thomas and Joe turned pale.

My brothers quizzed him for any further details. Then we quickly grabbed the last of the cakes in the display cabinet, thrust them in his arms and let him out the back door.

Trying not to panic, we jumped into action. Joseph called the men in the bakery from their end-of-day chores to come and help dismantle the precious awning, apart from Martin, who was dispatched round the corner to warn Samuel. As soon as the awning was down and stored, the shutters went up, the shop door was locked and barred and Thomas raced home to help Emma pack. He wanted her well away from likely trouble spots – three blocks was too close. Meanwhile, Mary Anne frantically gathered basics, mostly for the toddler.

Within half-an-hour of Ralph's warning I was also heading out the back door, with my sister-in-law and little niece. I'd been given the responsibility of escorting our women up to Mother's, in the quiet part of town.

Our departure was heartbreaking. Joseph kissed his fleeing wife and child farewell, not knowing when or if he'd ever see them again. Then, grabbing the tin box with the day's takings, he ran to hide in Mr Hicks's cellar. Hicks was one of the good guys; a staunch abolitionist, long-time member of the Committee of Vigilance, but not in the public eye. Thomas was to join Joseph in the cellar as soon as he'd helped Emma prepare to leave. My brothers wanted to stay near our home and business but out of sight. They knew better now than to try and stop a mob, but they could possibly prevent further damage if, for example, the attackers started a fire.

On the way to Mother's, Mary Anne and I called to collect Emma and her children. Just as well I didn't bother to bundle up any of my own possessions – I was like an overloaded donkey, burdened with baby paraphernalia for my sisters-in-law. Mary Anne pushed her fancy baby carriage, loaded with as much as she could fit in around the child. Emma had filled up a little cart Father had made for Henry, loaded with their essentials. Little Emma clung to her hand. Four-year-old Henry was given his favorite toys to carry in a small shoulder satchel.

As we walked up the hot and dusty streets we saw other similarly laden families. They were also heading away from the trouble spots. Frightened women. Crying children. Other little ones, like four-year-old Henry, thinking it was an adventure. It was a relief to see Mother's neat home and picket fence.

'Oh, thank goodness you're here,' she cried as we walked in. 'Alf, could you please go back now and help Ann. Get her here as fast as you can.'

I found my sister just about to leave her house and shouldered some of her burdens. Once we were safely back at Mother's and I'd dropped Ann's bundles in the hallway, I looked back out the door, wondering how soon I could get away. Mother read my mind.

'Don't you even *think* about leaving, Alfred Burnett. We need you here. I don't think the troubles will come this far up-town, but we need a man to protect us.' For a moment I was miffed. I wanted to run back and join Joseph and Thomas. See the action. Be there to help. But clever Mother hit the right spot. A man, she called me! That was a first. I will confess to a touch of pride.

'What about Father?' I had to try, for form's sake. Wouldn't do to look too flattered.

'Your father is in hiding elsewhere, thank goodness. That man is a magnet for trouble. I don't think his presence would be a help at all!'

I figured she was right.

My sisters took over. Jane took charge of the three little ones and Sarah hustled us into the kitchen to brew a cup of tea. I relaxed for the first time since Ralph had dashed through our door.

We were all safe – for the moment – but the poor blacks were not.

Chapter 53

Alfred
Cincinnati 3rd – 4th September 1841

By 8 o'clock that Friday night, the crowd had increased. About seven or eight hundred men and boys assembled by the market buildings close to our store, a goodly number of them from Kentucky, we were later told. From their hiding place in Mr Hicks' cellar, Joseph and Thomas could hear the angry buzzing of men's voices. It seemed that we and our premises were not their focus – yet. Nonetheless, my brothers took Ralph's warning very seriously. Kept well out of sight.

A ring-leader shouted above the noise. 'Listen up, lads. We gotta protect our rights. Gotta be able t' work. Gotta feed our families.'

There was a roar of approval from his audience. He continued, 'Here's the plan. We'll go over to Bucktown. Let's drive all the damned darkies out. Stealin' our jobs, they are. We want none o' the bastards in *our* city.'

No officials came to disperse the mob. From Fifth street market, the raggle-taggle crowd marched the four city blocks towards Broadway and Sixth, their numbers swelling as they progressed. Some came with clubs and other makeshift weapons. Others picked up stones or ripped boards off properties as they went.

Their first target was a Negro confectionary on Broadway next to Sycamore, smashing the doors and windows. More trouble-makers ran to join the mob, adding their yells and blasphemies to the frightening tidal wave of sound.

The Mayor arrived, all of a fluster. He and others tried to reason with the mob. They shouted him down with cries such as 'down with him!', 'run him off', and other imprecations.

The black community was ready. The events of the previous days had warned them to prepare for the worst. The besieged residents opened gunfire on their attackers. The battle ebbed and flowed until 1 o'clock on Saturday morning.

About this time, the aggressors procured a cannon from down near the river and loaded it with slugs, boiler punchings and any other dangerous debris they could find. Dragging it into the battle zone, they fired it several times. The Mayor again tried to stop them. Again, he was ignored. They located the cannon on Broadway, pointing down Sixth street. Two or three were wounded or killed – on both sides. By this time many of the black community had fled to the hills, especially the women, children, and vulnerable old people, their wagons, carts and carriages loaded with whatever essential possessions they could easily carry away. They were terrified for their lives. Afraid their homes would be destroyed.

Sometime after 2am the Mayor and police finally brought in the military, though it took nearly another hour before their combined efforts managed to quieten the riot. Why were the military so slow to act? Many believe it was because they were mobocrats themselves.

Joseph's journal entry for the next day, Saturday 4th September, paints a grim picture.

Yesterday sent Mary and child up to Mother's with Alf. Then got my money to start. But the mob came yelling down the back alley. Thought my time was come. Lewis was with me. I got Martin and Lewis to help shut up the store and made my escape to Mr Hicks. The mob had entire possession of the city.

While at Mr Hicks' a mob meeting was held in Fifth street market house. Thomas and I went by the scuttle ready to escape, listening to the yells of the devils with our hands up ready to defend ourselves. Got Mr Alley to get a barouche, disguised myself as well as I could. Thomas and I went to Mr Hopkins on Mt. Auburn.

This morning, clear and hot. Went to store early in morn. Father came down but thought it was not safe and advised him to go to Mr George Smith's on 8th street. He left just in time to save his life. Thomas and I returned to Mr Hopkins.

The mob started hunting every black man they could find, and put them in what they called a Negro pen.

That Saturday went down in history as one of Cincinnati's Blackest Days, for two different but related reasons.

First was an urgently convened meeting. While my brothers and father were hiding in fear for their lives, and I was stuck with all the women, a gathering of citizens was called for 10am at the Court House to discuss the events of the previous few days.

The very well-attended meeting was presided over by Mayor Samuel W. Davies and addressed by Judge Read, Sheriff Avery and others – well-known anti-abolitionists. A few reasonable citizens were also in attendance, but when they tried to keep the assembly focused on resolving the immediate mob violence, they were shouted down by inflammatory speakers who blamed the whole sorry string of events on we abolitionists.

Their resolutions were a scurrilous attack on us and our Negro friends. In short:

Resolved. That the Negroes who committed outrages on two white youths should be committed to jail for examination. *[The white boys started the whole thing. The Negroes only acted in self-defense. No mention of punishing the initiators.]*

Resolved. That the Township Trustees immediately execute the law of 1807, requiring Negroes and mulattoes to give bonds. *[This required any person of color to pay a bond of $500 for the right to reside in Cincinnati. It had not been enforced for some years. This was their devious way to force people of color out of the city. Hardly anyone could afford $500.]*

Resolved. That they would carry out the law to the letter until 'our citizens are relieved of the effect of modern abolitionism – and our southern brethren may be assured that this is no idle move, but will be carried out in good faith.' *[Slave owners, we've got your backs! Keep up the good work, and we'll do our bit by stamping out those pesky business-destroying abolitionists.]*

Resolved. That every Negro who escapes from his master and comes within our borders shall be delivered up. *[What's new?]*

Resolved. That the civil authorities, headed by the Mayor and Sheriff of the County, proceed at once to the dwellings of the blacks and disarm them of all offensive weapons. *[We, the men with power and might, are off to ensure those unwanted citizens of our city have no way to protect themselves.]*

Resolved. That patrols protect the persons and property of the Blacks during the existence of the present excitement, until they give the bonds required by the act of 1807, or leave the city. *[We'll put the black community under constant surveillance and intimidation. Make them pay that enormous amount of money or leave. Hopefully that will quit us of most of them.]*

Resolved. 'That we view with abhorrence the proceedings of the abolitionists in our city, we repudiate their doctrine and believe it to be the duty of every good citizen by all lawful means to discountenance every man who lends them his assistance.' *[Unleash the hounds of intimidation on every abolitionist.]*

Resolved. That the Mayor be requested to call by Proclamation on the parents and guardians of boys who'd been involved in stirring up the mobs, to keep them at home. *[Many of the worst mob stirrers were boys of the type I've described earlier. Good luck on that. When did such boys listen to reason? And did they have parents who'd care?]*

This outrageous list of resolutions was then distributed in hand bills around the town and published in the main papers. Dr Bailey printed it in the *Philanthropist* on September 8th. His publication and commentary were delayed for reasons soon to be revealed.

The second issue, which Joseph touched on in his journal entry, was even worse.

Someone decreed that the black men of the city should be rounded up into a cordoned-off area near the battle ground of the night before, guarded by sentinels, and held under martial law. Every black man that could be found was dragged there during the day by parties who scoured the city, assuming the authority of the law.

By the end of the day they'd rounded up about five hundred men and older boys. One paper reported: *Small bands, sometimes composed of mere boys with clubs and other weapons, went all over the city, instituting inquisitorial searches, demanding the persons of colored servants and driving them off like brutes to the Negro quarters.*

In the main, the kidnappers and sentinels were rioters, vigilantes, young thugs, vagabonds and loafers ready for any mischief. They were egged on by loud-voiced older men, a goodly number not known in our city, or so later reports said. Rough rivermen and fellows from across the river were blamed. However, knowing how abolitionists and Negroes were despised and reviled in the city, I suspect many city dwellers were just as guilty. But – I am endeavoring to stick to confirmed facts in this tale.

The roughly arranged enclosure was in the area between Broadway, Pike, New and Seventh streets and surrounded by armed sentries. Observers told us later that it was scarily reminiscent of southern slave auctions, where collections of frightened slaves would be penned up awaiting their turn on the auction block.

Some of the detainees tried to argue with the sentinels posted around the perimeter. Others slumped on the ground in despair. All were held against their will. The hot sun beat down. Screams, shouts and abuse punctuated the day. Occasionally someone would come with a bucket of water for them – but never enough.

Eventually, about 5 o'clock in the afternoon, the captives were placed between a slim line of military and conducted to jail – for their safety, it was said. They were surrounded and followed by an immense crowd, shouting and yelling all the way. At any time, further trouble could have erupted. The military were few; the mobocrats were many. Our experience of being dragged to jail nine weeks earlier, scary as it had been, was a pale version of what our black friends experienced that day.

Chapter 54

Alfred
Cincinnati September 4th 1841

When I heard about the arrest of all the black men and boys, for in truth that was what it really was, I began to worry about my friend John. Had he been caught in the roundup? Was he in prison?

Mother wouldn't let me try and find out. New lines of worry had etched pathways down her aging cheeks. She took hold of my hands, looked earnestly into my eyes, spoke very seriously.

'Alf, you can't go out this door. Too many people know you're a Burnett. Go near the prison to enquire for John and you might be clapped in irons, or worse. We've got enough to worry about with the rest of our men running for their lives. I can't lose you too.'

She wiped away a tear. It gave me a shock to see my mother cry. I stopped fussing and resigned myself to a truly difficult task – exercising patience.

As the day proceeded, thoughts of John were swamped by worry about our own family, for the news continued to worsen.

Our only source of information came from occasional well-wishers dashing in with updates. None were good.

'I'm sorry, ladies,' said one supporter as we all clustered around him, desperate for news. 'We have no idea where your men are.' Mother gasped, then went silent. Mary Anne and sister Ann cried. Emma looked terrified. Sarah made another cup of tea. And Jane and I tried to keep our nieces and nephew entertained, while all the time lending an ear to the reports.

Toward the end of the day, once the colored men had been taken to jail, we were told that things had quietened down. But it was a false peace – merely a lull before the mob turned to hurting us. The rioters were just waiting for nightfall.

By evening the mob was back on the streets. This time they were more organized. They spread themselves out to different targets, making it harder for the military and police to prevent further mayhem. Their targets this time were the abolitionists – and our extended family was top of the list. Ralph's warning was correct – their aim was to kill. When they couldn't find any of our men, they took out their evil intentions on the next best thing – our livelihoods and our family home.

First they went for Samuel's press in Patterson's Alley, between Main and Walnut, just around the corner from our place. A patrol of soldiers happened to be moving down the lane as the mob gathered outside the *Philanthropist* office. Reports varied. One said there was an exchange of words, a slight pause, the soldiers moved on and the rioters were free to continue with their original intention. Another one claimed that the mobsters appeared to disperse so the soldiers continued. Newspapers later claimed that the officer in charge chose to turn a blind eye to the crime quite clearly about to be committed. He denied it. But – actions speak louder than words. No guards were posted to prevent destruction of private property.

Lighting their way with candles and lanterns, and armed with sticks, clubs and sledgehammers, the rabble broke into the office, smashed up both of Samuel's presses and dragged parts of the machinery down to the river. We were told later about the frightening howls, screams, oaths and wild laughter as they pounded the machines with their implements. The only equipment that survived were the trays of type – Samuel had hidden them at a friend's place the night before.

Then they moved to our bakery and home. They didn't care that it was now Joseph's business, not Father's. Roars of glee were heard as a flood of villains burst into the building. For nearly an hour there was the sound of breaking glass, thuds, crashes, banging and chopping. Many of our possessions, especially the baking ingredients, were seen being rolled or carried down the street by elated opportunists. Presumably a lot of baking was done in their homes over the next weeks. Anything left behind was damaged or destroyed.

Their next attack was to be the home of Dr Bailey but they were assured that he resided out of town. So, seeking another target for their evil energies, they turned their attention to property occupied or owned by Negroes. Homes in the vicinity of the Negro settlement on Columbia, Sixth, Broadway and Western Row near the river were next. Even the Bethel church, beloved by its Negro congregation, was desecrated. Windows were smashed, doors broken down. Cowards that they were, with most of the black men either in prison or in hiding, it was easy to terrify the children and rape the women. Many victims were scarred for life by the atrocities.

Governor Thomas Corwin issued a proclamation calling for the end of the violence. It made no difference. Neither the official nor the temporary representatives of law and order – military, police, or the large number of short-term sworn-in deputies – were effective at stopping the rioters. It wasn't until quite late at night, because they were starting to tire, it was suggested, that the rampage was finally halted by the authorities. The looters had been about to destroy an abolitionist bookstore. About twenty of the leaders were arrested and the violence petered out.

Chapter 55

Joseph's Journal
Cincinnati September
4th – 13th, 1841

Joseph and Thomas weren't the only ones hiding from the vigilantes out at Mt Auburn. From Joseph's journal:

About tea time a colored man came to join us at Mr Hopkins' place, a Mr Anderson. Was very frightened.

We were all just ready to go to bed when Mr Macy arrived from the City and told us that the mob was going to search all the houses on the hill. So, Thomas, Anderson and I started north to Mr Mervill's, who put his horse in harness and drove us to Mr Smith's. Went to bed. Was awakened about midnight, and thought the mob was upon us. But it was Mr George Smith and Father from the city. They brought the news that the Philanthropist *press was destroyed.*

What Joseph didn't know, when he penned the words about our brother-in-law's printing press, was what had happened to his own business.

He wasn't left long in ignorance, as showed in his next entry:

Received very hot news. That my store was broken open and my property destroyed – and that they were hunting for Father. So, Father, Thomas and I started after dark for Mr Van Zandt's. Got there about 11 o'clock. Went from there to Mr Glen's. Thought we were not safe there, as he was threatened also. Started back past Mr Van Zandt's to Mr Conklin's. Got there about 1 o'clock.

Imagine driving from place to place in panic, hoping that the safe houses they'd used to shelter black fugitives so many times would now be able to shelter them. The saviors needed saving. No-one was safe. The main mob might have ceased harassing the citizens of the city, but a number of their cohort were terrorizing anyone in the country-side known to be an abolitionist supporter. They were determined to break the Underground Railroad.

I was totally frustrated at not being with my brothers. What I thought I could do, goodness knows, but being tied to the apron-strings of a gaggle of women did not please me. However, looking back, it was well that I was with Mother. One less person for her to worry about. I resigned myself to being the only male in the hen-house, apart from little Henry. And the women and babies did keep me occupied.

So we have to stick with Joseph's daybook for more details.

Monday 6th September

Staid at Conklin's all day. Mr Grainger came for me to return towards evening. Returned as far as Mt Auburn to Mr Hopkins'. Soon after I left, about 50 of the mob, a number of them Kentuckians, came near where Father and Thomas were. They searched Mr Van Zandt's through twice. Father and Tom hid in the woods.

Tuesday 7th September

Mary came to Mt Auburn with Sarah and Mr Grainger to consult as to what it was best to do. Sent Mary back to fix up and be selling.

Mary Anne just wanted out of Cincinnati. She'd reached breaking point.

From Wednesday to Friday Joseph continued to hide at Mr Hopkins' place.

Saturday 11th September

Father came this morn. And Mr Van Zandt. A runaway came and wanted our assistance. Made arrangements.

Father and Van Zandt started after dinner for the farm, leaving me to make further arrangements. Went to Mr Hopkins, who drove me into the city. Slept at Dr Miles.

It was another two days before he could safely go home.

Chapter 56

Alfred
Cincinnati September 1841

Our fellows were all still in hiding when the women and I first went back to the house. It was heartbreaking to look at the destruction. Even I cried when we saw what the rioters had done.

In the cellar, the few barrels left by looters were tipped over. The floor was a disgusting mess of flour, rice, sugar, molasses and golden syrup. Streaks of egg yolk had hardened on our once-pristine whitewashed walls. Spilled spices stained everything with red, yellow, brown and orange.

In the bakery they'd wrenched off the oven doors. Every piece of equipment pulled off its shelf or out of its drawer. Most of the shelves ripped down. Our hard-to-get large crockery mixing bowls smashed into hundreds of pieces. Also, all our other plates and bowls. Pots and cooking utensils thrown everywhere. Anything they could break, they'd destroyed or damaged beyond repair.

No meals would be coming out of the kitchen any time soon. Food supplies, utensils and everything we ate off or drank from – all were either stolen or strewn in pieces all over the room. Mary Anne cried the louder when she saw her favorite copper mixing bowl, passed down through her family for several generations, dented and damaged beyond repair. Even her shopping baskets, used every day to go to market, had been stomped on and smashed.

In the store, our beautiful wooden counter, so lovingly crafted by Henry Boyd, had been gouged by sharp instruments. The windows smashed in. The front door lock broken. Dangerous shards of glassware crunched underfoot. Sweets from our specially imported glass barrels strewn all over the room. The barrels themselves in a thousand pieces. And the awning shredded yet again.

In the parlor, curtains yanked down. Joseph's precious piano axed, the ivories ripped out, the lid caved in. Our books hurled off shelves. Covers pulled off and pages ripped out. Paintings my parents had brought from England torn off walls and knifed.

Footprints of flour and sticky substances were tracked everywhere. Ground into the parlor carpet. Tramped up the wooden stairs to the bedrooms.

Upstairs was just as heartbreaking, if not worse. We felt violated as we surveyed the destruction. The baby's cot and toys smashed. Her clothes torn. Mary Anne's heirloom hairbrush and mirror, given by her grandmother, buckled and broken. Linen ripped. Clothing dragged out of cupboards. Much of it ruined. Some stolen. We were later told of men parading down the street in Mary Anne's bonnets, cackling with hateful laughter.

Suddenly I remembered what I now thought of as my Abigail coin. It had become my most precious possession. I ran to my room. Panicking, I stood in the doorway. In the terror to get the women and babies up to Mother's last Friday, I'd completely forgotten it. Was it gone? My curios collection, carefully gathered and increasing since my childhood days in Utica, was strewn all round the room. My few clothes had been tipped out of the bureau. My tin soldiers, bent and buckled, lay scattered. But where was my coin?

I sank to my knees. Started scrabbling through the mess. Distress filled me. Would I never see Abi again? And then, a dark brown slither of metal caught my eye, lying on the floorboard under the window. Thank goodness – there it was. Carefully wrapping it in a handkerchief, I put it in my pocket until somewhere safer could be found.

It wasn't only our home that was destroyed. Both ours and Samuel's livelihoods had been smashed to smithereens.

The *Philanthropist* said it for us all a few days later, when their next issue was hastily printed on a friendly printer's machinery.

It may be asked what we intend to do now. The answer is easy. We consider that the Philanthropist *is identified with the right of free discussion in the west. By it then, we stand or fall. Two presses have been thrown into the river. Its editor and printer are in daily jeopardy. Our enemies are open in their threats. Prudent friends advise a suspension. But we give place to the mob? No, not for an hour. So long as the friends of liberty shall aid, by the help of our Father in Heaven, we hope to abide at our post. All we ask is, the* means. *Our Society is in debt. Our printer is a poor man, and he has lost all but his type. Perhaps eight hundred dollars will cover his loss and one hundred ours. We ask help for him and for the cause. Will our friends grant it, or will they at this crisis, by their neglect, do what no mob can do; put down the* Philanthropist?

Chapter 57

Abigail
Auckland February 2015

It was a few days after my last trip to see Alf, when he'd told of their experiences during the June attack and how the men had all been dragged off to prison. Mum texted as I was about to leave school.

'Please get baking dish from Aunt H on way home. Need it for dinner.'

Aunt Hanna had the dish ready. As she handed it to me, she said, 'I've just found a few more pages of the *Philanthropist* we've not yet read, Abigail. From the same year but a couple of months later. Have you time to read them tonight? It's such close type and my eyes are having enough strain reading the letters. Someone thought it was worth keeping these pages. You might like to have first dibs.'

I carefully slipped the folder she gave me inside an exercise book for safety.

After dinner, while Mum was out at one of her meetings, I carefully laid out the crinkly old pieces of newspaper on the table. With mounting horror I read the story of the September riots. What had happened to Alf? To all of them?

No matter how dangerous, I had to find out. Looking back later, I realized it was a foolhardy decision, but like my ancestor, I was sometimes guilty of acting first and thinking later.

As fast as I could, I clambered into my 'traveling' costume. Grabbed a shawl just in case. Then threaded the coin and slung it around my neck.

Blackout. Bang. And here I was again. I shook my head. It was always fuzzy on arrival.

I'd landed beside a canal. Quickly I scanned the environment. Shabby rough-painted houses, looking as though they'd been slapped together in a hurry and leaning in on each other, were about fifty yards away. Nearer was a cluster of rusty tin sheds, shaded by a couple of willow trees. On the other side of the waterway I could see a hard-packed path. The back end of a canal boat was disappearing round a bend. But no Alf. He usually showed up within seconds of my arrival. Odd.

I shook out my dress and waited quietly for a moment. Then I heard voices, coming from the other side of the sheds. One voice sounded like Alf's. Moving as quietly as possible, I stepped in that direction.

Alfred

It was near on a week before John and I found each other. I'd managed to grab a breather from clean-up duties by offering to go over to Bucktown to see how many of our network remained. Many families had gone permanently. I was wandering around the scarred buildings, trying to make sense of what I saw, when I spotted him.

We both started gabbling, delighted to see each other. Words tumbled out as we stood there on the street, sharing our stories of the terrors.

'Hold on, hold on,' I said after a couple of minutes. 'Let's find somewhere to have a proper discourse.'

We were quite close to the Miami Canal. A freight boat was heading out of town, for commerce was slowly getting back to normal, and nearby were a few tumble-down sheds, partly shaded by a couple of trees.

'There's a patch of grass over by those sheds, John. Why don't we sit down there in the shade?'

No sooner said than done. We made ourselves comfortable, leaning back against the least rusty of the sheds.

John picked at a nearly-healed scab on his knee as he began his story.

'Last Saturday started bad, right from the beginning. We were just finishing breakfast at the Woodsons. Mr Tinsley, Mr Woodson's assistant, had arrived for work. The men were trying to decide whether to open the doors of the carpentry shop. Everyone was very worried about the mobs and who they would next attack. They also didn't think I should risk going downtown to my Saturday job at Mr Watson's.

'Just then, we heard a loud hammering at the door. Gave us a terrible fright, it did. At first Mr Woodson was afraid to open up, 'til he recognized a neighbor's voice.

'The man came panting into the room. "You fellas all gotta hide, William. All black men and older boys are being taken prisoner."

'He looked at me and added, "You're probably not safe either, young John."

'There was a real how-de-do while they tried to think where they could hide. Finally, they fixed on the chimneys. They tried to get me to join them but I was terrible afeard for my brother Gideon.

'Ignoring their wishes, I ran out the back yard, jumped over the fence into the back alley and for as long as possible, kept off busy streets. But soon I had to turn onto Main Street to cross the canal bridge. All the time I was watching for danger. In the middle of the bridge I heard voices behind, ordering me to stop. I was terrified. Ignored them. Kept running.

'It's near a mile from Woodsons' place to Gideon's shop by Fourth and Main. I ran fast as I could. Was pretty well tuckered out by the time I got close, I can tell you.

'I was almost at Gideon's place, outside the drugstore next door, when I fell. The shop owners think I most likely fainted. Said running in the heat, plus terror, would do it.'

'Jumping Jehoshaphat, John. Could have been bad. What happened?'

'They're good people. I came to on their floor, a ring of kindly white faces peering down at me. They gave me water. Patched me up.' He gestured to his still-healing knees. 'Carried me to Gideon's rooms, and waited to make sure I was recovered. Then waited some more to hear the cause, in case we needed more aid.'

'Were the fellows who tried to stop you anywhere close?'

John gave a small smile of satisfaction. 'Nah. Gave those mongrels the slip.'

He continued. 'Gideon already knew and he and his five employees had found hiding places. His doors were well barred against entry. I could have saved myself the trouble. But it was all worth it to be with my big brother.' His eyes sparkled.

'We hid for hours. A couple of times, gangs came banging on the door. We sat still as mice in our hiding places. Even if they'd broken in, they'd not have easily found us. We were up in the attic, behind old shop fittings Gideon had thrown up there. But, thank the Lord, each time they gave up and went away. As they headed down the street looking for more victims, we heard them grumbling about cowardly niggers that ran away.'

I thought of our own horrible experiences. He didn't know the half of it yet.

'Those people are the scum of the earth, John. Call themselves the law. Law-breakers, more like.'

John nodded in agreement.

'How long did you hide?'

'Until dusk. By then we were fearsome hungry. Finally, Gideon sent me back to his neighbors to see if they'd help me get food from a confectionary just along the road. We couldn't risk trying to get to your shop.'

'As well you didn't.'

He didn't realize the significance of my remark. Went on. 'We'd not eaten by then for close to fifteen hours. It was safer to send me – as you know, I'm lighter-skinned than Gideon and sometimes mistaken for white. I've taken more after my father, people tell me. Plus the mobsters were less likely to grab a boy, 'specially in company with white people.'

'Are you all back to business yet?'

'Mostly. Because it's mainly white men who go to both Mr Watson and Gideon for their barbering, they were quickly back in business. Men need their shaves and haircuts. It will take a lot longer for Mr Woodson to recover. He works for both black and white clients, and many blacks are fixing to leave town. Not investing in their properties in case they lose them. Plenty people are talking about moving, even as far away as Canada. Too frightened to stay here now.'

'That I understand. There's some in our family thinking the same way. Tell me, when you were finally able to go out for food that Saturday night, could you hear the mob anywhere near?'

'Now you mention it, I did. Sounded like up in the next street. Hang on – that's your street.'

'Yep. And it wasn't just in our street. It was our house. And nearby, Samuel's press as well.'

John looked at me, distressed.

'Oh, I'm sorry. Here I am blathering on about our concerns. What happened?'

Just as I was about to start, I heard a small noise behind us. Holding my finger to my lips, I quietly stood up. Gently eased myself round the back of the shed. To my astonished eyes, I beheld Abigail, leaning up against the back wall, her head turned in my direction.

She gave a start. A shocked comment was about to slip out of my mouth, but just in time I remembered my young friend a few feet away. 'Stay there,' I mouthed.

As I returned to John, I reassured him. 'It's nothing. Maybe just a bird.' As I sat down I felt my pocket. Sure enough, the coin had gone again.

I filled him in on our own horrific dramas, knowing that Abi was also listening. How I was to get her back home through our normal coin exchange, I'd have to work out later. Right now, John expected a tale.

Finally, war stories exchanged, John stood up. 'I best be away. Mr Woodson will start to worry if I be gone too long. Everyone's scared of more trouble. Us blacks won't feel safe for a very long time.'

'Same at our house, friend! I'll just wander over to look at the canal before I head back.' We gave each other a boy hug and I watched his wiry frame and curly dark head disappear back amongst the houses. Relieved that I could now turn safely to my time-traveling descendant, I walked round the back of the shed.

Abi was anxiously waiting for me. 'Oh Alf, I heard all that! How's everyone now?'

'Let's walk along the canal for a bit,' I suggested. My legs had cramped up while sitting down with John. A thought occurred. 'Did you know any of this before you came?' I asked. 'You said you'd read about the June riot in the paper.'

'Sure did! I just read about it. Came immediately. Aunt Hanna only gave me the newspaper report this afternoon.'

'It'd be helpful if you read a bit ahead. Some warning would be good!'

Abigail looked worried. 'I've thought quite a lot about that, but I end up going round in circles. Like, if I've read about something, it's happened. If I was ever able to come back before some bad shit goes down,' as usual, she ignored my raised eyebrows at her bad language, 'and warn you, would that change history? And if so, how could I have read about it? It does my head in, quite frankly.'

We laughed about it. 'Well,' I said, 'maybe it's better not to know. A bit like knowing in advance when you're going to die. I don't think I'd like that.'

Just then I heard the Town Clock chime midday. 'Tarnation. If I'm not home for lunch, Mary Anne will get worried. I'll real sorry, Abi, but I have to go.'

A few moments later, she vanished. With the coin safely back in my pocket, I headed back through the damaged streets.

Chapter 58

Alfred
Cincinnati October 1841

As quickly as we could, we returned the bakery to a working operation, for it was our only source of income. It took longer, the best part of two weeks after the death threats ceased, to get the living quarters cleaned up and restored enough for us to move back in, although kind friends helped. Many of our little comforts, now gone forever, had been sentimental items of no great monetary value, but it gave a jolt every time we reached for something familiar, only to remember that it had been stolen or destroyed. And living in a place that had been so completely wasted was a strange sensation. We no longer felt safe in what had been our haven.

Little Mary was left a bit longer with her grandmother and doting aunts, until we'd restored as much as we could. Mary Anne was reluctant to bring her baby home too soon, in case of more danger. The rioters had gone to ground – but she, more than any of us, lived in fear that some other incident would bring them out of their holes, slavering again like wolves after their prey. Two-legged prey. Us.

The newspapers made a lot of noise about the riot, much of it very one-sided. The *Enquirer*, a loudly pro-slavery publication, laid the blame on we abolitionists. Disappointingly, even the *Gazette* and the *Republican*, who were usually more favorable to justice, were scathing about abolitionists and our extreme and radical views. As usual, our father was named as one of the ringleaders, along with Dr Bailey.

Further cause was attributed to Kentuckian rabble from across the river. According to the reportage, no 'worthy citizen' of our fair city was guilty of any inciting action.

Blame was given to idle youth, vagrants, the Irish, the blacks and the abolitionists. Even the proclamation produced by the Fathers of the city on Saturday 4th was apparently blameless of any incendiary behavior.

We knew differently, having been at the receiving end of 'protection' from our constabulary. Said 'protection' included the troop of soldiers who came upon the mobsters about to attack Samuel's printery but marched away, leaving the premises unprotected. And not all our neighbors were as innocent as they wished us to believe.

Joseph was talking to Mr Muller, who'd just replaced our bakery oven doors.

'That were a right disgraceful thing them mobsters done to you, Mister Burnett,' said the burly workman as he checked the doors were hung correctly.

'Thank you, Mr Muller. I appreciate your sympathy,' replied Joseph.

'Didya hear who done the damage? Or took your stuff?' was the next question.

'No. Joseph looked at him a bit more closely. 'Why do you ask?'

'Well,' drawled Mr Muller. 'Some of the fellas what run off wiv' your supplies didn' 'ave far to go to off-load. Me and me old lady was watchin' from our apartment. We reco'nized some of 'em. For sure, some're the scum of the earth you see hangin' round t' market. But others you'd be surprised at. Neighbors like.'

Joseph looked sad. 'There's been a lot of things surprised me this year. Mob behavior is very unpredictable, I've realized. Not everyone is as honest as they profess.'

It wasn't just baking supplies and equipment that didn't go far. Several times I was pretty sure I saw some of our clothing draping the frames of shifty-looking wall-loungers hanging around the streets. The wearers were not the kind you'd challenge. I had to just button my lips and walk on by, their jeering faces turning to watch me.

Late one afternoon after work, I was in my bedroom, taking a few quiet minutes to arrange what was left of my collection, when Abi landed on my bedroom floor.

'Oh, I'm glad I've arrived in a less conspicuous place,' she said as she straightened up her clothing. She always arrived disheveled. I laughed, delighted to see her. I was becoming very fond of my courageous relative. I wasn't sure I'd have the nerve to jump between centuries as she did, especially knowing what she did regarding the danger of my situation.

Quickly putting down my remaining arrow heads, I jumped to shut the door. 'Just talk real low,' I whispered. 'The family's downstairs.'

'I thought I'd come and see how things are now, Alf,' she whispered back. 'Is it still 1841? What's the latest news?'

'Yes. Only a month since the riot. News? I was hoping you might be able to tell me,' I answered. 'Have you read any more newspapers, or letters that tell you what's to happen?'

'No, I'm sorry. It's really busy at school at the moment. The teachers are piling on the homework, and I'm having to practice for our inter-school sports competition. I'm on the school athletics team. I can only tell you that from next year there are many more letters between you all than there have been for the last couple of years. Aunt Hanna and I think that someone must move away, or you'd not have reason to write. I haven't had a chance to read them yet. Who do you think might move?'

I thought about this for a minute. 'Well, I know Father's going nowhere. But Mary Anne is really unhappy. During the riot Joseph was talking about selling up. I thought it was just talk in the heat of the moment, but now you've got me wondering.

'We're all determined that we have to carry on the fight for justice, though. Father is of the opinion that one day the abolitionist view will prevail. I fear it might never happen in my lifetime, if the latest happenings are anything to go by. We're all shocked by the inhumanity of these supposedly civilized people.'

'Oh no, Alf. You'll see the end of it,' said Abi.

I looked at her in surprise. 'What do you know?'

Just then we heard voices from the stairwell.

'I better go,' she whispered. 'I'll come back as soon as I can.'

I was sitting on the edge of my bed, holding my coin, when Joseph popped his head in the door a minute later. 'Here he is, Mary Anne,' he called down the stairs. 'Dinner's ready, brother.'

What did Abi know?

Chapter 59

Alfred
Cincinnati October 1841

For the next few days I was like a terrier who'd lost a rat down a hole. What had Abigail been about to tell me? Meanwhile, Joseph and Mary Anne's future was the common theme at Fifth street. One night, over the pork casserole, they finally made a decision. It started with Joseph saying, 'Perhaps we could go back to Utica, love? You were happy there.'

'No. I'm sorry, Joe,' she said firmly. 'Back in Utica you've got Gerrit Smith and lawyer Alvan Stewart, plus others very active for the cause. There's as much opposition there as here.'

Joseph asked, 'What about New York? You'd be closer to your family.'

'You know I don't like New York. It's crowded, dirty and dangerous. It's fine to pay a visit, but not a place I want to raise our children.'

'Is there any other place you'd like to go? What about Pennsylvania?'

'I'm sorry dear, but there's conflict about slavery and abolition everywhere. Just think of that beautiful Pennsylvania Hall in Philadelphia. Built by abolitionists and meant to be a safe place for free discussion.' She looked sad. 'Burnt down by arsonists as soon as it was built. There's nowhere in this country I feel safe.'

'It feels like we're giving up,' Joseph replied. He really didn't want to leave.

She sighed. 'I'm very conflicted. I want to see the end of slavery at least as much as everyone in this family. But just as the poor slaves yearn to be free, I also want freedom – from fear. I'm desperate to raise my children in safety.'

It seemed like an impasse.

Joseph glanced over at me, silently eating my dinner, and brought me into the conversation. 'Alf, there's an extra matter we've not yet told the family. My dear wife is in circumstances again. You know how difficult that path has been for us. I'm prepared to sacrifice much to have her feel safe.'

He barely waited for my congratulations before turning back to his wife. 'I have an idea. What say we return to England? You left when you were but a child, and I was eighteen. But we do have loving family there. Aunt and Uncle Nolloth and cousin Caroline and her husband Tom Liffiton would greet us with gladness.'

After much talk, so it was decided. Our parents were *not* happy! I wasn't particularly struck on the notion either, for there was a distinct possibility that I'd be expected to live once more with my old parents and sisters. I didn't fancy the likelihood of being overrun with fussing women – again!

'Perhaps I could go to England with Joseph and Mary Anne,' I said to Mother. She was horrified. I figure she saw her comfortable semi-retired life slipping away.

'Lawks-a-mercy, boy! Don't even think about it. I know you've only been working in the business two years, but you're showing promise. We can't lose the only two with good business brains.'

Thomas and Father winced at her strong words, but I knew she was right. Father was always off on 'other matters' and Tom, though a good journeyman, didn't enjoy the management side of things. I, on the other hand, had discovered an aptitude for the work. I delighted in joshing the maids and matrons who patronized our shop. As they laughed, they were easily encouraged to spend a little more, and the shop takings increased accordingly. And, I often came up with ideas to expand and improve our operation. Before the riots there'd even been talk of opening more Burnett Confectionaries in other populous parts of the city.

Reluctantly, I had to shelve my ambition for more travel – for now.

A couple of days after the big decision, to my delight Abi showed up again. I was walking down Montgomery Pike after doing a delivery and found her sitting on the rock wall I'd rested at with Purity, the first day we met.

Abi smiled when she saw me. 'I figured you'd show up soon.'

'I'm so glad to see you!' I sat down beside her. 'You have *no* idea how frustrating it's been, waiting for you to come back! What were you going to say last time? About me seeing the end of slavery?'

She smiled. 'I told you we were to study American history this year. I've been taking particular note of events that will happen in this century. On New Year's Day 1863 a future president, Abraham Lincoln, will sign the Emancipation Proclamation to end slavery. But it will take another three years and the end of a terrible civil war, before it really ends on December 18th, 1865.'

My jaw dropped. I didn't know whether to focus on the emancipation or the war. This was the first time Abi had given me so much information about my own times. She saw my shock. Clapped a hand across her mouth.

'Oh, I shouldn't have said so much. Aunt Hanna says people are best not to know what lies in their future.'

She would give no more details about a coming war. But on the subject of slavery, she was encouraging. 'You mustn't lose heart in the work. What you're all doing is making a difference, even though it doesn't seem so at the moment.'

I looked at her sadly. 'Well, that's good to know, but it's at a huge cost to us. Joseph and Mary Anne are fixing to sell the business and return to safety in England.'

Abi looked at me sympathetically. 'You'll miss them, won't you?'

'I hate the thought. For the last five years Joseph's been father, brother, employer and a really good friend. I'm right cast down at the thought of them departing.'

To my surprise, Abi chuckled. 'I'm not far enough through the family letters yet – my Aunt Hanna has read further ahead than me – but she just told me last night that it's Joseph and Mary Anne who eventually end up moving to New Zealand. I wouldn't describe the latter end of the 19th century in New Zealand as exactly peaceful, but they must have survived or I wouldn't be here to tell you about it. I wonder if you'll ever come visit them?'

I had no concept of what she was talking about. I knew nothing about this unknown country of New Zealand apart from the squiggle on the map and what Abi had told me, but in a bizarre way, her comment was comforting.

We visited for a while and then, noting the sun's descent, I figured I needs must get back to work.

Standing up, I said, 'Abi, I greatly hope this isn't the end of your unannounced arrivals. You're an odd one, to be sure, but I do enjoy conversing with you.'

She gave a cheeky grin. 'We don't know if this little coin exchange number will keep working, but for sure I'll give it my best shot. Getting to know you has been the most awesome way to learn history. Far more exciting than any textbook or history lesson, that's for sure.'

She reached out and gave me a big hug before pushing the edge of the coin towards me.

A moment later, she was gone.

Chapter 60

Abigail
Auckland February 2015

Back home, as always, I carefully put the cord away and checked that the coin had done its own time-travel and was back in the old tobacco tin.

With difficulty, I settled down to history homework, my thoughts still with Alf in Cincinnati. Over the last six weeks my interest in history, especially American history, had exploded. No longer was it something interesting but of no real modern-day relevance. Now it was alive. Vivid. Dangerous. Frightening. And exciting.

I pulled out my laptop to begin a 500-word essay on the causes of the American Civil War, wishing I'd not mentioned it to Alf, twenty years into his future.

Flicking between internet pages to examine what different experts gave as the causes, I noted several. The rights of the states to control themselves instead of being controlled by federal government, the economy and, as we'd discussed in class, slavery.

As I was looking for inspiration on how to start, a picture caught my eye. It was Abraham Lincoln shaking hands with a small woman. The caption read: *Lincoln meets Harriet Beecher Stowe.*

My attention sprang to full alert. Lincoln was alleged to have said to her, when they met: *'So you're the little woman who wrote the book that made this great war!'.* Although a number of authors cast doubt as to whether it really was said by Lincoln, they all noted the seismic shift in public opinion, in favor of abolition, that her book caused.

I thought of Alf's stories about her, and what I'd learnt when I read *Uncle Tom's Cabin*. How amazing to think that my ancestors had known her, been part of her life, maybe even the source of one or two of her stories. Pulling out the coin, I placed it on my desk for inspiration.

An hour later, I took a break from the keyboard and picked up my precious and magical pass to that other world. 'What will I see, next time I use you?' I said, then smiled at the silliness of talking to a piece of metal. Clutching it carefully in my hand, I walked out onto the porch for a stretch and a breath of fresh air before settling back to the essay.

Just at that moment, as I stood looking over the garden, a terrified ginger streak came racing towards me. It was Macavity, with a Rottweiler right on his tail. Macavity took a flying leap into my arms. Startled, I dropped the coin. It rolled away. All hell broke loose. The cat spat and screeched, the dog snarled and snapped, I screamed, and the harassed owner, pounding down our drive, shouted.

Cat calmed and dog dragged away – why didn't the stupid owner have it on a leash – I tried to find my precious coin. Where was it? I searched in every corner, shifted every pot plant, swept the porch, sifted through the garden below – but it was nowhere. I was devastated.

For the next two weeks I looked. And looked. And looked. Nothing. For months I still kept hoping it would miraculously find its way back to me. Finally, I gave up.

My only way of getting to Alf was lost. I grieved. It felt like a death. As though I'd lost a loved one. And in so many ways, I had.

I made a promise to Alf – and to myself.

'This is not the end of the story, Alfred Burnett. I'm proud to have known you. I hope I see you again, but if I don't, I'm going to learn more about your story through the things you left behind. And – one day I will tell the story of you and your family.'

Epilogue

There was a lot of discussion about who would take over the business. Joseph's preferred option was to sell it before they left for England. It was agreed by all that, despite my promising start, I was too young to take responsibility. Father had become used to the freedom of having his sons run the business, and wasn't interested in again being a full-time baker. His focus was now firmly on his abolitionist activities. And Thomas didn't want to take over. After working with Joseph for two years he realized how much work there was in being an owner. Didn't want the hassle. So, conversations went round and round, looking for a solution. Should they put it on the market? Who would want to buy a business twice targeted by mobs? Would prospective buyers consider the premises tainted?

One night, about a month after things had returned to some semblance of normality, the whole family assembled at Mother's for Sunday dinner. As the roast lamb and mint sauce were passed around, Samuel suddenly said, 'Joseph, if you're definitely going back to England, what do you think about selling your bakery to me?'

Ann sat there quietly. Clearly they'd discussed it beforehand. None of us had ever imagined Samuel in the bakery trade, let alone running a store. However, in many ways, it made sense. Although the readers of the *Philanthropist* and members of the Ohio Anti-Abolition Society responded to Dr Bailey's plea to dig deep in their pockets so Samuel could buy another press, and he was happy to continue as their printer, he wanted a fallback position. Now he was a married man and had a family starting, just like Mr Pugh in 1836, he didn't want his family's future to be reliant on such a volatile enterprise. Thus, the printer also became a baker.

Informers infiltrated Father's Committee of Vigilance so, most reluctantly, we disbanded it in 1842. We were all at risk of being thrown in prison again and, more importantly, couldn't guarantee the safety of fugitives passing through our network. However, we all continued working for the cause, but in a less visible way. Our belief in the rightness of all men and women to live free never wavered.

Eventually the work paid off. A surprisingly short number of years later, the mood of the city changed and abolition ceased to be a dirty word. And, as Abi predicted, by December 1865 all slaves were freed. Although many injustices continued, we'd been useful foot soldiers in the ranks of freedom fighters, helping win the first major battle – for emancipation. Equality, however, we never saw. That battle was left for future generations.

Father passed away in 1851 of apoplexy, only sixty-three and still active in the work. He was greatly mourned by his many friends, both black and white.

Samuel was a poor baker and businessman and never finished paying Joseph for the business, so Joseph and his family returned to Cincinnati in 1843. He quickly turned it back into a profitable operation. But then came further tragedy. Their dearly beloved little Mary, aged only four, died of croup. That broke him. He and Mary Anne hightailed back to England, never again to live in America. This time Mother took over his store, with me to assist her.

For some years I engaged in the bakery and confectionary business. As well as working closely with my dear mother, I also opened my own premises. This did very well, but the exciting world of theatre called. Mother and Mr Dorchester, you were wrong. Clowning around pays *very* well, as I will tell one day in another tale.

In 1856 Joseph and Mary Anne did indeed sail to New Zealand, on the other side of the world, seeking a better life. They ended up in the district of Whanganui, where they and their family prospered. However, they never forgot their years in America, and often talked with their children and grandchildren about the American chapter of their lives. They built a beautiful home and named it Oneida, after the county in which Utica was the principal city. They even built a special room to store the family letters and journals. They wanted to be sure that the dramatic events they lived through, the sacrifices made by so many, and the lessons learnt, would be passed on to future generations.

After the riots of 1841, Abigail vanished. And though she disappeared as suddenly as she'd arrived, I never forgot her. It was a comfort to know that our stories were cherished, copied, saved and shared.

We fought for freedom for all. Freedom to choose. Freedom to think. Freedom to live.

Good people who believe in and fight for justice
can change the world,
if they just refuse to quit.

THE END

Watch for Alf's further adventures in the next book in the
Freedom Series.
For more on Robyn's books, both fiction and non-fiction,
check out https://www.robynpearce.com

She publishes her fiction under Robyn R Pearce.
(It's an Amazon algorithm thing! Don't ask!)

If you've enjoyed this book, it would be incredibly helpful if
you could leave an honest review on Amazon,
or wherever you purchased it.

For independent authors swimming in the deep ocean of
online publishing, reviews are our life-blood!

If you love historical fiction and would like to keep up with
Robyn's future books, just go to www.robynpearce.com to
get occasional spam-free news and interesting tit-bits (plus
giveaways, special deals, and great reads by other authors).

For Those Who Want to Know More

Many players in this story were real people, and represented as accurately as is possible in a fictional work. This includes all the Burnetts, their extended family, employees and the abolitionists listed, both black and white. Except for Mr Herbertson, Mr Thompson and the Olsens, the runaways helped were named in either the quoted newspaper accounts (dates and publications as shown in italics in the story) or the Burnett family papers. However, I took poetic license with Benjamin Wallace and his sons, who arrived for help August 29th 1841, just before the city-wide riot. Joseph's journal records that his wife was with them. The account I give of why Benjamin ran was a typical story, but not his.

A few of the key abolitionists and conductors on the Underground Railroad, both black and white, have been extensively written about, and most deservedly so. However, many more deliberately kept a lower profile, or were not well-known outside of their own immediate time and place. I like to think of this tale, although it is primarily of one family, as also being the possible saga of every active abolitionist family.

The Burnetts and their associates were just one cog in a huge army of steadfast people, of all colors and creeds, who fought to end slavery in the United States. However, they were possibly unusual in the amount of material the family retained, for if Joseph and Mary Anne Burnett, their descendants and other relatives hadn't kept an enormous repository of family letters, journals and relevant newspaper cuttings, this story would have vanished.

When Joseph and Mary Anne emigrated to New Zealand in 1856, they were accompanied by his first cousin, Caroline

Liffiton, her husband and children. Both families settled in Whanganui. Caroline Liffiton (nee Nolloth) was my great-great-great-grandmother.

I'd love to say I was able to time-travel to chat with Alf, but with such rich primary resources and an abundance of real-time travel and research, he came to life for me.

Other historical characters

- In Utica: Gerrit Smith, philanthropist – and he did live to see slavery abolished; Alvan Stewart, lawyer, and James DeLong, influential business man. All were staunch abolitionists.
- The *Philanthropist*: James G. Birney, first editor; Dr Gamaliel Bailey, second editor; Achilles Pugh, first printer; Samuel Alley, second printer and son-in-law of Cornelius Burnett, as portrayed. In popular online references to the *Philanthropist*, Alley is rarely mentioned, but was as central to the story as Mr Pugh.
- Harriet Beecher Stowe and her family.
- Rev John Rankin and his family, of Ripley, Ohio, abolitionist and preacher.
- Salmon P. Chase, lawyer and future Secretary of the Treasury for Lincoln & Chief Justice of the USA, 1864-1873, plus many other positions and honors.
- Cincinnati abolitionists named, both black and white: Gideon Langston, Henry Boyd, John Van Zandt, Mr Grainger, Mr Hicks, Mr Hopkins and the others listed on the Committee of Vigilance Constitution.
- Other notable members of the black community: John Woodson, landlord of John Langston for the first six months of his time in Cincinnati; William

Watson, barber, bathhouse owner and second landlord to John.
- Dignitaries and City Officials named.

Fictional characters

The principal fictional characters are Abi, her mother and Great-Aunt Hanna; Eli and Hetty; the Wetzel family and crew; Purity and Will. Supporting fictional characters are Joseph's Utica assistant Sam; Alf's friends Seamus (in Utica), and Ralph.

Sources

I've endeavored to be as accurate as possible with historical facts, and following are some of my main sources. Any mistakes are mine.

All the newspaper quotes and sources are as stated and can be seen in the Hamilton Public Library, Cincinnati. For the sake of easy reading, very minor changes have been made to a few of them.

Even though the Burnetts left an enormous treasure-trove of letters, and the first draft of this book included many extracts, by the time the story had gone through multiple drafts and rigorous edits, very few letters remained. Instead, many of them, with their extensive social commentary, morphed into dialogue and action. For those who like to know fact from fiction, the first letter Abi reads, dated January 14th, 1837, is original Cornelius except for the last two paragraphs, which were invented by me. The second letter, dated September 14th, 1837, is all my invention. The sentiments expressed in those two examples, however, were constantly repeated in extensive family correspondence. Other snippets in italics are direct quotes.

The excerpts described as coming from Joseph's Day Book or journal are indeed from that source, with very minor alterations for ease of comprehension. Many of the originals can be viewed at the Alexander Turnbull Library, a major collection of the National Library of New Zealand. Several handwritten volumes of Joseph's journals and family letters, transcribed by his son Cornelius, the baby Mary Anne was carrying at the time of the September 1841 riots, can be seen in the Whanganui District Museum, New Zealand. They include both the remarks about the trip Joseph and Alf took in 1837 from Cincinnati back to Utica, and his understated observations about running from the mob in 1841. Of course, conversations are entirely from my imagination.

The Constitution of the Committee of Vigilance was copied exactly from the family papers.

Details about the Erie Canal in New York State and the Ohio Erie Canal in Ohio, the resistance to the 1836 Abolition Convention in Utica and the two riots that the Burnett family found themselves at the center of are based on extensive research and as many primary sources as possible.

John Langston's experience of the 1841 riot is based on his description of events in his autobiography *From the Virginia Plantation to the National Capital,* (1894) and the extensively researched and annotated article *Culture and Kinship: John Mercer Langston in Cincinnati: 1840-1843* by William and Aimee Lee Cheek, (1989).

The full list of resolutions passed by the city fathers on 4th September can be found in the *Philanthropist* 8th September 1841 under the sub-heading *'Citizens' Meeting'*. Alf's summary is my handiwork.

The Harriet Beecher Stowe Center is on Gilbert Avenue, Cincinnati and was the home of the Beecher family. Harriet's most famous book, *'Uncle Tom's Cabin'*, was written as a result of her exposure to the horrors of slavery in Cincinnati and Kentucky. It was first serialized in 1851 in *The National Era,* in book form in 1852, and is still in print today. Her story of Eliza, the runaway mother who crossed the iced-up Ohio River and was helped by the Rankins, was based on a true event told her by the Rankins. It's also told in the Rankin family papers. *Uncle Tom's Cabin* created an enormous shift in public opinion.

I was first introduced to the Rev Rankin and his family through Ann Hagedorn's well-written and carefully researched book *Beyond the River.* The Rankin House at Ripley, upriver from Cincinnati, is now a National Historic Landmark and well worth a visit. Their inspiring story is also told in a 25-minute film *Brothers of the Borderland* which you can see at the National Underground Railroad Freedom Center. The story is introduced, and segments linked, by Oprah Winfrey.

The National Underground Railroad Freedom Center is located on the waterfront of Cincinnati. It's a brilliant source of information on all matters relating to slavery, not only in Alf's time, but also in ours. Tragically, slavery still exists today in many countries around the world.

What happened in history after 1841

The abolition of slavery took another twenty-four years and a bloody civil war before slaves were emancipated. However, even abolition did not bring equal rights. The only thing the colored people won in that violent conflagration was the right to not be enslaved. It wasn't until a hundred years later, in the Civil Rights Movement of the 1960s, that they won basic human rights.

John Mercer Langston, depicted in the story as Alf's friend, is an example of the inequities colored people experienced. Langston left Cincinnati to be educated at Oberlin College, became the first African American lawyer in Ohio, in 1855 was the first man of color to be elected to public office in the United States and the first colored lawyer. He was a brilliant orator, highly educated, and held many important positions in the business and educational world of the times, along-side white colleagues. He was a personal friend of General, later President, Ulysses S. Grant and Salmon P. Chase. He also served two years in Congress 1890-91. However, an increasing number of racist 'Jim Crow' laws were brought in around the time of his election to Congress. As a result, from March 1901 for nearly thirty years, no African Americans served in Congress. Watch for more about John in the next Alf story.

Lawyer Salmon P. Chase was tireless in his fight for the rights of colored people, both free and enslaved, and the abolitionist movement and its supporters. Later he became very influential in American political life. He served as US Secretary of the Treasury (1861-64) in President Lincoln's wartime Cabinet and was the 6th Chief Justice of the United States (1864-73). He also had two terms in the US Senate and was the first Republican governor of Ohio (1855-59), the party he helped to found in 1854. Abolition of slavery was a major Republican platform – it was the most progressive political party of those times.

Major elements made up to enhance the story:

- The explosion on the Hudson River. Many explosions happened during the days of paddle steamers, but not to the Burnetts, as far as we know.
- Alf's writing in the 'Freedom Journal' and his book. He was a prolific writer and contributor to a number of publications. However, this one was all my invention.
- Alf's escapade at Albany, although if he had got lost, Albany was a likely spot to misplace an inquisitive boy. The descriptions of the canal, the discomforts of travel, and the type of craft are based on extensive research.
- The grounding of the *Ben Franklin* steamer. There was a steamboat of that name but it didn't go aground

at the time of Alf's second journey to Cincinnati. Groundings were quite common, however.

- The family's involvement with the Beechers and the Stowes. This I cannot verify, but they definitely would have known each other. As regards Joseph's involvement in helping the Stowe's runaway maid escape, (an historical event, although some sources put it as happening a year earlier than I portrayed) there also I worked on possibilities. It would have been logical for the Stowes to enlist the help of a known abolitionist who knew where to go, for in the period this story covers, Harriet and her family were not active abolitionists.
- The incident with the re-captured slave on the banks of the Ohio when Alf got too absorbed with fishing.
- Alf's friendship with John Langston. They would have known each other and it's very possible that they would have been friends, but I don't have proof.

A few explanatory notes:

I used 'black', 'nigger' and 'colored' in the way of the times. I apologize if any offence is taken – it is not intended.

In much of the 1800s and especially in Victorian times, legs were considered extremely private. For example, in polite conversation they used 'limb' instead of 'leg'. To say 'trousers' or 'pants' was not polite either. Instead, they used phrases such as 'sit-down-upons', 'inexpressibles' or even 'unmentionables'. The last was also used for underwear.

'Removed'. We would say 'moved', 'shifted' or 'relocated' to another place, but in the Burnett letters they always talked about 'removing' to somewhere else.

If you thought the editors had missed correcting 'street' to a capital 'S', no. In all the correspondence and newspaper reports of the time, it was spelt with a lower 's'.

'Good-sister' was a common term for a sister-in-law.

A Jacob's Ladder was a popular toy. It is a series of wooden blocks held together by tape or ribbon. Still available today.

Montgomery Pike, the main road to Lane Seminary, is today named Gilbert Avenue.

Uncle Sam's Tooth Pullers were vessels operated by the US Army Corps of Engineers. They removed obstructions from the rivers and canals with a winch and crane system positioned at the front (prow) of the boat.

If you're familiar with the major abolitionist names of the region, you may wonder about the omission of Quaker Levi Coffin. He didn't move to Cincinnati until 1847.

New Zeeland. The first known European explorer to discover New Zealand, Abel Tasman, called it 'New Zeeland' after the Dutch province Zeeland, and Australia he named 'New Holland'. When Abi and Alf met in 1837, there was no town by the name of Auckland. This vibrant South Pacific city, the largest in New Zealand, came into being in 1840.

Huge thanks and acknowledgements

The story could not have been told without some wonderful supporters, helpers and sources:

- Peggy Vause, my amazing aunt (96 when this book was finally finished), without whom this story would never have been written. She's suggested, coaxed and gently nagged me for years! She was my inspiration for Aunt Hanna and years ago fished a swag of old family letters out of a tin trunk.
- Robin Burnett Ward, tireless transcriber of nearly two centuries of the Burnett family papers and a direct descendant of Joseph and Mary Anne. I would never have known Alf's story without Robin's amazing work. Many of the original Burnett materials are located in the Alexander Turnbull Library, Wellington and also

the Whanganui Regional Museum, New Zealand. Others are still in *her* tin trunk!

- Mimi Daria, researcher extraordinaire, volunteer at Harriet Beecher Stowe Center, Cincinnati when I met her, and an enormous help. Her friendship and enthusiasm for the story has added a whole new dimension to historical research.
- Captain Jerry Gertz, Erie Canal Cruises, Herkimer www.eriecanalcruises.com – a wonderful source of valuable information about the original Erie Canal. Take his tour!
- Janice Reilly, Oneida County History Center, Utica, NY. A contributor of highly valuable information about early Utica, as well as pointing me to John J. Walsh's invaluable *Vignettes of Old Utica* (1982). I had a lot more about early Utica in earlier versions of the story that will hopefully come to light in future work. Editing is a harsh process – you have to kill so many darlings!
- Carl Westmoreland, Senior Researcher and Historian, National Underground Railroad Freedom Center, Cincinnati. I first met Carl in 2004 when I began seriously researching the Burnett family, just before the Freedom Center opened. When I explained my connection to the story he replied, '*Cornelius Burnett was a friend to our people. He is not forgotten.*'
- Also from the National Underground Railroad Freedom Center, Interim President Dan Hurley (2017/18). He had just written an article referencing Cornelius Burnett in *Reflections on Leadership* a month before my 2017 visit to Cincinnati. http://cincy-magazine.com/Main/Articles/Reflections_on_Leadership_5316.aspx

- The Genealogy & Local History department of the Cincinnati Library are awesome in answering long distance questions.
- Research Librarian Jim Mainger, also at the Cincinnati Library, was exceptionally helpful when I virtually camped in the library for a week in August 2017. The library holds a great repository of books and newspapers of the times, including papers on both sides of the abolition divide.
- George Ebey, Ohio & Erie Canalway Coalition, Akron, OH. ohioeriecanal.org for his patient answering of endless questions and for directing me to Canal Fulton to take a packet ride. discover-canalfulton.com/
- The Erie Canal Museum, Buffalo, NY is a wonderful resource. eriecanalmuseum.org/
- My Writing Group and local Book Club members – thank you, dear friends, for your eagle eyes and insightful critiques. I hope I've eliminated most of the clunky 'telling instead of showing' bits!
- My granddaughters Brianna, Olivia and Bethany and your wonderful parents for being my final proof readers. You guys rock!
- Judith White, for your insightful editing of the final version. I've learnt heaps from you.
- Kirsten Bryant, for making me so welcome at Oneida House, Fordell, Whanganui, the beautiful historic home built by Joseph in New Zealand in 1870. Burnett family members lived there until 1975, and it was bought by the Bryant family the following year. I'd planned to include Oneida in this book, but stories have a habit of taking over. Look for it in a future tale. The name comes originally from an Indian tribe, and, as mentioned in the Epilogue, is also the county in which Utica is the principal city.

About the Author

Robyn R. Pearce lives in South Auckland, New Zealand. Her peaceful waterside home is a wonderful creative place to be, whatever is going on in the world!

From when she was a small child, she's been in love with stories that bring history to life. This was fostered as a child, when every school day she looked at the oldest European wooden house and the oldest stone building in New Zealand. Their stories romanced her.

Then, in her adult years, older family members began to share letters and journals of intrepid ancestors who'd sailed for a far land, leaving sometimes difficult, sometimes terrible, situations on the other side of the world, all in the hope of a better life for their children. With such a heritage, no wonder freedom is one of Robyn's core values.

Before she began writing historical fiction, she had a long and successful career as an international time management and productivity specialist, with eight books on the topic. More about them at https://www.robynpearce.com

www.ingramcontent.com/pod-product-compliance
Lightning Source LLC
Chambersburg PA
CBHW021059110726
47900CB00007B/1943